GLITTER GIRL

A Swamp Yankee Mystery

James Y. Bartlett

Copyright © 2022 by James Y. Bartlett

For information contact;

Yeoman House Books
10 Old Bulgarmarsh Road
Tiverton, RI 02878

www.jamesybartlett.com

Cover design by Todd Fitz of Fuel Media

ISBN: 978-1-7363930-2-4

First Edition: January 2022

Second Edition: February 2026

10 9 8 7 6 5 4 3 2 1

For Sheppard Bartlett

1924-2021

PROLOGUE

THE UNIT SHIPPED out of Talaqan before dawn that morning, heading north along the D-Road that went all the way up the valley and through the mountains to the city of Chichkeh near the Tajikistan border. Near Talaqan, the valley was broad and green, the well-kept farms looked prosperous and peaceful. But looks could be deceiving. And this was Afghanistan.

As the squad reached the end of the valley, the mountains narrowed on both sides, the road changed from paved to rocky dirt and the men in the back of the armored personnel carriers began to sit up, gear up and pay attention. The normal joshing conversation and the loud Spotify playlist stopped and they all began to listen hard. Up here, the enemy--Taliban, ISIS-K and any of a dozen other sects and fighting groups--were in control.

The mission that day had been explained as a simple S&O: Surveillance and Observation. The chin-strokers back in Kabul wanted a status report on how out-of-control northern Takhar Province was. And unfortunately for the men in Gus Haddock's unit, the only good way to find out was to ride up there and see who or what shot at them.

The convoy consisted of two Cougars, front and rear in the

column, with a few up-armored M1114 Humvees in the middle. Haddock, the unit's lieutenant, had twenty men along for the fun, all experienced Special Forces, well trained, well equipped and ready to rumble.

The rumble started about forty-four clicks outside Talaqan AFB, one of the northern outposts of the allied NATO forces in Afghanistan. The first surveillance point was a small village where the D-Road crossed a rocky stream spilling out of the mountains. The plan was to send some soldiers up to high points on both sides of the highway and peer ahead into the steep valley to look for enemy activity.

But as usual, the Taliban, or the enemy forces of whatever name, had other plans. About a klick south of the village, an RPG came screaming down from the steep rocky cliffs above the roadway and exploded in the dirt ten yards in front of the lead Cougar. The 21-ton armored carrier bounced a bit in the shockwave, but kept on going.

"No harm, no foul," Gus cracked. No one laughed, but everyone buckled the chin straps on their helmets. Gus nodded at Gonzo, the chief gunner, who flipped on his CROWS II weapons system, activating the heavy, remotely controlled M2 .50 calibre machine gun affixed to the top of the Cougar and began sending withering fire into the hills. From inside the air-conditioned cabin, the men heard, and felt, the thud-thud of the gun firing, and began to smell the burning gunpowder of its discharge. They'd all heard, and smelled, it all before.

The convoy kept rolling and soon pulled up outside the brown mud huts and buildings of the village. There were no people around, which told Gus that the enemy had known they were coming today.

It was uncanny, he thought for the millionth time, how they seem to know when and where we go.

When all the trucks were inside the village, Gus barked orders through his headset and the men poured out of the trucks and took up defensive positions, taking cover behind the mud walls and fences alongside the highway. Gus stayed inside the lead Cougar and radioed in a report, noting the welcoming committee which had fired the RPG, and notifying Mission Control that air support might be needed.

As he climbed out of the thick reinforced metal walls of the Cougar HEV, Gus was greeted with the sound of small arms fire coming from the hillsides above on both sides of the highway. He and his men crouched down behind the mud walls and listened to the sound of the lead wasps as they called them--the angry zipping sound of Russian Kalashnikovs being fired from above.

"Bucky?" Gus called to his sergeant. "You got a location?"

Bucky was peering up into the hills, watching for tell-tale signs of the enemy firing at them: the clouds of dust blown up by the explosive recoil of the weapons being fired or the slight flash from the barrel of the Russian-made rifles. One of Bucky's men said something and pointed, and he nodded.

"Just slightly west of the road, Fish," he called out. "About eighty meters up the hill."

Gus turned to Cranks, his mortar man. "You hear that?" he asked. Cranks nodded and unslung his mortar, quickly set it up to point up the mountain and slipped a charge into the front barrel.

"Mortar out!" Gus called.

Cranks fired a round, the launcher making a dull thump and they all waited and watched. A few seconds later, a puff of white smoke appeared up on the mountainside, followed by a muffled boom as the sound wave echoed through the valley. Working methodically, Cranks laid down a pattern of mortars--short, long, left and right--hoping to flush out the enemy snipers. It seemed to work, as the incoming rounds from above ceased. At least for a while. Then the firing started up again, this time coming from the other side of the highway.

"Call it in Rush," Gus called to his radioman. The guy's name was actually Charles, but everyone called him Rush Limbaugh, or Rush for short, because he was the radio guy. Rush called in the GPS coordinates and got an immediate confirmation back from air control.

"Three minutes, Fish," he called over to Gus.

The unit sat there and let the enemy waste ammo with its fitful small arms fire until, exactly two minutes and forty seconds later, they all heard the thin high screaming of an F-16 jet blasting up the valley from the south. The jet loosed a couple of rockets on its first pass, circled around and sent a couple more into the hills on the other side of the highway. Above the village, clouds of smoke and dust billowed upwards as the jet's missiles exploded against the rocky hillsides. After the jet finished its two passes, the valley was quiet. The gunfire ceased.

Gus and his men stood up and came out into the open.

"We goin' up to check?" Bucky asked the lieutenant, nodding at the towering slopes. "Clean up the mess?"

"Nah," Gus said, shaking his head. "Today we're only doing S&O. Our orders are to look but not touch today."

"Fine by me," Bucky said. "Lotta caves up there. We'd be here for weeks trying to clean all those rat's nests out."

Gus smiled at him and went back to the Cougar. He radioed in an updated report and, after a short delay, was ordered to turn the convoy around and return to base. "But be careful, Fish," the tinny voice said over the radio.

Gus disconnected and was about to order the men back into the vehicles when he noticed several of them scramble into shooting positions, pointing their AK-47s up the road. He looked out through the yellow tinted glass of the bulletproof windshield.

Two children, a girl and an older boy, were coming down the dusty highway. The boy, maybe ten years old, was waving a white kerchief and the girl, who looked to be a couple years younger, was holding his hand. They looked like brother and sister.

"Hold fire," Gus ordered. The men kept their rifles leveled and ready to shoot. They had all been in theater now for more than a year and they all knew what could happen. Most of them had seen and all of them had heard stories of children used by the Taliban to carry out suicide missions against the allied troops.

They all watched as the children continued to approach. The boy was waving his white flag frantically as if it were the Fourth of July and there was a prize at the end for the most enthusiastic.

Gus called out, "Where's Hakeem?" He was the unit's Afghan liaison and the only one fluent in the language. Hakeem came forward, near the open doorway of Gus' Cougar, and watched the approaching children with narrow, suspicious eyes.

"Whaddya think?" Gus said, speaking softly.

Hakeem's eyes never wavered, studying both children, what they were wearing, how they looked, how they were acting.

"Hard to tell," he said finally.

"Tell them to stop," Gus ordered. Hakeem called out a command in the harsh guttural patois of the Afghan language. The children pulled up short in the middle of the road. They were about a hundred yards from the front end of the Cougar.

The boy kept waving his white flag. His other arm was wrapped around his sister's back, holding her close. Her face was shrouded by her head scarf. The soldiers could not see her eyes or expression.

Hakeem barked a few more words at the children. The boy smiled broadly, nodding his head and shouted something back.

"He says they want candy," Hakeem said to Gus. "Americans always have candy."

"Tell him to drop the white thing and show us his hands," Gus said to Hakeem. "Her, too."

Hakeem relayed the message. The boy smiled and nodded enthusiastically. But he didn't do what he had been told. He continued to grasp both his white flag and the hand of the girl at his side. The girl looked at him and said something. The soldiers could not hear what it was.

Then, she pulled away from his side, pulled her hand free with a wrenching movement and turned and started to run back down the highway in the direction they had just come. The boy turned and shouted something at her.

"Shit!" Gus said.

Simultaneously, the boy looked back at the soldiers, said something to himself and then the road exploded. The shock wave was loud and it rocked some of the soldiers back on their heels, but the children were far enough away that nobody was hurt in the blast. Except, of course, for the children, who pretty much vanished into thin air as the boy's explosive vest detonated. Before the shockwave receded, the gunfire started again, again from the surrounding hillsides. One of Gus' men, who had been standing there watching, took a bullet in his wrist: he said a bad word and spun away into cover behind a mud wall.

For a long moment, Gus was motionless and silent. Like the others gathered around, he could not believe what he just witnessed. Two young lives ended in a flash and a bang and a spray of blood and matter. It was incomprehensible. And yet, it was real. It had happened. Right in front of all their eyes.

"Right," Gus said finally. His voice was hollow and cracked. "Everybody OK?"

There were murmurs and sounds of assent from his men. They were as emotionally drained as their leader.

"Chicken Wing," he called to the soldier who had been hit by the bullet. "You gonna live?"

"Fuck yeah, Fish," the man called Chicken Wing responded. "It was a through-and-through. I didn't need all that blood anyway." He was busy applying a field dressing to his wound.

"What next, Fish?" asked Bucky, Gus' sergeant.

Gus didn't answer, staring down the road at the blackened depression. Thinking of the two young lives that had been there just a few minutes ago.

"Gus?"

Gus blinked and forced himself to come back to the reality of the present. He shook his head as if to clear out the bad stuff. "Right," he said, nodding at Bucky. "Set up a perimeter. Anybody who manages to pot one of those sonsabitches up there will get extra ice cream for dessert tonight."

"You got it, Fish," Bucky said, and he crawled out of the Humvee to begin positioning the squad.

The men were stuck there in that empty village for another two hours or so, exchanging gunfire with the enemy. None of them ventured down the road to look at the blackened crater in the middle--the small arms gunfire kept them pinned behind their cover. Gus called in two more air strikes, but it was midafternoon before the situation was calm and quiet enough for Gus to round up his squad, load them in the trucks and head back to Talaqan.

It was a long and quiet ride back to base. Everyone was thinking about the small boy with the white flag and his younger sister.

CHAPTER
1

GUS HADDOCK PULLED his squad car into an angled parking space in front of the Commons Cup. Before he shut it off, he thumbed the radio button.

"Mornin' Dottie," he said. "I'm at the Cuppa. Goin' in for a brew. Can I bring you anything?"

The radio squawked briefly and Dorothy Adams, the police dispatcher, responded.

"Thanks, Chief," she said, "But I'm good. Brought in my Thermos today. But I heard Betty's baked up her cranberry scones today. If there are any left, you oughta jump on it. Out of this world."

"Roger," Gus said. "I'll be right in."

It was a glorious October morning and Gus allowed himself a moment to enjoy the view of the triangular village green of Little Penwick, Rhode Island. The spire of the Congregational church pierced the bright blue and cloudless sky, while the bright white clapboards of the old church contrasted with the gray, tilted, mossy headstones in the surrounding church yard. The leaves on the tall trees that ringed the village green—mostly maples and oaks—were starting to turn to their autumn colors of yellow and red.

Gus Haddock paused for a moment longer. He really wanted a cup of coffee, but he really didn't want to undergo the scrutiny of the other people of Little Penwick, several of whom were probably inside, sipping coffee and munching on cranberry scones while they gossiped about everyone else who lived in this strange little corner of Rhode Island. And Gus was sure they would be talking about him, and his family.

But the need for caffeine won out. Gus pulled open the door to the place and strode inside. A quick glance around showed Gus that the usuals were in place. The president of the town council, Bob Murtha, was sitting with Louise Cox, the town clerk. Each had a steaming mug of coffee and a paper plate with a partially eaten scone on the table in front of them. The Barkleys, an old couple who lived down near Harbor Point, occupied another table and had their noses buried in the morning newspaper. Clancy, one of the Public Works drivers, was sitting at the counter, trying to flirt with Rebecca, a girl in her late teens who was the current server. Since Clancy was pushing fifty and wore a greasy sweatshirt that barely covered his prodigious beer gut, Gus did not believe the flirtation was going to prove ultimately successful. Back in the small kitchen prep area behind the counter, through a pass-through window, Gus could see Betty Billingsly, the owner of the Commons Cup, pencil tucked behind her ear, frizzy gray hair shooting off in all directions, while she deftly assembled a breakfast sandwich for somebody.

All of them, although not all at once, looked at Gus Haddock as he came in. They saw a tall, rangy man, hair kept short in the military style, although not quite as close-shaved as when he was in the Army. He had broad shoulders, long arms, and a solid, fit-looking body. He was clean shaven, with a strong square chin and deep-set gray eyes. He wore a pair of dark khaki slacks and a white uniform blouse, with epaulets on the shoulders, two pleated pockets on the front with two-inch flaps. There was a gold badge affixed over his left breast. No necktie. Gus Haddock hated wearing neckties.

Rebecca immediately ended her conversation with Clancy—it had not been much of a two-way discussion—and came over to the take-out counter, behind which Gus Haddock was standing.

"Mornin,' Chief," she said, giving him a bright toothy smile. "Whatcha have?"

"Large coffee," Gus said. "One sugar. No cream. To go, please."

"You got it," the girl said and turned to fill one of the white cardboard containers. "You wanna scone with that?"

"Two," Gus said. "Please."

"You got it," she said again, and, after fixing the lid on the coffee, she snapped open a small brown paper bag with a practiced flip of her wrist, lifted the glass cover from the baked-goods tray on the counter and dropped two of the golden brown scones, dotted with red cranberries, into the bag. She folded the top of the bag down neatly. She carried the coffee and the bag over to the cash register, punched a few buttons and the machine hummed while it spit out a couple of inches of receipt. "Four forty-two," she said. "Including tax."

Gus handed over a five. "Keep the change," he said, nodding at her. She gave him another big toothy smile.

"You doin' all right then, Gus?" asked Betty, who came out from the kitchen with a plate which she put down in front of Clancy. "Gettin' settled in?"

"Doing fine, Betty," Gus said.

"How's Julius?" she asked.

"Well as can be expected," Gus said.

"You tell him we miss him, you hear?" she said.

Gus nodded, picked up his order, and turned to go.

Bob Murtha headed him off before he could get out the door.

"Mornin' Chief," Murtha said.

"Bob," Gus said noncommittally. Murtha was in his sixties, dressed in slacks, a white shirt and a sweater. His body was round, his hair mostly missing, and his reading glasses dangled on a chain around his neck. He was the head of the five-man town council, and had been for probably twenty years now. Other members of the council came and went, but Bob Murtha was always re-elected and always named as council president. Gus had an almost reflexive dislike for the man, having been raised by a father who frequently came home complaining about whatever the town council had done, but he knew better than to deliberately do anything to make an enemy of him. Murtha had control of too many levers that could affect the police department, and both men knew it.

"We still on for our eleven o'clock?" Murtha said.

"Unless armed terrorists choose today to storm Horseneck Beach," Gus said.

"Ha-ha," Murtha chuckled. "Good one."

"What is it we will be discussing?" the chief asked.

Murtha looked around the small cafe filled with citizens of Little Penwick and frowned.

"I think it's better if we wait to talk about that in your office," he said. "It's mostly about some paperwork."

"Great," Gus said, smiling. "I love paperwork. The more the merrier. All of us crime stoppers love the paperwork part of the job."

Murtha looked at Gus blankly. "Right," he said finally. "See you around eleven."

Gus put the paper bag in his teeth, freeing up his right hand to push open the sticky front door of the Commons Cup and made his way outside. The sun was still shining brightly and the view of the village green was still spectacular.

"Ooo, he's so hot," Rebecca said to Betty as they watched through the shop window as Gus climbed back in his car, backed it up and drove away. "He's not married, right?"

"Down, girl," Betty said, going back in the kitchen, getting the grill ready for the lunch crowd that would begin filing in soon. "Gus has a lot on his plate right now. He's only been the chief for what…six months?"

"Less than that," said Clancy, who had been eavesdropping from his stool at the counter, eating his egg sandwich. "He got here around the middle of June. Got out of the Army in May, I think. Special Forces. Anbar, Fallujah, Syria. All them fun places."

"He did three tours," Betty said, nodding. "Then his Dad asked him to come back home. Take over the family business."

"Chief of police is not a hereditary position," Bob Murtha said, back at his table with Louise. "The council appointed him acting chief. Though it was on the recommendation of his father."

"Was that before or after old Jules was hauled off to the state pen?" Clancy said with a smirk, twirling around on his stool to confront Murtha.

"During, Mister Clancy," Murtha said. "Julius Haddock wanted to ensure continuity in the police force in the town, and felt that his son was the right candidate to ensure that. After all, he'd been on the force since he was twenty, before he joined up with the Army five years later. We interviewed him, in public and in executive session, and made the conditional offer of employment. He's acting chief. We will evaluate his performance in nine months."

"Pretty damn convenient, you ask me," Clancy said, mostly under his breath. But Murtha heard him. The Commons Cup was not a big place.

"Think what you will," Murtha said. "But the results so far are excellent. Gus Haddock was a leader of men in the Army, and he's doing a fine job leading the department now. He'll make an excellent chief of police."

"If you say so," Clancy said. Finished with his sandwich, he tossed a few bills down on the counter and left.

Gus drove the three hundred yards from the Commons Cup to the public safety complex around the corner and just off the town triangle. The relatively new brick building contained Little Penwick's police and fire departments. The building had been built twenty years earlier after a Little Penwick patrolman pulled over a car operated by a South African gangster who worked with an international cartel to import Pakistani hashish into the United States on fishing trawlers. The result of the bust was that the town of Little Penwick was able to confiscate about $10 million in dirty drug money, as long as it spent the funds on law enforcement. So the town voted to build the fancy new public safety complex, which was one of the most modern in the state. The arresting officer got a nice Christmas bonus that year, as well.

Gus entered the door on the left, which opened onto a long central hallway. On the left, through a plate glass wall, was the squad room, with four metal desks covered in computers, phones and stacks of paper. Down the hall, towards the back of the building, was the holding area, with three small barred cells. And Gus' office was to the right, opposite the door to the squad room.

There was only one person in the squad room, Buzzy Franklin, the town's chief of detectives. In fact, he was the only detective. Little Penwick's police department was small, like the town itself. In addition to the chief, the Little Penwick Police Department consisted of Lieutenant Commander Barry

Callahan, Sergeant Jessica Martin, Detective Sergeant Franklin and eight patrolmen. As is the case in many small town departments, four of the patrol officers were probies—probational officers in their first year of service, fresh out of the Rhode Island Police Academy in Warwick, on the other side of the state. The other four officers had records of service that ranged from four to eighteen years. Gus tried to pair one of the new guys with an experienced hand when he could as he set up the working shifts to cover both day and night patrol.

Gus walked down the hall and pushed into the almost entirely dark dispatch office. Dottie Adams was sitting behind her desk, a curved affair with multiple monitors, a keyboard, a radio microphone and nothing else, save for her cup of coffee. Dottie was a silver-haired senior, round and solid, dressed in jeans and a casual top. She'd been the town's dispatcher for police and fire forever, it seemed. She was chatting away with someone apparently on her telephone, her headphones covering her ears, and the boom mic arching around from her headphones. Gus grabbed a tissue from a box on the credenza behind Dottie, reached into the paper bag and took out one of the scones, which he placed at Dottie's elbow. Without missing a beat in her conversation, Dottie blew him a kiss.

Gus went into his office next door, closed the door behind him, and sank into the leather chair behind his desk. Unlike those in the squad room, the chief's desk was bare of clutter. It had one of those blotter pads in the middle of the desk, a telephone on the left, and a computer keyboard and monitor to the right. Dottie had left a small pile of pink While You

Were Out message slips tucked into the margin of his blotter. The walls of the office were covered in rows of photographs, mostly of local sports teams—softball, youth basketball, soccer—the police department had sponsored over the years, along with some citations and ribbons. Gus had not touched the walls since he moved into the office: all this stuff had been hung by his father, Julius Haddock, during his twenty=plus years of service as the town's chief of police.

Gus sat down, took a bite of his scone, peeled the top off his coffee cup and tossed it into the wastebasket under his desk. He scanned the message slips and decided none of them were so important as to interrupt his coffee drinking time. He clicked his computer open with the mouse and did a quick survey of the news of the day. Nothing was happening in Little Penwick, very little was happening in Newport County, of which Little Penwick was one of six towns, and not much more was going on in the other 38 towns and cities in the entire state of Rhode Island. Gus nodded approvingly as he sipped at the coffee: he liked it when nothing was happening.

He next checked the State Police website, logging in to the intelligence and crime report section reserved for law enforcement. He scanned quickly through the overnight arrest reports which, as usual, were dominated by entries from the state's bigger cities and towns: Providence, Pawtucket, Central Falls, Newport, Warwick and Cranston. A couple of shootings, some car thefts, breaking and entering, and the usual DUI list, which last night had been twelve arrests. Nothing unusual. Pretty typical for the small state of just over a million residents, not counting the illegal immigrants living in the state because nobody counted them. Unless they committed a crime, Gus thought to himself, which they frequently did.

There was a knock at his door and Buzzy stuck his head in.

"Got a minute, Chief?" he asked, eyebrows arched upwards. Antone "Buzzy" Franklin had been a police officer in Little Penwick for fifteen years and had been promoted to chief detective five years ago. He was a short, stocky, fireplug of a man, with no discernible neck, buzzcut hair, bulging arm muscles and a fleshy face that ranged from bright pink to fiery red depending on his mood.

Gus motioned him to come in, and Buzzy, holding a green-covered case report, flopped down in one of the two guest chairs in front of the chief's desk.

"S'up?" Gus said.

"You remember that abandoned pick-up we found about a month ago?" Franklin said. "Down by the Weetamoo Swamp?"

"You mean, just outside the property line of Danny Ferro," Gus said.

"Yeah," Buzz nodded. "Of course, there are two other property owners whose lines are near that spot, too, but Ferro's land starts about ten yards from where we found that truck."

Neither man needed any further discussion. The Ferro family had lived in and around Weetamoo Swamp practically from the time the glacial melt had receded leaving behind the wet and rocky terrain of southern New England. And that had been a few hundred thousand years ago.

And both men had been out to the Ferro place numerous times, since roughly half of all the crimes committed in Little Penwick could be traced back to one or another of the Ferro family. Every town, Gus knew, had a bad-seed family like the Ferros. No good explanation why—it was just the way things were. There was a standing order at the police department that no officer could visit the Ferro place alone. Two squad cars and four officers were required, even if they were just serving papers. It was a policy necessary both as a show of force and for the safety of the officers. The Ferro land was well over a hundred acres, even though much of it was swampland, and the extended Ferro clan occupied about a half-dozen trailers and a few houses stuck here and there among the thick trees. There were dozens of rusted out old cars, five or six energetic pit bulls on chains and God only knew how many firearms, legal or otherwise, could be found out there. When the Little Penwick PD visited the Ferro property, they did so in force. With eyes wide open and heads on a swivel.

"So what about the pick-up?" Gus said.

"As you know, we found out it had been stolen over in Hartford about a year ago," Buzzy said. "There was no registration, plates or anything in the vehicle, so we had to trace the VIN. But there was a crumpled Coke can in the back of the cab. We got some partial prints off it."

"And?"

"And the state crime lab just said there's an eighty percent probability that the fingerprints belonged to Angelo Ferro, Senior," Buzzy said. He sat and watched for Gus' reaction.

"No shit?" Gus said. He kept his voice level. "The same Angelo Ferro who's gone missing?"

"Yup."

"And who the staties think was offed by Julius C. Haddock, former Chief of Police and also known as my dad? Who is currently held in jail and charged with obstructing a state investigation?"

"Yup."

"Well that's interesting," Gus said. "There's no way one can tell the age of a fingerprint, correct?"

"Not really, no," Buzzy nodded. "I mean, you can draw some conclusions based on the condition of the print. And there are some academics out there who think that you can measure the migration of the biomolecules in a fingerprint to get a fix on its age. I'm sure the FBI lab rats are working on that. But generally, no: we can't tell the exact age of a print. And, again, the ones on the Coke can were just partials. Part of a thumb and almost all of the right forefinger."

"So we don't know when Angelo Ferro was holding the Coke can," Gus said. "Whether it was before or after ... the time he disappeared."

"Nope," Buzzy said. "Coulda been two weeks ago or two years."

"No other prints in the vehicle?"

"Nah," Buzzy said. "The Ferros musta wiped it clean before they dumped the truck. Of course, being Ferros, they missed the can under the seat. It could have been sitting there for weeks before we got the call to deal with it."

"OK," Gus said. "Update the files. Keep looking."

CHAPTER 2

POLICE BLOTTER
NEWPORT COUNTY NEWS

6:25 p.m. Little Penwick Police reported that a Nissan sedan, driven by Robert S. Gerden, collided with a deer on Easterly Road.

Mr. Gerden's car sustained damage to its front left bumper. The collision with the deer caused the driver to lose control of the vehicle, which swerved off the road, spun around and crashed into a stone wall, causing further damage to the rear bumper.

Police responded and found Mr. Gerden shaken, but unhurt in the incident. He was escorted home and his vehicle was towed.

GUS HAD TAKEN over a late shift from one of the patrol officers that afternoon. Jerry Hanlon had driven a prisoner over to Newport late that morning, and then was scheduled to appear in the District Court on Washington Square to testify in two preliminary hearings on some DUI cases that had finally worked their way through the court docket.

So, as he often did in those circumstances, Gus filled in for Jerry on the late afternoon patrol shift. Other than some residents returning home from their office jobs in Providence or Fall River or Newport, traffic was light. There was not much going on, which was exactly how Gus liked it.

But in the gloaming of the autumn evening—the sun was setting earlier and earlier every day—Bob Gerden, a sixty-something man returning home with the groceries for his wife Mabel, never saw the large buck jump out of the woods on Easterly Road. The fall rutting season was in full bloom, and the thousands of deer that lived in the woods and swamps of Little Penwick were horny. The bucks were chasing the does, and the does were on the run.

So Gerden didn't see the buck until it was right off his left quarter. He hit the brake in a panic stop, but there was no time to do anything. The deer hit the front bumper with a sickening thud, and then Bob was fighting to maintain control of his car. The collision plus the panic braking set the rear end free and it began a slow spin around to the left, while the car drifted with the screech of tires, off the road to the right. When the wheels hit the soft dirt and grasses of the verge, it finished its spin and then drifted backwards and to the right, until the car's rear end swung around with another screech of the tires, crunched into the stone wall and stopped.

Bob was more than a little shook up—the entire incident lasted maybe five seconds, tops—but there was nothing physically wrong with him. His car was a mess, but he seemed to be OK. He managed to fish his cell phone out of his jacket pocket and called 9-1-1.

Dottie called Gus on the radio and he was at the scene within three or four minutes. Gus pulled his Ford Navigator, blue lights flashing, around the body of the dead deer in the middle of the road and stopped next to Bob Gerden's crumpled car. He called Dottie with the initial incident report and then got out.

Gerden was out of his own car by then, looking first at the front, and then the rear sections of his car, shaking his head.

"You OK, Bob?" Gus asked.

"Goddam deer," Bob replied. "Gonna need new bumpers front and rear and a little body work on the front panel."

"But you're OK, right?"

"Mabel is gonna kill me," Bob said. "She always thinks I drive too fast."

"How fast were you going?"

"Oh, hell, Gus, I don't know," he said. "Not that fast. Damn thing just leaped out of the woods. Nothing I could do. Goddam deer."

"You had anything to drink tonight?" Gus asked. He knew this was a question that could set someone off, especially someone whose car had just been damaged. But he had to ask, anyway.

"Not yet," Bob said. "But ask me again as soon as I get home. 'Cause I fully intend to knock back a few."

"I hear ya," Gus said.

He went back to his squad car, opened the passenger door and pulled out his notebook. He fished around until he found an accident report form, clicked his pen open and began writing. After he filled in all the squares and ticked all the correct boxes, he called in to Dottie and asked her to send a tow truck out.

"Get your groceries," he told the older man. "I'll run you home. You can have your cocktail and things will look better in the morning. They always do."

Gerden began moving his grocery bags into the back of the squad car. Gus put on a pair of gloves, then grabbed the rear legs of the deer and dragged the carcass out of the road, leaving a smear of blood across the center line. It was not a large buck, Gus estimated it at less than three years old, but it still weighed around ninety pounds. He had never taken physics at school, nor veterinary medicine, but Gus knew that ninety pounds of living flesh had no chance against two thousand pounds of sheet metal traveling at around 50 mph.

"Too bad nobody can eat the damn thing," Bob said, watching. "At least somebody would get something of value."

"Don't worry about that," Gus said, peeling his gloves off again once the deer had been moved away from the road. "I'll call the Department of Environmental Management later tonight, but they won't send anybody out until morning, at the earliest. But there are several folks here in town who monitor the police radio. I'll bet a couple of them are already on the way over here. This deer will be butchered and in somebody's freezer by midnight."

"No shit?" Bob said. "I don't know if I think that's great, or disgusting."

"Nothing goes to waste," Gus said. "If the humans didn't come get him, the coyotes and other critters would be all over it. By the time the DEM got here in the morning, be nothing left but a few bones."

Bob Gerden stood and looked at the dead deer in the tall grass by the side of the road, his hands on his hips.

"Goddam deer," he said again.

He got in the squad car and Gus Haddock drove him home.

CHAPTER 3

Just after eleven, there was a knock at the door.

"Come," called Gus, who was methodically working his way through a pile of reports, overtime requests, purchase orders and other routine paperwork.

The door opened and Bob Murtha came in, followed by a young woman.

"Chief Haddock," Murtha said, "I want to introduce you to Maggie Wells. She's an assistant district attorney with the AG's office in Providence."

Gus stood up and reached across his desk to shake hands with her. The woman had a head of curly brown hair, sparkling dark eyes and gave Gus a brief smile of greeting. Not unfriendly, but noncommittal. She was of medium height, probably around five eight or so, proportional and shapely and looked to be fit. She held a slim brown leather briefcase under her arm and was wearing a conservative business suit: a tailored gray skirt that fell down to just past her knees, matching suit coat, white silk blouse and just a few silver jangly bits around her neck. Gus motioned the two visitors to sit.

"I understand you recently got back from a few tours overseas," Maggie said to Gus as she settled in. "Thanks for your service."

Gus nodded. He was always a bit uncomfortable whenever someone said something like that to him. And it was said a lot. He wasn't sure how to respond, so he usually kept silent. "What brings you down to Little Penwick?" Gus asked, tilting his head in Maggie's direction.

"At the request of the Attorney General, Ms. Wells has been appointed by the Superior Court in Providence to be Special Master," Murtha said.

"Well, congratulations," Gus said. "What does that mean?"

"The Special Master will be, in effect, the overseer of your department until further notice," Murtha said. "She will approve all personnel decisions, oversee the progress of all investigations, and ensure the Little Penwick Police Department is operating within the boundaries of Rhode Island law."

There was an uncomfortable silence in the room while Gus stared across his desk, first at Murtha and then at Maggie Wells.

"Did you request this?" Gus said, finally, addressing Murtha.

"No, I did not," Murtha said.

"The Attorney General was concerned about the situation with your father," Maggie said, sitting forward on the edge of her chair.

"The situation with my father was entirely created by the Attorney General," Gus said. "My Dad's in jail because the Attorney General put him there."

"That's not entirely accurate," Maggie said, shaking her head. Her ringlets of hair vibrated when she moved her head. "Your father, the former chief of police, refused to cooperate with a state approved investigation into the disappearance of Angelo Ferro. That refusal resulted in a contempt citation by the Superior Court, a trial before a judge, and your father's incarceration. Julius Haddock can walk out of the ACI today if he tells us what he knows."

"He's told you what he knows," Gus said. "You have chosen not to believe him."

"Regardless," she said, "The Attorney General has decided he is, umm, uncomfortable with the former chief's son running this department without oversight. Especially since your experience at this job is quite limited. So he asked the Court to appoint me as Special Master."

"I've been an officer in this town's force for more than five years," Gus said. "I was deputy chief for six months before I joined up. I grew up in this town. So you can tell the Attorney General that I know the job, I know the town, I know the people, and that I know more about policing in Little Penwick than he does. Tell me, when was the last time the AG came down here and looked around? I'm guessing the fifth of never."

"The Attorney General is fully cognizant of your background, Chief Haddock," Maggie said. She was trying to keep her tone modulated and even, as tempers were beginning to percolate in the chief's small office. "He told me that he sees my role simply as backup. I'm not going to try and micromanage your department, I can assure you."

"Great," Gus said. He picked up some papers from the stack on the desk in front of him. "Let's see … Patrolman Jamie McMaster is asking for three days off next week because his wife is about to give birth to their third child. It's their third one, right Bob?"

"Yes," Murtha said.

"That OK with you, Ms. Master?" Gus continued. "How about this one?" He picked up another paper. "We need new tires for about half our squad cars. It's been two-plus years. The low bid came in from Tire Warehouse over in Newport, but Sammy White down at the BP station wants the contract, too, and his bid is about a hundred bucks more. Whaddya think? Give the business to a local guy, or go outside the town and save a hundred bucks? Can't wait to hear what Special Master Wells wants to do with that."

"Gus…" Murtha tried to interrupt.

"Oh, hang on, here's a good one," Gus continued as if Murtha hadn't spoken. "The Little Penwick Church Basketball League wants to know if we're gonna buy the back-page ad for the annual program again. We usually take a picture of the entire force in front of the building here and say 'With Compliments of Your Police Department.' You think that'll fly, or do you need to get approval from the Superior Court in Providence first? There may be some pressing issues about the separation between church and state that will keep you asshole lawyers busy for weeks."

"I understand ..." Maggie started to speak.

"No," Gus said sharply. "I really don't think you do understand. You come waltzing in here thinking you can just take over this department and everything will be super swell. You think my officers will take orders from you?"

"It's not my orders," Maggie said. "The orders come from the Superior Court."

"Which judge?"

"O'Rourke," she said. "Frederick O'Rourke."

Gus blew out his breath in a snort.

"Jesus," he said. "Freddie O'Rourke. How old is he now, a hundred and six?"

"I believe he's eighty-two," she said.

"Still mobbed up to the gills?"

"That's a defamatory statement," she said.

Gus smiled at her. "So sue me," he said.

"Listen, Gus," Bob Murtha decided he had to play peacemaker. "I know this has got to be upsetting. I didn't like it very much when I heard about it."

"Which was when, Bob?" Gus retorted. "You knew this shit was coming and didn't let me know? Whose side are you on?"

"I'm on the side of the town," Murtha said sternly. "If we don't agree to this temporary probationary period, there's an excellent chance the state will cancel our accreditation. You and the entire department could get laid off. All cases that are brought by this department, whether a traffic stop or a drug bust, could get thrown out of court. They'd bring in the State Police to patrol the town, and I know you don't want that any more than I do. Those guys are the real assholes."

Gus turned and looked at Maggie Wells. She stared back at him defiantly.

"That true?" he said. "You would close us down?"

"That would be a decision made by the Attorney General," she said. "But, yes, I think he would."

"Would you like to hear my opinion of the Attorney General?" Gus said.

"I don't think so," Maggie Wells said. "I'm guessing it's equally defamatory. And I was told to come down here today and make a connection. Which would be better than me having you arrested for spreading calumnies about the top law enforcement officer in the state."

Gus huffed out a breath in response to that, but otherwise stayed silent. Bob Murtha nodded at him approvingly.

"How does this work?" Gus said.

"How does what work?" Maggie responded.

"This Special Master bullshit. You gonna come down here every day and sit in that chair and second-guess everything I do? Or do I have to fill out my paperwork in triplicate now and haul my work up to Providence every other day so you can supervise my decisions from there?"

"I have no intention of trying to second guess your decisions, chief," she said. "I think you should go ahead with the Church League program, give the patrolman time off for paternity leave and buy the tires from the local guy. Or don't.

My job is to make certain the department is staffed properly and provide some oversight into any investigations your department may launch."

"Like against the Ferro crowd?"

"Yes," she said, staring at him. "Especially against the Ferro family. They are, we've heard, planning to file a major lawsuit against the town of Little Penwick and the state of Rhode Island, claiming police malpractice and worse in the disappearance of the patriarch of the family, Angelo Ferro. We don't want to give them any further ammunition. So I want to be read in any time you think about doing anything with them."

"Ah," Gus said, nodding to himself. "I think I'm beginning to understand, The AG is worried someone is going to sue his finely tailored ass. That wouldn't be a good look for when he runs for governor next year, would it? You got a big new job lined up with the campaign? I've heard that for a little state, there's a whole lotta cash floating around in Rhode Island's political circles. And every wheel needs some grease, am I right?"

"No," Maggie said, frowning. "I'm not into politics. I work for the state and plan to continue doing so."

"Right," Gus said. "And the Ferro family isn't offering to toss a few hundred grand into the AG's campaign kitty if he keeps the Little Penwick PD off their back."

"Again," Maggie said, "I don't do politics. But something happened to Angelo Ferro last January and I'm sure the family wants to know what that was. And your father seems to be the only person in the state who knows what happened."

"Swell," Gus said. "My detective, Buzz Franklin, told me an hour or so ago that the state crime lab found a fingerprint belonging to Angelo on a can of soda recovered from an abandoned and presumably stolen pick-up we towed from a public road that was about fifteen feet outside the property line of the Ferro compound."

"Really?" Maggie said, sitting up straight.

"Yes," Gus said. "But there is no way for us to tell how old the fingerprint is. It could have been made before Angelo disappeared, or after."

"What are you planning to do with this evidence?" Maggie asked.

"Not sure you can call it evidence," Gus said. "It's a can of Coke with a partial print that seems to belong to Angelo Ferro. Found in a vehicle, reportedly stolen, that had no other identifying evidence inside or out. Parked on a public street, not private property. If I could find Angelo Ferro, I could ask him if he stole the pick-up, or if he dropped a can of Coke inside the vehicle, which might qualify as littering. Either way, I suspect he'd break out in laughter. Assuming he's still alive and capable of laughing."

"Do you know if he's alive?" Maggie said, eyes narrowed and lips pursed.

"No, I do not," Gus said.

"Are you looking for him?"

"The department has a bulletin posted to be on the lookout," Gus said. "So far, it's been more than ten months and no one has seen hide nor hair. Which many of us consider to be a good thing. Angelo Ferro was, or is, not one of the better angels, you know."

"Again," Maggie responded hotly, "Whether he is an angel or not, he has all the rights that belong to any citizen."

"Well maybe as Special Master, you can find his sorry ass and tell him that yourself," Gus said. "I got more important things to work on." He motioned at the stack of paper in front of him.

"Thanks, Gus," Bob Murtha said, rising. "I would be happy to try and be an intermediary here, if either of you want that, or think it's important. My door is always open and I stand ready to help both of you find a way to make this work."

Gus said nothing. He was still angry about not being told what was coming down. Maggie Wells also said nothing, but stood, picked up her briefcase, and walked out behind Murtha.

Once they had left the building, Gus continued to sit behind his desk, steaming. Having recently been in the military, he understood the concept of chain of command, the need for hierarchy, and how to obey orders, even if he felt those orders were total bullshit. So he knew he'd have to suck it up and deal with this one. Even if that made him furious.

There was another knock at his office door. He looked up and saw the head of his second-in-command, Barry Callahan, peer in. Gus waved him in impatiently.

"Bad time?" Callahan said coming into the office. The lieutenant wore a full snappy uniform, as was his habit. Striped blue pants, fancy white dress shirt with navy colored epaulets on the shoulders, gold badge over the heart. Unlike Gus, Callahan always wore his thin black necktie, held in place with a gold tie pin right at the nipple level. He usually wore his high-peaked officer's cap as well, with its gold oak-leaf filigree on the glossy black front brim, but not when he was working inside.

Gus sighed. "It's always a bad time around here," he said.

"Yeah, I heard about the new Special Master," Callahan said. "What's she like?"

Gus thought about that for a moment. How did he hear about Maggie Wells before I did? he wondered. He decided not to ask.

"Just met her," he responded instead. "We'll see how it goes."

"Well, if there's anything I can do, just holler," Callahan said. Then he remembered why he had come into the chief's office in the first place. "I've got the new list of the autumn training classes over at the Police Academy," he said. "I've taken the liberty of drawing up a schedule. Basically, we'll be down one officer a week for the next two months, until they all get through the program."

He put a folder down on Gus' desk. Gus looked at it sadly. It looked thick.

"OK, thanks Callahan," he said. "I'll take a look."

"Right, Chief," Callahan said. He pivoted smartly and left the office.

Gus sat there and stewed in silence for a few minutes. The business with the state butting into his department's operations was troubling enough. He wondered what the real reason for appointing a Special Master was. He didn't believe for a second he was being told the truth. And then there was Callahan. Nobody ever called him Barry, for some reason. It was always Callahan. Gus knew that Callahan had been expecting to be named chief after his father had been arrested and sent to jail. Murtha had warned him to be aware of the older man's resentment. So far, their relationship had been cool, but professional. Gus hadn't detected any overt attitude problems. But you never knew what went on behind the scenes and out of sight. He even wondered, for a moment or two, if it had been Callahan driving the move to bring in Maggie Wells. That kind of sleight-of-hand-action would have been exactly the kind of thing an old veteran would pull off.

After sitting there and stewing for several long minutes, Gus finally got up and walked down the hall, pushing his way into the men's restroom at the end of the hall. He off-loaded the morning's coffee, then washed his hands in the sink. He looked up at his image in the mirror handing over the sink. The man looking back at him seemed angry: his face was red and sweaty, and his lips were turned down at the corners.

Gus ripped a few paper towels out of the container mounted on the wall next to the sink, dried his hands and tossed the wads into the trash receptacle. Then, he turned and punched the wall. It was a short punch, fired from the hips, shoulders rotating hard, his right fist following a short, straight path into the wall. He was lucky that he missed the metal stud upon which the slab of sheetrock had been affixed, and his powerful blow caused the sheetrock to buckle inwards.

"Fuck me," he hissed through clenched teeth. He looked at the hole in the wall without seeing it, and walked out of the restroom.

CHAPTER
4

GUS HAD THE dream again, Sunday morning. He awoke
before dawn, bathed in sweat, his sheets and pillow sopping.
It was those two kids, the ones from the valley north of Talaqan. In the dream, they had walked down the road and right
into the village. They were smiling and happy and the men
gave them candy bars, which made them smile all the more.
Everyone was smiling and happy and feeling good. And then
the little girl, the one who was about six or seven years old,
who had looked up at Gus, mouth wreathed in melting choco-
late, and she said "Allahu Akbar," and that's when Gus awoke,
drenched in flop sweat. He had that dream, or some close
variation, about once or twice a month. Sometimes it was the
girl who spoke, sometimes her brother. But Gus always woke
up before the next thing happened. Before the button was

pushed and the bomb went off. He felt lucky, but only a little bit, that he didn't have to relive that part of the nightmare, over and over again.

He had gotten out of bed, stripped the sheets and put them in the washing machine down the hall and taken a long hot shower. He closed his eyes and let that hot water pour onto his back. Then he made some coffee, scrambled a couple of eggs, popped some bread in the toaster and sat down to eat. He put on the radio and listened to music while he ate. But he was only half listening. He was picturing the depression that the blast had left in the middle of the hard-pack dirt road. Black, ashy. And no sign of what had been two kids, just seconds before.

He went outside and checked in the back seat of the squad car to make sure he hadn't left anything in there. While he was straightening up, an older woman came walking up the long driveway, a long haired Irish setter at her heels. When the dog saw Gus, it leaped forward, tail wagging furiously.

Gus saw it coming and turned to greet the animal, bending down low and scratching behind its ears. The dog wrapped itself around Gus' legs and let him scratch and pat and murmur approving words at it.

"Morning Gus," the woman said when she reached his car. "You going up to see Julius?"

Gus looked over at her, nodding. "Hey Miz P," he said. "Yeah, pretty much a standing appointment for Sunday at noon."

Vera Phillips was Gus Haddock's landlord. When he got home after the Army, his father had mentioned that she had a nice little bedsit over her garage. He'd gone over to look, decided it would suit his needs perfectly, and had put a deposit down that day. Vera Phillips had lived in Little Penwick her entire life, knew everyone in town and where they came from, and was now living out her retirement years quietly and happily in her comfortable home in the woods. Mrs. P's husband—he'd been a successful banker up in Providence—had died about five years earlier, but she loved her house and had no intentions of even considering living someplace else. Gus knew—because she had told him—that she liked having someone like him living in her garage apartment, "just in case," was the way she put it. She was only in her mid-70s, Gus estimated, and probably had years of healthy life left, but one never knows.

"Well, you tell your father that we all think he did the right thing," she said. "Angelo Ferro is a common criminal and Julius Haddock is worth seven of him. Maybe eight."

Gus smiled. Vera P was from old-school Little Penwick, and most of the people in town thought that if the chief of police said he didn't know what had happened to Angelo Ferro, then he didn't know. And putting him in jail for that was outrageous.

Gus gave the dog a last pat on the head. "Thanks, Miz P," he said. "I'll do that."

A few minutes later, Gus was on the road up to Providence, picking up a highway in Fall River, Mass. He then swung south on I-95 heading along the western shore of Narragansett Bay and exited at Cranston. A few blocks to the west sat the huge, imposing, almost Gothic structure known as the

Adult Corrections Institute, or ACI. Julius Haddock had been an inmate there for six months. The sprawling jail complex was built with heavy blocks of gray granite taken from a nearby quarry a hundred years ago, and would have been imposing in architectural terms even if the formidable facade had not been ringed with thirty-foot tall fencing topped with razor wire. The ACI looked like a place that, once they put you in, you were not getting out any time soon.

Gus was driving his squad car, but he was dressed in civilian clothes—khaki pants, a blue shirt and a light jacket. The October day was overcast and chilly. Prison rules said no uniforms were allowed inside on visitor's day. And Gus understood that someone dropping in dressed in full police regalia would be like waving a red flag in front of a bull. Or, in front of about 3,500 bulls, which was the approximate male prisoner population at the ACI.

Still, because he was a cop, Gus' badge got him the benefit of a few shortcuts, skirting past the long lines where all guests and family members were being searched and patted down for contraband or weapons. He nodded to the guards he knew, and after he was wanded and waved in, he took a seat on a bench set against the white tiled hallway outside the visitor's hall, and waited. Waiting was something everyone had to do in prison, visitor or inmate. The prisoners waited for their release; their visitors waited to be herded into the large hallway filed with metal tables fixed with four plastic seats each. As more and more people crammed into the hallway, the ceramic tile walls and cement floor reflected their voices, creating an echoing din that assaulted everyone's eardrums.

Finally, at the stroke of eleven, two of the guards opened the entrance doors to the visitor's hall, and the people streamed in, rushing to claim one of the four-seated tables. One of the guards noticed Gus sitting on the bench, and nodded at him to follow. He led Gus to one of the private interview rooms set on the side of the hall, and unlocked the door for him. Inside there was a Plexiglas half-wall above a wooden shelf, a metal chair, and a similar desk and chair on the other side of the glass.

Gus sat down and waited. Out in the larger hall, the inmates who had visitors were beginning to file in, amid shouts of recognition and joy, and the background din became foreground sound, even in the little interview space where Gus sat behind the closed door.

There was motion behind the glass and Julius Haddock, accompanied by one of the guards, sat down in the chair and smiled wanly at his son. Now in his mid-sixties, Julius Haddock was still a powerful-looking man. He was a few inches over six feet and had a thick and powerful upper body. His graying hair was close clipped, like his son's, and he wore a pair of bifocal reading glasses on a halyard dropped around his neck. He was wearing his prison uniform of orange canvas shirt and pants and slip-on orange walkers. The guard went and stood against the far wall, arms folded across his chest. Julius picked up the telephone. Gus did the same on his side.

"What's the latest?" Julius said. He was never one for small talk, personal conversation or idle chit-chat about the weather, the Red Sox or politics.

"The AG appointed a Special Master," Gus said. "To watch over the department and make sure we don't go to war with the Ferro clan."

"Yeah, I expected that," Julius said, nodding. "No offense, but they couldn't let my son run my department without sending someone to look over your shoulder. Who's the lucky guy?"

"Maggie Wells," Gus said. "Assistant DA."

"Hubba hubba," his father said, a small smile playing on his face. "She's a looker."

"Ya think?" Gus said. "I didn't notice."

"The hell you didn't," Julius said. "When was the last time you got laid?"

"Bagram. 'Bout a year ago," Gus said. "She was a major, attached to the Intelligence Division. I think she was bored."

"Didn't I teach you how not to bore a woman in bed?" Julius said, grinning now.

"She wasn't bored in bed," Gus said. "Bored with being stuck in Bagram with nothing much to do."

"What happened after? No follow-up? Women hate it when you screw 'em and screw, y'know."

"Thanks for the fatherly advice," Gus said. "I shipped out the next morning on assignment into Helmand. When we got back a week later, she had moved on. Back to the States, I think."

"You got her number, at least?"

"Nope," Gus said. "But I know her name and she knows mine. She's in Intelligence. She can find me if she wants, and since she hasn't, I figure she doesn't want to."

Julius shook his head sadly. "You kids today," he said. "It was different in my day."

"Yeah," Gus said. "Free love, flower power and lots of STDs. Thanks, but no thanks."

Julius stared through the glass silently for a moment.

"What happened to your hand?" he said.

Gus reflexively covered his right knuckles, still sore and slightly swollen, with his left hand. "Nothing," he mumbled.

"Doesn't look like nothing," Julius said.

"It's nothing, Dad," Gus said. "Drop it."

"Okay, whatever," Julius said, surrendering. "What's Bob Murtha think about this Special Master stuff? Has he got your back?"

"I don't know," Gus said. "He knew it was coming before I did. Didn't tell me. Neither did Callahan. I think he knew."

Julius waved his hand dismissively. "Political games," he said. "All those people like to play them. You just need to keep an eye peeled to make sure neither of them are passing info on to this Special Master. Backstabbing. That's the second-favorite sport, after playing politics."

"Now, about this Maggie," his father said, "You understand that she's reporting directly to the AG, right?"

"Yeah, I figured that one out all by myself," Gus said.

"And the AG is trying to protect the Ferro clan, because they give him a lot of money."

"Donations?"

Julius Haddock looked at his son through the Plexiglas window and smiled.

"Well," he said, "That's what they call it, I suppose. Others may call it a percentage, vigorish, a payoff or get out of jail free money."

"That sounds illegal," Gus said.

His father didn't respond.

"Is that what all this is about?" Gus said. He nodded his head at the surroundings, the jail. The place where they had put his father.

His father remained silent. But his eyes remained fixed on his son.

"The AG thinks he's got you tied down," Julius said. "Got his little eyes and ears in place to keep him up to date. Thinks that he's in control. Might be just the right time to show him he's not. Like put a little squeeze on the Ferro boys and see what happens. Be fun to find out who squeals like a little piggy."

"You ever gonna tell me what went down between you and Angelo?" Gus said.

Julius was silent.

"Swell," Gus said. "Glad I came up today. If I hurry, I can get home in time so I can watch the second half of the Pats game."

"They're gonna win," Julius said. "One of the guys on my cellblock knows the goombahs in Vegas. He said the Pats are a dead solid lock today."

"To win? Or just cover the spread?"

Julius shrugged. "What's the difference?"

"I'm old fashioned," Gus said. "I like it when my team actually wins."

The two men were silent. The din in the hall next door was still there.

"You OK?" Gus asked. He didn't have to specify what he was talking about. They both knew.

Julius Haddock shrugged. "It is what it is," he said. "Like Belichick says. Not a lot of fun, but I'll get through it."

"Miz P said to say hello," Gus said. "Said everyone in town is behind you."

Julius smiled. "She's good people," he said. "Known her since you were in kindergarten, I think. Most of the people in that town are good people. 'Cept for the bad apples."

Gus smiled. That was one of his father's most oft-expressed adages. Most people are generally pretty good people, he always said, Except for the bad ones. And there's always a few bad apples."

"Can I do anything for you?"

Julius smiled at his son through the Plexiglas wall.

"Watch your ass," he said.

CHAPTER 5

Police Blotter
Newport County News

9:10 p.m. Officers responded to a call from a resident on Ocean View Drive concerning a woman creating a disturbance, confronting and attacking passing autos and shouting at neighbors. Officers spoke to the woman, managed to calm her down and transported her to a local hospital for evaluation.

Gus was at home, watching the Monday night football game when his phone rang. It was Dottie Adams, the police dispatcher.

"Evening, Gus," she said, "Who's winning?"

"The team with the most points," he said.

"Hardy har har," she said. "Listen, Carl Lincoln just called in. Sheila Barnsworth has gone off her meds again. He's over there now and wondered if you were available. Said Sheila will listen to you."

"Aww, crap," Gus said. But he flicked off his television. "Tell Carl to hold down the fort. Reinforcements on the way."

"Ten-four," Dottie said and rang off.

Fifteen minutes later, Gus pulled onto Ocean View. There wasn't any ocean in sight, but it was a nice neighborhood of low ranches with green lawns, upgraded landscaping and solid middle class citizens. He drove down the street for a few hundred yards until he came up on Carl Lincoln's squad car, its blue lights flashing.

Carl was standing in front of his car, illuminated by the headlights. He was talking and gesticulating with someone Gus couldn't see, someone standing in the shadows of a couple of large oaks that framed the walkway leading to the front door of the Barnsworth place.

Sheila Barnsworth was well known to the entire police department of Little Penwick. Bi-polar with a little added dash of schizophrenia, Sheila went off her meds about twice a year, something that usually sent her round the bend and resulted in a visit from the police. Her husband, Frank, was a tiny frail guy, now in his late 60s, who had pretty much given up trying to care for her. A visiting nurse stopped by every other day or so to check on her, but if Sheila missed her pills three days in a row, her brain would short circuit and she would begin to act out.

Tonight, she had apparently decided to take on everyone in the neighborhood. She had run outside, taken up a position in the middle of Ocean View Drive, and began haranguing everyone she saw. She had thrown some logs at passing cars. She had screamed at Wendy Jackson, who lived next door and had come outside to try to do what she could to help. Sheila had lifted up her dress and urinated in her front yard. Now, she was standing next to the trunk of one of the twin oaks and was listening, but not really listening, to Carl Lincoln try to convince her to come with him for a ride.

"She's been mostly catatonic for about a half hour," Carl told Gus. "Which is something of an improvement, I guess."

"OK," Gus said. "I'll try talking to her."

He walked slowly up to the tree where Sheila stood. She was shaking slightly, like she was cold.

"Hey Miz Barnsworth," Gus said, "Gus Haddock. You know me, right?"

She didn't respond. Just stood there shaking a little, one hand stroking the rough surface of the tree's bark.

"Listen, Sheila, I want to take you over to the doctor's office," Gus said, keeping his voice low and calm. "He wants you to come in and see him. He has some things he needs to say to you."

She turned her head slightly and her eyes slowly focused in on Gus's face.

"You're the police chief," she said. Her voice was low and strained. "Are you arresting me?"

"Arresting?" Gus said with a chuckle. "No. Of course not. You haven't done anything wrong, Sheila. I'm just here to give you a ride to the doctor's office. He really needs to talk to you as soon as possible. Will you come with me?"

"No," she said. Her voice was suddenly strong again. "No, I will not. No. NOOO!" The last was a scream, loud and piercing, echoing off the nearby homes.

"Okay," Gus said. "That's fine. We don't have to go right now. We can just wait a minute until you're ready. Is that all right with you?"

She looked at him, but her eyes were unfocused. She shook her head, as if to clear away whatever cobwebs were clogging up her brain.

"We can just stand here and talk for a while," Gus continued, keeping his voice low and calm. "And then, when you feel ready, I'll run you over to the doctor. OK?"

"No," she said, shaking her head. "No, no, no."

"How's Frank?" Gus said, trying to keep the conversation going. "He enjoying retirement?"

"He drinks too much," she said. "He's a drunk."

And for good reason, Gus thought to himself.

"Maybe I should arrest him," Gus said.

"Yes," Sheila said, a smile playing on her face. "Yes. Yes. Yes."

"Well, here's an idea," Gus said. "You come with me right now to see the doctor and I'll come back and arrest Frank for being drunk. Sound like a deal?"

Gus watched her closely as Sheila thought about that. It took a while for the idea to work its way into her fog land of a brain. But eventually, she began to nod.

"Yeah," she said. "Yeah. Yeah."

"Good," Gus said. He walked up to her and gently took her arm. "Would you like to ride with me, or with Carl here? He's got the car with the blue lights."

"I like blue," Sheila said. But she kept walking as Gus led her toward the squad car, holding her arm.

"Okey doke," Gus said. They walked through the head-light glare and Carl opened the rear door. "Maybe Carl will turn on the siren for you, too. Would you like that?"

"Yes," she said. "Yes. Yes. Yes." She climbed into the back seat. Gus leaned in and made sure her seat belt was clipped around her hips.

"There you go, Sheila," he said. "You go talk to the doctor. I'll take care of Frank."

"Shoot him in the ass," she said. "Right in the ass."

Gus was smiling as he gently closed the door. He turned to Carl. "Take her to St. Anne's up in Fall River," he said. "They got all her records up there."

"Right, chief," Carl said. He got into his car and drove away.

CHAPTER
6

Gus went into his office early Tuesday morning. He spoke to Dottie, sitting as usual at her dispatch post, poured himself a cup of coffee in the break room and closed the door behind him in his office. Sitting down behind his desk, he opened one of the large desk drawers, flipped through the files and found the one marked "Ferro." It was heavy, a couple of inches thick.

Opening the file on his blotter, he sifted through the pages until he found the document titled "Incident Report," which was dated January 8, earlier that year. One of the boxes on the report was checked next to the category "Missing Person," and the name Angelo Ferro typed in. Gus had read this report before, many times over. Sipping his coffee, he began to read it again.

Angelo Ferro, age 66 years, had been reported missing on January 8th by one of his sons, Daniel Ferro. The younger Ferro told the police that two days earlier his father had taken one of the Ferro family's commercial fishing boats—they had three of them moored at Little Penwick harbor—out of port late in the evening of January 5, around 10:30 p.m. Asked if that was unusual, Daniel Ferro had said no, a late departure like that was commonplace, especially when the destination for the fishing trip was the Dump, an area of shallow undersea canyons about sixty miles offshore. The boat, named the Lizzie B, was forty feet long, about a hundred tons, set up with trawling nets off the stern. The target at the Dump was bluefin tuna, cod and haddock.

What was a little unusual was that Angelo Ferro left Little Penwick harbor all by himself. If he had been planning on doing any serious fishing out there at the Dump he would have at least one hand aboard, and probably two or three. Angelo Ferro was in his sixties and while a single hand could conceivably handle all the nets and windlasses and lines by himself on a heaving deck in the middle of the Atlantic, it made more sense that a man of his age would stay in the enclosed warmth of the bridge and let the deck hands do all the hard outside work. The original investigators of the case had noted this anomaly in their report.

The exact time of departure was unknown. There was nobody at the harbor at 10:30 on a frigid January night, so nobody saw Ferro and the Lizzie B leave the port. The Little Penwick police had checked with the U.S. Coast Guard base at Castle Hill Station outside of Newport. They had recorded one electronic signal from the Lizzie B, an automatic ping between the fishing boat's onboard electronic GPS gear and the Coast Guard station. That had come in at 11:12 p.m. on the night in question. The Coast Guard had not been able to pinpoint the location of the Lizzie B on the basis of that one ping. There had been no further pings. Either the onboard electronics had malfunctioned, or someone had shut them off.

After that, there had been no further contact with Angelo Ferro, the Lizzie B or anyone else. The fishing vessel was never seen again. Neither was Angelo Ferro. His cell phone was unresponsive. The initial conclusion by the police and the Coast Guard was that the Lizzie B had suffered some kind of catastrophic failure and was lost at sea with all hands.

But Daniel Ferro had complained to the police that the record was incomplete. He had told the police that his father, Angelo Ferro, had encountered the Little Penwick chief of police, Julius Haddock, earlier on the evening he disappeared. He said there had been words between the two men, harsh words. He said threats had been issued. Daniel Ferro told the police that he, and his family, believed that Julius Haddock had killed his father that night, put the body on the fishing boat and taken the boat out to sea, where he had scuttled the vessel and somehow returned to shore.

Those accusations had been included in the Missing Persons report, followed by notations by the police to the effect that there was no evidence to support the accusations. Chief of Police Julius Haddock had submitted to an interview, said he had seen Angelo Ferro at The Roadhouse at about eight o'clock on the night of January 5th, spoken to him normally with no angry words or dispute between them, and then had gone home and was in bed by eleven. The investigating officer had interviewed the bartender at The Roadhouse who was working that night who said he remembered Angelo Ferro coming in that night and having dinner with a couple other members of his family. He also said he recalled Chief Haddock stopping by around eight o'clock, but did not speak to the chief and, because he was busy that night with a nearly full house, and he did not recall noting when either the chief or the Ferro party had left the premises. Examination of the credit card receipt from the Ferro party indicated that they had paid their bill at 8:52 p.m. The other two members of the Ferro family who had been dining with Angelo told the police that all three had returned home from the restaurant. The other two went off to their homes and Angelo to his. Nobody saw him again. The case was thus filed and closed, pending further developments. In the intervening months, there had been no further developments. Angelo Ferro had disappeared off the face of the earth.

Gus paused, drained the dregs of his now lukewarm coffee, and stood up to stretch. He went and looked out the window of his office, which overlooked the front parking lot. There was nothing going on: the lot was empty, an occasional car drove past the station house, carrying someone to work. It was still early, a little before eight. He went back to his desk and resumed reading the file.

Two weeks after the disappearance of Angelo Ferro and the Lizzie B, two Rhode Island state police officers and a representative of the Attorney General's office in Providence had arrived in Little Penwick to conduct an interview with chief of police Julius Haddock. The town's chief of detectives, Buzzy Franklin, sat in on the interview and took notes, which were later appended to the investigation file.

The assistant DA, an aggressive young lawyer named Agatha Barr, had begun by asking Chief Haddock to recount the details of his meeting with Angelo Ferro on the evening of January fifth. According to notes taken and later typed up by Buzzy, Haddock told the staties that he ran into the elder Ferro at the Roadhouse, a honky tonk-like bar and grill out on Overland Road. The chief said Angelo Ferro had been dining with some associates and, when he saw the chief walk in, immediately approached him and became belligerent. "He got in my face," was the way Chief Haddock had described the interaction. Asked what the reason for the belligerence was, Haddock had laughed and said "Everything for the last twenty years." Asked to explain, Chief Haddock had recounted the long history of contacts between the Little Penwick PD and the Ferro family. Various members of the Ferro family had been arrested and charged with crimes ranging from domestic abuse, public drunkenness and traffic violations to more serious matters including drug trafficking, smuggling, auto theft, arson and suspicion of murder. Several of these cases had been litigated in the courts and several members of the Ferro family had served time in the ACI.

The chief was asked what happened next.

"I went home," he said.

Where did Angelo Ferro go?

"I have no idea," the chief said. "I went home."

Can you corroborate that?

"No," Chief Haddock said. "I live alone. My wife died fifteen years ago."

You were in the bar that night, but the bartender doesn't recall serving you. Can you explain that?

"I didn't buy a drink," Chief Haddock said. "I wasn't inside the place for more than ten minutes. Angelo got a little heated, so I left."

Did you follow Angelo Ferro to the harbor?

"No."

Did you cause any harm or violence to the person of Angelo Ferro?

"No."

Assistant DA Barr had said "This appears to be a significant case. The family of the victim claims that you and Angelo Ferro were enemies. You were the last person to see him alive. There are many unanswered questions here."

Chief Haddock had responded.

"This appears to be a pretty simple case, to me. Mr. Ferro and various members of his family have been engaged in unlawful activities as long as I have known them. The multiple criminal records on file indicate that to be true. I was not the last person to see him alive. I left Mr. Ferro inside the Roadhouse where about twenty to thirty other patrons were eating and drinking. Two bartenders, several waitresses and I don't know how many cooks out in the kitchen. All of them potentially were the last ones to see Angelo Ferro alive, not me. I went home. And finally, the Lizzie B was not the first, and likely will not be the last, fishing vessel to sink in the North

Atlantic, if that is, in fact, what happened to her. It's a dangerous business, fishing, and shit happens. Sudden squalls, engine failure, swamped by a rogue wave in a following sea, he could have hit a floating cargo container, he could have been sunk by a passing Russian sub. I could come up with a million hypotheticals. But I don't know what happened. I was home in bed."

The interview had come to a close soon after. The two state cops and the assistant DA had packed up their papers and returned to Providence. Buzzy Franklin had updated the Incident report, Chief Haddock had initialed it, and it was filed away with the rest of the sheaf of papers in the Ferro file.

Done and dusted, thought Gus to himself, as he closed the file on his desk. It had all been done by the book. Or had it?

Because it had been less than ten days after that interview by the state police and the assistant DA that Julius Haddock had been informed that a grand jury sitting in Pawtucket had voted to indict him. The charge was misappropriation of funds. The state of Rhode Island charged that Julius C. Haddock, chief of police of Little Penwick, Rhode Island, had taken $25,000 in state grant funds appropriated for an anti-crime educational effort designed for the state's high school students and instead placed those funds in the general revenue account in the town's bank account.

There had been a hearing, six days later, in Providence Superior Court, the honorable Frederick O'Rourke presiding. Julius Haddock, represented by a police union lawyer, pointed out that the town of Little Penwick, Rhode Island did not have a public high school, and instead sent its hundred or so high school-aged students by bus to the high school in the nearby town of Portsmouth. So Chief Haddock had placed the state grant, designed to educate high schoolers about crime and how the police can help, into the general funds.

"That's right, Chief," said Judge O'Rourke. "And that's exactly what the grand jury has charged you with. So I take it you are pleading guilty?"

"No, your Honor," Julius had said. "I am not."

"Well, I and everyone else in this court room just heard you admit that you misappropriated those funds," the judge said. "I therefore will record and accept your plea of guilty to these charges. I sentence you to one year of incarceration in the Adult Correctional Institute. Dismissed!"

And Julius Haddock had been taken away. An appeal had immediately been filed, but a new hearing on the case was still months away. It was likely that Julius' sentence would be served long before he got back into a courtroom.

THERE WAS A knock at his office door. "Come," he called out.

Lieutenant Callahan came in and closed the door behind him. He took one of the guest chairs in front of Gus' desk. Then he sat there and look at Gus for a moment or two.

"What's up?" Gus asked.

Callahan blinked once or twice, then looked away. Then looked at the chief again.

"This isn't easy," he said.

"Spit it out," Gus said. His internal warning lights were flashing brightly.

Callahan reached across the desk with a long arm and dropped a single sheet of paper onto Gus' blotter. Gus picked it up and began to read.

"Order for Psychiatric Evaluation," he read out loud. His eyes dropped to the bottom of the paper. "Signed by our beloved Attorney General. What the fuck is this Callahan?" He looked across the desk at his second in command.

Callahan looked uncomfortable. His face was flushed and he kept moving around on his chair as if his buttocks were being attacked by voracious fire ants.

"As the second in command of this department," he said haltingly, "It has fallen to me to give you this order. They're ordering you to go see this shrink lady up in Brockton…"

"Dr. Susan Maloney," Gus said, reading the name on the form he was holding.

"Yeah," Callahan nodded. "I've heard of her. She's supposed to be pretty good, has a lot of cops come in. She's a specialist in PTSD problems."

"The AG thinks I have PTSD?" Gus said.

Callahan shrugged. "They must have heard about the hole in the men's room wall," he said. "You and I know that's nothing, but this guy apparently has a raging hard-on for you, so …"

"Who told him about the hole?" Gus said. "Was it Special Master Wells?"

Callahan shrugged again. "I don't know, Chief, I really don't. Could have been her, or it could be anyone else on the force. If you see something, you're supposed to say something."

"Did you drop a dime on me, Barry?" Gus used the man's first name to let him know he suspected that it had been Callahan who had reported the incident. It was just like him: cowardly, backstabbing, an action full of latent resentment for being passed over for the top job. Gus could think of no one else, even Maggie Wells, who would have done such a thing.

"No, Gus, it wasn't me," Callahan said. "Look, Gus, I was in the service, years ago, although God knows I was never in combat like you were. Hell, I spent my time in the motor pool in Frankfurt for God's sake. Only thing that drove me crazy was too much pilsner and not enough frauleins."

He paused, hoping Gus would laugh, but he didn't.

"But I have seen and worked with guys who came back from the Mideast and needed some help afterward," he continued. "There's no shame in it. When you're in the middle of it, like you were, you see things and hear things and do things that no ordinary man has to do. I know you don't talk much about what went on over there, but we all know what you went through. Stuff like that's gotta have an effect on your mental outlook. Nobody thinks you're crazy or even mentally ill. But I've known guys who found it really helpful to have someone to talk to, hash things out. Like a relief valve. Like I said, I've heard this Doc Maloney is pretty good. I know some guys up in Fall River who've seen her. One of 'em, it saved his marriage."

"I'm not married," Gus said.

Callahan grimaced. "You know what I mean. Look, this is a legal order from the state," he said. "I had to give it to you because I'm next in rank. I agree with you that this sucks. I agree with you that the AG up in Providence is a flaming ass-hole and probably corrupt as hell. But I don't think it would hurt anything or anyone if you went to see this doc. Even if you don't think you have any aftereffects from the war, maybe you do. You wouldn't be the first, and won't be the last, and it's not your fault if you do. Plus, you're dealing with your Dad being in jail and all the rest. I'll support you whatever you want to do, but if you want to know what I think, as a friend more than as your lieutenant, I'd say go. Talk to the lady. What do you have to lose? But if you don't go, they can suspend you or even have you dismissed. I don't want that. So I think you should go."

Gus was silent for a bit, thinking about what Callahan said. What he hadn't said was that a psyche evaluation would go on his permanent record. And if the town council was considering whether or not to keep him on as chief of police in six months or so, it might crop up again and be considered a black mark. Which would put Lt. Barry Callahan in the cat-bird seat to be appointed the next chief. Gus folded the paper in half again and tucked it into his blotter.

"Okay," he said. "Thank you for your honesty. I'll take it under consideration."

Barry Callahan heaved himself out of the chair and left the office.

CHAPTER 7

Maggie Wells arrived at the station after lunch. She checked in with the duty officer in the squad room, and he called Gus in his office.

"Ms. Wells from the AG's office is here," he said.

"Send her in," Gus said. He had spent the morning catching up on paperwork, one of the constants of his job. But all the while, he had been fuming about his psyche appointment order. Despite his doubts about Lt. Callahan, he didn't want to think that anyone at the LPPD had dropped a dime on him to the AG. He suspected it had been Maggie Wells. She had seen his raw knuckles, and had probably heard the station scuttlebutt. Did she turn him in because she was part of a plot to get him out of the chief's office? Or did she tell the AG about his temper tantrum because she was genuinely worried about him and his mental condition? Neither alternative made him happy and the first would make him crazed, but he didn't know. He'd have to wait and see.

His door was open. She peered around the corner.

"Hi, Chief. OK if I come in?" she said.

"Sure thing," Gus said, waving her into the office. She came in and sat down in front of his desk. She looked at him with a smile, but that faded away when she studied the look on his face.

"What's the matter?" she asked, cocking her head to one side.

He didn't respond. He picked up the letter he had been given earlier and tossed it across his desk at her. She picked it up and read it. Her face turned red. When she was finished, she handed the letter back. He noticed that she didn't look him in the eyes.

"You got anything to say?" Gus asked.

"I didn't know about that until last night," she said. "The AG told me he was sending it down this morning."

"Thanks for the heads up," Gus said. "You didn't tell him anything about me? Didn't happen to mention this?" He held up his right hand, still a little red and puffy around the knuckles from his punch against the wall.

"No," she shook her head and sat forward in her chair. "That did not come from me, I swear."

"And I should believe you?" he said. "Based on what? Our long and fruitful friendship of about five days? The enduring trust we've built up from you being installed as my special master? I'm sorry, Ms. Wells, but I'm not exactly feeling all warm and fuzzy here."

She sat there for a moment or two, biting her lower lip, thinking. Trying, Gus knew, to figure out a way to weasel out of her predicament.

"Look," she said finally, "I understand how you feel…"

"Do you?"

"Yeah, I do," she continued. "You feel blindsided. I get that. I should have called you last night. My bad. Won't happen again, promise. But you've got to believe me, I had nothing to do with this."

"Somebody dropped a dime on me," Gus said. "I don't think it was anyone in this department. And I can't think of anyone else with the knowledge, the motive and the ability. That creates a trust issue. Which makes it very difficult for me to see how you and I can continue to work together. I'm gonna have to formally request that the AG assign another special master, someone I can share sensitive information with and who I can trust not to go blabbing to everyone up in Providence with the latest station-house gossip."

She sat back as if someone had slapped her. But her face hardened into a look of resolve.

"You can do that, Chief," she said, "But I seriously doubt if the AG will agree. He sent me down here because he was worried about the way this department was being operated. He is not going to let the subject of his concerns dictate who gets to look over his shoulder. It doesn't work that way. I was appointed Special Master and I'm afraid you're stuck with me."

Gus stared across his desk. Anger rose inside him, but he managed to keep it tamped down.

"For what it's worth, I agree with his recommendation that you go see a professional," she said. "I've known lots of cops with PTSD, including a few who never served in the military. It can happen to anyone, and it's not your fault. I'm sure you'll find it helpful to talk it out with a trained professional."

"I'll be sure and tell the doc that a young female lawyer with no medical training has diagnosed me as having PTSD. She'll no doubt be thrilled that she doesn't have to actually use her own medical training to make that determination. Saves a lot of time. Maybe I'll start by telling her about all the people I work with who don't seem to have my back," Gus said. "That should be good for a few sessions."

"That's totally unfair," she protested.

"And totally true," he said. "Look, why don't you go use the Interview Room? You can work in there. Frankly, I'm kinda done with dealing with you right now."

She had nothing to say to that, so she collected her things and walked out of his office.

Gus went back to his stacks of paper, slowly working his way through them until the piles were less imposing and looked, at least, more manageable. It was boring, routine work, but it kept his mind occupied and let his blood pressure drop back down out of the red zone. After a couple of hours, he sat back with a sigh, and looked at his watch. It was quarter to four.

There was a knock at his door, tentative sounding.

"Come," Gus boomed out.

Maggie opened the door and poked her head in.

"Can I come in? Or are you still angry?"

"More disappointed than angry," he said but he waved her to come in. She came back in and sat down in the same chair. She was carrying a file covered in a stiff brown cardboard. Gus recognized it as one of his department's investigation files.

"I've been reading the Angelo Ferro missing persons file," she said. "Got a minute? I have some questions."

Gus reached over, opened one of his desk drawers, flipped through some tabs and found a file which he pulled out and positioned in the center of his desk blotter.

"I got one of those, too," he said. "I read it about once a week. Always looking for anything we might have missed before."

"Doesn't tell us very much, does it?" she said.

"Sometimes a file that doesn't tell you anything is telling you everything," Gus said. "That's why I keep reading it."

"Have you been back to interview the witnesses again?" Maggie asked.

"Well, first of all, I have had nothing to do with this investigation to date," Gus said. "All this happened while I was still in Afghanistan. I pulled the pin in May, which was six weeks after Dad went to jail. Came home, re-upped with the force here, and the council tapped me as chief at the end of June, first of July. So none of the actions this department has taken have come from me in any way, shape or form. I just want that on the record between us."

Maggie looked at him across the desk. Gus thought he could see some sadness and regret in her eyes, but told himself he was just making that up. Like his father had warned, Maggie Wells worked, first and foremost, for the Man up in Providence.

"I understand," she said, her voice quiet. "Do you think we should interview the witnesses again, is what I meant."

"At The Roadhouse? We did two interviews back in January, when it first happened," Gus said. "Buzz Franklin talked to Charley Clarke, the bartender, and to the two other Ferros who were at the bar that night. Then, couple weeks later, we sent Freddie Benes, one of our senior patrolmen, over to speak to them again. Check the stories, see if there were any discrepancies, loose threads. There weren't. They told us the same thing the second time they told us the first time."

"Any sense that the story was rehearsed?" Maggie said. "That they agreed to tell us the same thing?"

"Nope," Gus said.

"Which Ferros were there that night?"

"In addition to Angelo, now apparently deceased, there was Cosme Ferro, Angelo's younger brother; and Emilio, one of Cosme's sons. They were eating fried clams and drinking beer. And probably thinking up some new ways to break the law."

"I've seen the rap sheet on the Ferro family," Maggie said. "It's a long one. They don't seem to be a law abiding bunch."

"So why is your boss trying to protect them?" Gus said.

"He isn't," she said.

"Really?" Gus said. "Angelo Ferro disappears one cold January night. Your boss and the staties seem to think Dad had something to do with that disappearance. He says he didn't, so instead, Preston Knox creates this bullshit misappropriation charge and gets Dad out of the way. Putting him in the ACI was a real asshole move, by the way. Preston Knox and Freddie O'Rourke know what happens to cops who go to prison. My guess is they hope it happens to Dad. But either way, they got him out of Little Penwick and out of the Ferro family's hair for a year. I can't think of any reason why they'd do that, except to protect whatever the Ferros are currently up to. Which, if the past is any kind of prologue, would be no good. Then, to add insult to injury, he sends you down here to spy on me."

"I'm not spying on you, Chief," she said hotly. "And my boss thinks your Dad is covering up something in regards to the disappearance of Angelo Ferro."

"Without proof," Gus said.

"No hard proof, just a lifetime of motive and a long cold night of opportunity," she said. "Sometimes that's more than enough."

"In this country, you need proof beyond a reasonable doubt," Gus said. "Other places I've been, like Iraq and Afghanistan, all you need is high-level suspicion to toss a guy in jail for years. Is that what we're going for now, here in little Rhody?"

"That's just unfair," she said.

"But true," he came back. "My Dad gave his testimony about what happened that night and it hasn't changed. There's zero evidence that says Dad had anything to do with Angelo after he left the Roadhouse. But because your boss wants to get rid of a chief of police that he thinks is bothering a regular donor to his political campaigns, he's charged him with corruption and gotten some bent old judge to railroad him into the clink. The full Rhody, as they say: corruption, money and power politics."

Maggie Wells shrugged. Gus wasn't sure if that meant she agreed with him, or just didn't want to argue with him. But it was clearer now than ever that Maggie Wells and Gus Haddock were on opposite sides of the fence. And that was not likely to change.

At four o'clock, the shifts changed. The evening patrol came in, while the daytime shift returned to base to check out, file any reports, and go home. As always, there was a lot of loud joshing and back-and-forth between the outgoing and incoming officers, and the sounds of laughter and sports argument drifted into the chief's office.

"I want to interview the witnesses again," Maggie said. "The bartender and the two Ferros."

"How come?"

"New set of eyes, new perspective," she said. "You never know. They may let something drop."

"Waste of time, in my view," Gus said. He looked up at Maggie and noted her frown.

"But it's fine with me. You want me to come along as backup? Charley Clarke at The Roadhouse won't give you a hard time. But those two Ferro guys might. It's in their DNA."

"Sure," Maggie said. "You can come with me. Be good for us to get to know each other a little better."

"Yeah," Gus said. "Good."

GUS DROVE THEM out to The Roadhouse in his squad car. It was a little early for the happy hour crowd, but there were a few customers in the place. Gus nodded at two older women he knew were members of the town's library board who were sipping on Bloody Mary's and finishing up a plate of sandwiches. Ladies who lunch, he thought to himself. Long, boozy lunch.

Behind the long wooden bar that ran down one whole wall of the place, Charley Clarke was drying and stacking some glasses that had just come out of the steaming dishwasher. Clarke was probably in his mid-sixties, and his long straight gray hair was combed back severely and tied in a pony tail type thing at the back. He had a bushy mustache, twinkling blue eyes framed in rimless glasses, and looked like he was probably one of the last survivors of Woodstock, or maybe a veteran of a couple long years on the road following the Grateful Dead.

Gus and Maggie perched on two of the round stools set in front of the bar. Charley, seeing Gus out of the corner of his eye, finished up with the glass he was working on and wandered over.

"Afternoon folks," he said. "Get you anything?"

"Just some information," Maggie Wells said. "We want to talk to you about last January. The night Angelo Ferro disappeared."

Charley looked at her for a moment. It was an appraising look that clearly defined her as outsider. As in, not trustworthy

… different … from away. After giving her the up-and-down, he turned to Gus.

"I'll have a Coke, please, Charley," Gus said. He fished around in his pocket and toss a couple of ones down on the bar when Charley brought back his tall glass, filled with ice.

"Sure I can't get you anything?" he asked Maggie, giving her one more chance. She shook her head. Charley shrugged.

"Mr. Ferro did not disappear as far as I'm concerned," Charley said. "He was here, large as life, with two others from his family. They had some dinner, a couple of drinks. Sat over there…" He nodded towards the far corner of the restaurant, at a round table for six set up underneath a broad paned window.

"It was busy that night, so I wasn't exactly sitting around keeping track of everyone in here and what they were talking about, y'know?" He looked up at Gus with raised eyebrows. Gus nodded at him to keep talking.

"It was around eight when Julius….I mean, when Chief Haddock came in," he continued. "I saw him walk in, look around the restaurant and then he walked right over to the Ferro table."

"Do you think he came in specifically to see them?" Maggie asked. "To see Angelo?"

Charley shrugged and began wiping down the top of the bar. It was perfectly clean and without spills, but he did it anyway. Like a reflex. Keep moving. Never stand still. Stay busy. He'd been a bartender for years.

"Not a mind reader," he said. "Have no idea why he came in or what he wanted. He didn't tell me. He walked in, looked around, saw Angelo, headed over to his table to speak with him."

"What was he wearing?" Gus asked.

"Who? Julius?" Charley scratched his chin. "Let me think. Leather jacket, I think. Does he have one with like a gold insignia or something on the front? Maybe on the arms? I seem to remember something like that. Wooly hat. Not a police hat. Like a ski cap. It was pretty cold that night."

"Did he look like he was about to head out to sea?" Gus asked. He felt Maggie shoot him a glance, but didn't look at her.

"Julius?" Charley said with a chuckle. "Nah. You plan to go out on a trawler in early January, you're gonna be wearing several layers, thick boots, and your sou'wester gear. Serious weather out there in January. Chief Haddock knew enough to layer up if he was going out to sea. He looked like he came in after processing a fender bender or something. He looked like the town cop. Which figures, because he is." He glanced over at Gus, frowned. "Or, was."

"Gloves?" Gus kept pressing.

Charley scratched his chin again, thinking. Then he shook his head. "Can't remember any," he said. "Sorry. It's been a while. And again, I was busy. Didn't really have time to take notes on what my customers were wearing."

"What do you remember about the conversation he had with Angelo?" Maggie asked.

Charley shrugged again. "Nothing," he said. "They were way over there—" he motioned again at the table across the room. "We had a good crowd in here that night, pretty busy. Someone was working the juke box, so it was kinda loud in here. Hey, our customers like their tunes, y'know?"

"So you didn't hear anything they said to each other?"

"Nah," Charley shook his head. "After Julius came in, I lost track anyway. Had customers to take care of right here at the bar. Right after New Year's, y'know? People like to try and keep the holiday spirit going for a few more days. I think Julius went over to their table, stood there for a minute or two. Can't swear, but I kinda remember Julius pointing at Angelo."

"What kind of point?" Maggie said. "Was he angry? Mad?"

"Sorry," Charley smiled at Maggie. "I really couldn't say. I really wasn't paying close attention."

"What happened next?"

"Next time I looked up, Chief Haddock was gone," Charley said. "Left the bar. Angelo, his brother and nephew were still sitting over there. They stayed about another hour, then got up, paid the bill and headed out."

"Was Angelo Ferro dressed for the sea?" Maggie asked.

"Howsat?" Charley said, cocking his head to the side.

"Well, you were quite convinced that Julius Haddock was not wearing the right kind of clothes to go out to sea on a freezing January night," Maggie said. "So I'm asking…what about Angelo Ferro? Was he wearing lots of warm layers, thick boots and a yellow rainslicker?"

Charley stared at Maggie. Gus could tell he didn't like her much. Seems like it had been an instant reaction, probably to the tone of her first question. Or her refusal to order anything. But then, the folks in Little Penwick didn't react warmly to most people from away. On principle.

"I think he had on pants, shirt and sweater, and loafers," Charley said. "Same with the other guys with him. He was dressed for a casual dinner at the Roadhouse. No, I would say he was not dressed for a fishing trip."

"Did he say anything when he left? When he paid the bill?"

"Yeah," Charley said with a smirk. "He said good night."

MAGGIE AND GUS sat in his squad car for a minute outside in the parking lot of the Roadhouse.

"Learn anything new?" Gus asked, cutting his eyes quickly at the woman sitting in his passenger seat.

"Sounds like Angelo was not planning to go to sea that night," she said. "Wasn't dressed for the occasion. Which means somebody could have forced him onto his boat. Driven him out to sea. Scuttled the boat."

"That's a lot of assumptions based on the fact that he wasn't wearing full nautical gear while having dinner at the Roadhouse," Gus said. "If Angelo left here at around nine, and the Coast Guard got a ping from his boat at a little after eleven, that leaves plenty of time for him to take his brother and nephew home, change clothes, throw on boots and gloves, get down to the harbor, cast off and steam away ... all by himself. And a lot of the commercial fishermen I know keep their cold weather gear on board. They'll change clothes before they steam out of the harbor. So you can't make any assumptions based on what they were wearing here while eating dinner."

Maggie was silent.

"Let's go find the other two Ferros and ask them what they remember," she said.

Gus shrugged and turned the key. He picked up his dashboard mic and thumbed the switch.

"Dottie?" he called, "Gus here. Ms. Wells and I are heading over to the Ferro place. Is anyone free?"

There was a slight delay and then Dottie's voice came over the speaker.

"Sure, Chief," she said. "Jerry is watching traffic up on Main Road."

"Roger that," Gus said. "Have him swing by the Ferro place in about thirty minutes. I'll wave at him if everything is good."

"Ten-four," Dottie said.

CHAPTER 8

The sun was beginning to set when Gus drove his squad car up the long dirt and crushed-clamshell drive into the Ferro compound. The dying sun cast long shadows across the drive and had begun to paint the western sky in a brilliant shade of pink. There was something about the atmospheric conditions in late fall in Little Penwick that turned out lovely sunsets almost every clear night.

The entrance to the Ferro place was off Weetamoo Road in what was almost the geographic center of the town. To the east, the remnant of a long granite ridge that ran north-south was probably the ancient boundary containing the waters of the Sakonnet River, that slow-moving tidal estuary that might have been an actual river a million or so years ago. Now, it was just a broad and protected body of water that joined

Mount Hope Bay to the north with the Atlantic, defining the east-facing shoreline of Aquidneck Island. Aquidneck, which was bounded by Narragansett Bay to the west, Mount Hope Bay to the north and the open sea to the south, contained two towns, Portsmouth and Middletown, and one city, Newport.

But here in the middle of Little Penwick, the land was low and marshy, in what everyone called the Weetamoo Swamp: dark, murky and shallow ponds bordered by tight narrow stands of oak and pine. In between the trees grew the vinous stalks of pucker brush, a nasty strain of weed that quickly took over the forest floor with underground runners and sent out strong shoots of green vines covered with thick, sharp, spiny inch-long thorns.

The swamps and the pucker brush helped keep wandering visitors off the Ferro land, and that family liked it like that. A family engaged in various illegal schemes and activities did not like uninvited people wandering onto their land. The Ferros actively discouraged it.

Gus' car tires crunched on the crushed shells as he slowly wound his way along the drive, passing a couple of the swampy ponds along the way. Maggie stared out the car window as they passed a rusty old double-wide trailer set back twenty yards off the drive. A bit further on, there was an old wood shack, its boards turned gray with age and weather, the windows black and opaque. There was a dusty gray pickup parked outside.

"I'm getting a Gothic vibe," Maggie said as they continued down the drive.

"Oh," Gus said, "It gets better."

After another quarter mile, the drive rose slightly onto a bluff and entered a broad clearing, some three hundred yards across. The drive continued up the center of the clearing, and there were five dwellings scattered near the clearing's edges, on both sides. Three of the dwellings were trailers, sitting on concrete blocks; two were actual houses. They were built next to each other, and the smaller one looked like it might have started life as a garage for the larger house, before someone turned it into a living space. Behind the large house, Gus could see a one-story building that looked vaguely like a garage. It had corrugated metal panels around the outside, no windows and a flat roof. There was a roll-up metal door on the front, which was closed, and a light fixture extending out over the top of the door. Unlike the other buildings in the clearing, the garage looked like it had been erected fairly recently.

The large house was two stories, covered in white clapboards, the windows framed in black shutters. There was a covered porch across the front with chairs and tables grouped at the far corner. On the side of the house, a large German shepherd ran to the front, affixed by a long leash to a metal cable strung between two trees, and began barking at the car, rearing back on its hind legs and then making hard circles.

Gus pulled to a stop in front of the main house.

"This was Angelo's," he told Maggie. "I'm guessing his son Dan lives here now."

"Do you think Angelo had a will?" Maggie asked. "Have you checked to see if it's been probated yet?"

Gus laughed. "Do members of most crime syndicates draw up wills?" he said. "But no, we haven't heard about any filings in Probate—my understanding is that the family refuses to admit that Angelo is really dead."

The front door to the white house opened and Daniel Ferro came out and stood on the front porch. Two more big dogs came out of the house with him and ran over to Gus' squad car. They began barking, too, matching the sound from the dog on the cable at the side of the house. Ferro was about forty, with long black hair and the beginnings of a middle-age paunch at the belly. He was wearing jeans and a sweatshirt. He shaded his eyes with one hand as he looked out at the squad car. The sun was even lower on the horizon, now behind the trees. Ferro whistled loudly and the two loose dogs returned to the porch and stood at his side.

"Do we have a strategy?" Maggie asked. Her voice sounded a little strained. Gus imagined that it had been a while since a big city lawyer like Maggie Wells had done any actual investigative field work. Especially any that involved calling on a thief's den in the middle of a swampy morass, where bodies could easily be submerged and lost forever.

"Nah," Gus said. "Just play it by ear. If Danny Ferro threatens to harm you in any way, I'll just shoot him. I'll probably have to take out his dogs, too."

"Shouldn't you wait for my command on that, chief?" she said.

"Okay," he said. "When you tell me 'Fire!' I'll empty my clip into the nearest Ferro. Or dog. Whichever comes first." He chuckled, then threw his door wide open and stood up. Maggie got out of the passenger side and together they walked up the sidewalk and climbed the wooden stairs onto the porch. The two dogs maintained their position at Ferro's side, but one of them cocked his head to the side and growled.

"Well, lookee here," Daniel Ferro drawled as they approached him on the porch. "If it ain't our junior chief of police. What brings you out on this fine afternoon?"

"I have a few questions I'd like to ask," Maggie said. Her voice was firm and strong. Taking control of the situation. Policework 101.

Daniel turned his head and looked at her. Did an up-and-down scan. Smiled a little smile to himself.

"Do you now?" he said. "And who are you?"

"Maggie Wells," she said. "Assistant attorney general. Here's my first question: is your uncle Cosme or your cousin Emilio at home at the moment? They are the ones I really want to talk to."

"I'll bet you do, Assistant Attorney General Wells," Daniel said. "Are you the Maggie Wells who has taken over the Little Penwick Police Department from Junior Dumbass here? Somebody told me that the state sent down a hot chick to ride herd on Junior."

Maggie didn't respond. She just stared at Daniel for a few moments.

"Cosme?" she said, raising her eyebrows. "Emilio?"

Ferro pulled his cell phone out of a rear pocket, punched at the screen and held it to his ear. They waited while it rang. Gus could hear the call signal buzzing. Then there was a click and a muffled answer.

"Cos?" Daniel said. "Couple cops are over here. Hot young thing from the AG's office in Providence wants to ask you a few questions. Emilio, too."

He was silent while Cosme said a few things.

"Yeah, can you grab him and come over? We always want to be cooperative with our local law enforcement."

Cosme said something back and Daniel's face broke out into a grin. His fingers punched the phone and put it back in his pocket.

"He'll be right over," he said. "Do you want to tell me what this is about?"

"No," Gus said.

"That's not very cooperative," Daniel said. But he was still grinning when he said it. He sat down in a cushioned porch chair. Both dogs came over and laid down at his feet, but their eyes never left the two strangers. Gus and Maggie remained standing a few steps away. They waited.

It took about five minutes before a bright red Ford pickup came barreling down the drive and skidded to a stop outside Daniel's house. There were two men inside, and they each climbed out of the cab and walked up the walk to the porch steps. One of the dogs stood up, went over and nuzzled the leg of one of the older man of the two, who had hair graying and thin on top; the other was in his late twenties, sporting a full, bushy mountain-man beard. Cosme and Emilio Ferro.

"What the hell, man?" Cosme, the older one, said. "I was in the middle of something. Don't have time to sit around chit-chatting." He reached down and scratched the ears of the dog.

Emilio, the younger man, stared at Gus and Maggie as he perched on the edge of the porch railing, crossed his arms in front of his chest and waited.

Maggie took the lead.

"You two were having dinner with Angelo Ferro on the evening of January 5th at the Roadhouse restaurant," she said. "Chief of police Julius Haddock entered the premises at approximately 8 p.m. and came over to your table, according to witnesses. What did Chief Haddock talk about with Angelo?"

"That was ten months ago, lady," Cosme said, holding his hands out wide in protest. "How in the hell are we supposed to remember that?"

"It was the night Angelo Ferro disappeared along with his fishing boat in the North Atlantic," Maggie said. "I would think that, given those events, you might have replayed the scene in your mind once or twice. What was discussed when Chief Haddock was standing at the side of your table?"

Cosme shook his head. Maggie looked at Emilio, perched against the railing.

"How about you?" she said. "Is your memory any better?"

Emilio grinned at her, his teeth showing through his bushy black beard.

"He said 'I'm gonna kill you and sink your boat so no one find your body,'" he said. "How's that?"

"It's a felony crime to make a false report to the authorities," Maggie said. "And what you just said sounds like a false report. You wish to reconsider?"

"Meels," Cosme said in an undertone, warning the younger man.

"OK," Emilio said. "He didn't say that. But he probably thought it, since that's what he did. But to answer your question, I don't recall. It was months ago."

Maggie stared at both of them. Then she shook her head.

"You were right, Gus," she said. "They're both a couple of assholes."

"Hey!" Cosme turned to confront Maggie. "You can't say something like that to me."

"I think I can," she said. "Because I just did. Here's something else I'll say. You all don't seem to give a crap about what happened to Angelo that night. If you'd talk to us truthfully, we could investigate. But you won't, because you're all lifelong criminals and scumbags. So we're never going to find out what happened, and we're never going to find Angelo Ferro. And sooner or later, they'll let Chief Haddock out of jail because there won't be any further reason to hold him. So keeping your traps shut isn't helping. In fact, it's helping Chief Haddock's case. Maybe if you weren't such inbred morons, you'd understand that."

Emilio stood up suddenly, as if the porch railing had somehow become electrified. His eyes narrowed and his forehead creased.

"Why, you little bi—"

Gus turned to face Emilio, chest to chest. He didn't say anything. He just put his face up close to Emilio's and kept it there. Emilio's hot eyes had been fixed on Maggie, and there was a hot retort forming in his mind. But then he glanced at Gus Haddock's steely blue eyes. And did a double-take. And held his tongue.

At that moment, the front door to the house swung open and a young woman came out onto the porch. One of the two dogs went over to her and stood waiting for a response. Everyone standing there turned to look. She was tall, all arms and legs with long blond hair falling straight down her back. She glided over to the stairs leading down to the walkway and paused there, one long lissome arm reaching out to grasp the post that framed the porch and stairway railing. Despite the chill in the air, she was wearing a tight pink T-shirt and a pair of denim short-shorts that encased her rear end like a pair of surgical gloves and which ended just below the crease between her buttocks and her legs. Her face was glowing with youthful health, eyebrows perfectly manicured, lips painted a cheerful red.

She turned to look at the group standing a few feet away, all of whom were now staring back. Her eyes were a crystalline shade of blue, piercing, bright. As if seeing the others for the first time since she glided out of the house, she frowned, as if she had never seen other human beings standing in a group nearby before.

"Hello," she said, softly. Her voice was throaty and came out in a sultry whisper.

Gus Haddock took a step towards her. He nodded.

"Don't believe I've had the pleasure," he said. "I'm Gus Haddock, chief of police. And you are …?

Daniel Ferro leaped to his feet almost kicking the resting dog at his feet out of the way. "Janine," he barked. "Go back in the house."

The young woman's frown deepened. It turned into a pout. But she blinked once, bent over and cooed something at the dog, then turned and glided back across the porch, pulled open the front door with a lissome arm and disappeared inside. The dog looked at the closed door as if in disbelief, then came walking back over to Daniel and sat.

There was silence on the porch after she left. Each person there was processing what they had just seen.

"Well, I'm sorry you folks had to drive all the way out here to the Swamp, only to come up empty," Daniel Ferro said, breaking the spell. "Guess nobody here can remember anything that was said that night last winter. What a shame. Guess you cop assholes will have to look for evidence somewheres else."

"Thanks for your time," Gus said. "If you think of something that might be helpful to our investigation, please let us know."

They all heard a car accelerate and turned to watch as a Little Penwick squad car came rushing up the drive. It was Jerry Hanlon, following orders from Dottie to provide backup at the Ferro place. The car crunched to a halt next to Daniel's walkway. Jerry stayed in the car.

Gus moved back half a step. He glanced at Maggie and nodded. He walked down the length of the porch, she followed. They descended the stairs and on the walk, Gus made a signal with his hand toward Jerry in the squad car. They saw Jerry nod back. The tethered dog at the side of the house was going nuts again, barking and straining against his restraint. Jerry shifted the car into drive and wheeled away, his rear wheels scattering the crushed shells behind. He pulled forward a bit, did a quick 180 and headed back the way he came in, engine growling.

Gus and Maggie got into his squad car and they drove away as well. The three Ferro men stayed where they were and watched.

"Well, that went well," Gus said as he drove back down the drive.

"You were right," Maggie said. "Bunch of assholes."

"Little Penwick's finest," he said.

"Who the hell was the bombshell?" Maggie asked.

"No idea," Gus said. "Never saw her before."

"Maybe you should find out," she said.

"Maybe I should," he said.

CHAPTER 9

Dr. Susan Maloney's office was in an office condo development just outside the grimy streets of downtown Brockton, one of the many old mill towns that still dot the New England landscape. Long brick factories with towering smokestacks gave way to narrow city streets, block after block of rickety tenements, once known as company housing, a green park or two, crisscrossed by sidewalks and shaded by old trees, a few equally impressive stone churches of the Roman Catholic flavor, and a huge city hall built with orange bricks with a five-story terra cotta tower, arched windows and a brass clock face.

Gus found the doctor's address in a small cul-de-sac of two-story buildings that looked like modern apartments or condos. Aluminum siding in alternating pale pastel shades, simple black doors framed by windows on both sides, and curving walkways surrounded by well-landscaped plants. There was ample parking everywhere.

He arrived a few minutes before his scheduled appointment, and walked into the Dr. Mahoney's waiting room. There was a black leather sofa, an upholstered chair, a stack of magazines on the coffee table, framed prints of nature scenes on the wall and an aquarium filled with colorful fish against one wall. *Perfectly designed to instill peace and happiness in the minds of crazed patients*, Gus thought.

Gus sat down and began leafing through a travel magazine, which seemed to think that Peru was just the place to visit this year. It had mountains, it had the ocean, it had big cities with great restaurants. And the Peruvians were swell people, too. Gus was dressed in his usual business casual: pants, dress shirt without tie and a sportcoat. The coat was partly to indicate his station in life and partly to hide the SIG Sauer pistol in its holster on his right hip.

After about ten minutes, the door to the inner office opened and a middle-aged woman dressed in gray came out. She was clutching a white tissue in her left hand and her face was a little red. She seemed to have been crying. The woman quickly exited out the front door.

A minute or so later, another woman came out of the inner office. She saw Gus sitting on her sofa and smiled at him. She was in her sixties. Her hair was short and gray. She wore a plain blue dress with a colorful scarf around her neck and sensible flat black shoes.

"Chief Haddock," she said, extending her hand for him to shake. "I'm Susan Maloney. Please come in."

Gus followed her into the inner sanctum. There was a brown wooden desk with two brass lamps on either side of a central blotter. Behind the desk, two large framed diplomas hung on the wall and told Gus that Dr. Maloney had degrees from Emory University and Harvard. The walls were painted British racing green, probably because of that color's soothing qualities. There were two tub chairs in front of the desk, covered in a dark gray fabric. Dr. Maloney motioned for Gus to sit down in one, so he did.

"No couch," he said, smiling.

"That's a very old stereotype," the doctor said, sitting down in her own leather desk chair behind her desk. "We're all mostly face-to-face these days. Better to take things head-on. At least that's the underlying philosophy."

She reached into a desk drawer to her right and pulled out a manila file folder. She put the folder on the blotter, flipped it open with the tip of one red-painted fingernail, and studied the contents inside for a minute. Gus watched. There was a soft whooshing sound, coming from the HVAC fans blowing air into the room through the ceiling vents.

"Augustus Haddock," Maloney said, reading out loud. "Chief of Police of Little Penwick, Rhode Island."

"At your service," Gus said.

She looked up and smiled. Then resumed reading.

"Five years service with the department. Then three tours of duty in Afghanistan and Iraq," she continued. "Army Rangers. Second lieutenant. Extensive combat."

"Rangers don't sit around at the rear," Gus said. "We're usually the point of the spear."

She looked at him again. "Yes," she said. "So I understand." She continued reading the file. "Your father, Julius Haddock, was the chief of police then. Is that right?"

"Yes," Gus said. "He served as chief for more than twenty-five years."

"Did you resent that?" she asked.

"Resent what?"

"That your father was chief of police."

Gus laughed.

"That's a very old stereotype," he said. "Father resentment. No. My father's been chief of police for much of my life. It was his job. Why should I resent what he did for a living?"

"You ran off and joined the army," she said, "After working under him for several years. No resentment?"

"I joined up to serve my country," Gus said. "My dad approved. Told me I'd have a job when I came home. I appreciated that."

"What was it like?"

"What was what like?"

"The Army," she said. "Afghanistan. Iraq. Serving. Combat. Did you like all that?"

Gus shrugged. "When you join the Army, you kinda don't worry much about liking or not liking things," he said. "It is what it is, as Coach Belichick likes to say. You learn how to deal with it."

"How?"

"How what?"

"How do you learn how to deal with it?"

Gus shrugged again. "Well, first you go through basic training," he said, "Then you go through Ranger school.

There, they teach you how to jump out of airplanes, swim across oceans, climb mountains in the snow. You learn how to kill people, as fast and as efficiently as you can. You learn how to survive without food or water for three or four days, out in the wilderness. You learn a lot of stuff. But what you learn most of all is how to deal with life as it happens. If you learn that, and can handle all the physical stuff, they let you continue to be a Ranger. If you don't learn how to deal with it, you get to go home and be a cop in Little Penwick again. So I learned. And stayed."

She looked at him for a moment or two. She picked up a pen and made a note on the page in her file folder. Then she put the pen down again.

"How are you sleeping?" she asked.

"Mostly at night," Gus said.

She looked at him, without expression.

"Sorry," he said. "I sleep fine."

"Nightmares?"

"Sometimes," he said. "Mostly about not being ready for a math test in high school. Because I never was."

"Do you ever dream of being back in combat? Being shot at? IEDs? Things of that nature?"

"Very rarely," Gus said. "I usually wake up if I have a dream like that."

"Night sweats? Feelings of anxiety?"

Gus shook his head. "Naw," he said, "Not really."

The doctor wrote a few more lines, then looked into the file again.

"It says here that your father is in jail," she said. "He used to be the chief of police in Little Penwick. The job you hold now."

"I'm acting chief," Gus said. "Temporary assignment."

"How do you feel about that?"

"About being acting chief?"

"No," she said. "About your father being incarcerated."

"Oh, that," he said. "Yeah, that makes me unhappy. I'm trying to get him out."

"How are you doing that?" she asked.

"Investigating the case that put him in, mostly," he said.

"Are you making progress?"

"Not as fast as I'd like," he said.

"Does that make you anxious?"

Gus paused. "I'm not sure I'd use the word 'anxious,'" he said. "Of course, I want to get my Dad out of jail as soon as possible. It's a dangerous place for a cop to be. It's also ridiculous for him to be incarcerated in this case. There are political elements involved, and dealing with those things is always frustrating to a cop. But investigations always run at their own pace. Sometimes, there's not much you can do but let it run its course. Eventually you get to the truth, even if it's not as fast as you'd like."

"That sounds like something an experienced police officer would say," Dr. Maloney said. "It's not a perspective I would expect in an officer of your age and experience."

"I was a cop for five years before I joined the Army," Gus said. "And my Dad's been a cop his whole life. If you're good, you watch, listen and learn things."

She looked at him across her desk.

"Is your Dad a good cop?"

"I think so," he said.

"Even though he's in jail for malfeasance of office?"

Gus shrugged. "Like I said, it's political bullshit."

"Isn't that an excuse for misbehavior?"

"It could be," he said, "If there was any misbehavior involved. I haven't found any yet."

"But you're still looking," she said.

He shrugged again. "Of course," he said.

She went back to his file, reading it silently. He waited.

"You punched the wall in the men's lavatory last week," she said. "Can you tell me why?"

"Yes," he said. "I was frustrated. My father's in jail. The state appointed a special master to oversee my job performance. My top lieutenant would like to have my job and I'm not sure if he's taking active steps to accomplish that goal or not. It was a confluence of events that pissed me off. I went into the men's room and let off some steam."

"Do you think that kind of behavior is normal, or not?" she asked.

"Given the circumstances, I'd say it was very normal," Gus said.

"You often punch the wall?"

"Only when I'm really frustrated," he said.

"How often is that?"

"I dunno," he said. "What does it say in my file? Have I punched dozens of walls in the time since I got out of the Army? Or was this the first one?"

She pursed her lips. Nodded to herself slightly. Then, using the same brightly painted red fingertip, she flipped his file closed.

"I think you're on the PTSD spectrum, Chief Haddock," she said.

He smiled. "Say it ain't so, doc," he said.

She continued as if he hadn't spoken.

"There are basically two ways we have to treat these symptoms," she said. "The first way is either CPT or PE therapies..."

Gus must have looked confused.

"...better known as talk therapy," she continued. "You can come in here once a week and we'll talk about your experiences in combat and find out how deeply rooted those memories may be in your psyche. We'll also talk about your job and life and any frustrations you're dealing with. By talking about them, and doing some other kinds of exercises, we can confront both those past memories and current frustrations, learn how to deal with them and, hopefully, alleviate whatever stress and tension they may be bringing to your life and work."

"Okay," Gus said. "What's the other way?"

"Pharmacotherapy," she said. "I can prescribe various kinds of medications, antidepressants, SSRIs, other things. Again, these are targeted at your anxieties and stress."

"Fine chemicals for better living," Gus said. "Which of the two alternatives are you leaning towards?"

"I think talk therapy is indicated for your case," she said. "I'd like to get you started on regular visits. Can you come in once a week?"

He thought about that for a minute.

"Can we do it once a month?" he asked. "It might be easier to fit that into my schedule. I don't know that I can carve out an hour a week. Three hours, actually, given the travel time up here and back."

She nodded. "That's reasonable," she said. "Let's start a monthly session program and we'll see how it goes."

Gus nodded. "Fine," he said.

Dr. Maloney turned to her desktop computer and opened an appointments app. She called up the calendar for November and scanned through the open dates.

"How does November 20th sound?" she asked. "It's a Tuesday."

He nodded so she typed in his name and hit save. Taking an appointment card from a tray on her desk, she filled out the information and handed it to him.

"We'll see you in a month's time," she said. "If you feel like punching a wall in the meantime, or if anything else crops up, please don't hesitate to give me a call. I can usually squeeze a patient in for emergencies."

Gus got up to leave. Then he paused, looked at her across the desk.

"Can I ask a question?" he said.

"Of course," she nodded. "In this room, you may always talk about anything that's on your mind."

"Where did you get that file?" He nodded at the manila folder on her desk blotter, now closed.

She cocked her head to the side. "What do you mean?" she asked.

"Somebody compiled that file on me," he said. "It has lots of very personal information in it. Stuff about me. Stuff about my dad. There are only one or two people who even know that I punched the wall in the men's room. So where did that file come from?"

Gus was certain that Dr. Maloney's face reddened. Not a lot. But spots of color came up in her cheeks. She seemed a little embarrassed, as if she had been caught out.

"Your file was sent to me by the Attorney General," she said finally. "He recommended that I see you and do an evaluation."

"Huh," Gus said. He suddenly had an urge to punch the wall again, this time making a nice round hole in the soothing and calming British racing green sheet rock next to her Harvard diploma. "Does that mean that anything I say in this room will get back to the AG?"

"No, no," she protested, holding up a hand in a stop motion. "The conversations we have in this room are confidential and protected by law. It would be entirely unethical for me to share anything from our sessions with a third party."

"Even if the third party is the law?" Gus said.

"Absolutely," she said. "Illegal, unethical and unheard of. Our conversations are inviolate."

"Okay," Gus said. "Got it."

But as he left the doctor's office, he wondered if that were true.

CHAPTER 10

4:20 pm— Police in Little Penwick broke up an unruly gathering of teens outside the town Recreation Center on Friday. The group had apparently returned on the afternoon bus from Portsmouth High School and stayed on in the parking lot.

Police had been called after receiving a telephone call reporting that some students were smoking, drinking what looked like alcoholic beverages and behaving in a loud and boisterous nature.

An officer dispersed the teens, but

> *cited two of them for being non-cooper-*
> *ative.*

GUS HADDOCK HAD just finished up a late afternoon meeting with Mr. And Mrs. Lovell, parents of Jason, one of the kids who had been a little rowdy a few days earlier at the Rec Center. Jack Lovell, who owned a construction company in Newport, had come in breathing fire. He told Gus that a bad mark on Jason's record could mean he wouldn't get into the college of his choice. Mrs. Lovell just looked embarrassed. Jason, who was with his parents, looked scared.

"Okay, folks," Gus had said when everyone had said their piece. "I'm going to discharge the citation without prejudice." He looked at the boy's father. "That means there won't be any marks against Jason's record. But Jason, you should consider this to be your one and only bite from the apple. If you act out like this again, we can, and will, use this discharged citation as evidence of a pattern of behavior, and act accordingly. That means we can arrest you, or ask a court to take further actions as warranted. And that, young man, will go onto your permanent record. Where are you thinking of going to college?"

Jason shrugged. "I dunno for sure," he said. "Maybe Quinnipiac, maybe Holy Cross."

"What do you plan to study?"

He shrugged again. "I dunno. Probably business."

"How are your grades?"

"Okay," he said, looking down at the floor.

Gus looked at his mother.

"They could be better," she said. "He's gonna take the SATs again next month."

"Right," Gus said. He turned back to the boy. "Jason, you should think of doing nothing but hitting the books and getting your applications in, OK? That should be Job One for you right now. Horsing around with the guys at the Rec Center is not going to get you into a good college. You are old enough now to take responsibility for your behavior. You're almost legally a man. Time to start acting like one. OK?"

Jason, still looking down at his shoes, nodded. Jack Lovell looked like he wanted to say something, but his wife placed her hand on his arm and he stayed silent.

Gus hesitated, but then decided what the hell. "One more thing, if I may," he said. "I completely support your plan to attend college. Higher education is important and can help you get ahead in the world. But if you're not quite ready to make that move, if you're still trying to figure out who you are and what your mission in life is supposed to be, you might think about joining up with one of the military services. Couple of years investment, good work experience, time to grow and learn about yourself, and, when you come out, Uncle Sam can help with the college tuition. It's not for everybody, but some find it really helpful. And serving your country is always honorable. I hope you'll think about it, and if you have any questions about what it's like, or anything else, please give me a call at any time."

"Thank you, Chief Haddock," Mrs. Lovell said.

The three of them got up and left the chief's office. Gus had about two minutes to think about what he should do next when Buzz Franklin knocked and came into the office.

"Any luck with tracking down our mystery woman?" Gus asked.

Franklin shook his head and plopped down in a chair in front of the chief's desk.

"I flipped through some of the old reports on the Ferros," he said. "Nobody named 'Janine' popped out. We know most of the family members who live in the Swamp. None of the women we know about fits the description of young, blond and beautiful."

"So she's not a Ferro," Gus said.

"Doesn't seem so," the detective said.

"So who is she?"

"I can help answer that," said a female voice from the door. The two men looked up and Maggie Wells stalked in. She was wearing a black down parka from L.L. Bean and a woolen hat, carrying a briefcase on a strap over her shoulder. The weather had turned chilly. Probably chillier near the ocean in Little Penwick than it was up in balmy Providence.

"Whatcha got?" Gus said. Maggie shed her outer coat and hat and dropped into the second guest chair in front of his desk.

"I ran the name 'Janine' through our various data bases," Maggie said, pulling some papers out of her lawyer's briefcase. "That's kind of a long shot, usually, but it's not all that common as a woman's name. I filtered the search to include all Janine's that also matched with Little Penwick. We got a few hits."

"Such as?" Buzz Franklin sounded dubious.

"Janine del Grazio," Maggie read the first name. "Born in Newport in 1987, once listed a home address in Little Penwick. Current whereabouts unknown. Has an arrest for shoplifting in Westchester County, New York, in 2005."

Buzz Franklin looked across the desk at Gus.

"There was a del Grazio family lived over in Terrace Heights," he said. "Don't know if they still live there. I can check it out."

"She'd be in her thirties today," Gus said. "The Janine we saw at the Ferro place looked like she was about twenty." He looked back at Maggie. "Who else ya got?"

"Janine Brown," Maggie read the next name on her list. "Got a speeding ticket in Warwick five years ago. Gave her address as Middletown. Gave her DOB as 1998."

"Age is about right," Gus said. "Where is she now?"

"No idea," Maggie said. "She didn't pay the fine. Notices sent to the given address came back undeliverable."

"Skipjack," Buzz said.

"Don't think it's her," Maggie said. "Her citation said she had brown hair and brown eyes."

"Our Janine had clear blue peepers," Gus said. "And blond hair."

"Hair color can be changed," Maggie said, nodding. "But you can't change your eyes. Even wearing tinted contacts, you can tell."

"Not our girl," Gus said. "Any more?"

Maggie flipped over to the next page of her list. She smiled and nodded to herself.

"Janine Constance Stone," she read. "Showed up a little over three and a half years ago. Age sixteen on the arrest record, so that'd make her about twenty-one now. Picked up on a sweep through the Daddy Cat Lounge, based on a tip derived from a Providence P.D. investigation."

"The Daddy Cat? The strip club?" Buzz said.

"Yup," Maggie nodded. "That night there were four under-age girls in the club, including Janine Stone. Alleged to be working the private rooms."

Buzz looked at Gus. "That's where you can get a hand-job for a C-note," he said. "Totally illegal, of course. But if they're using teenagers, that's even more heinous."

"Club lost its license for three months," Maggie read. "The girls were sent to Family and Children's Services. A few days later, they were all released to one Margaret F. Almeida of Little Penwick, Rhode Island."

"Marge!" Gus and Buzz said the name simultaneously. Then laughed.

"You know her?" Maggie asked.

"Notice the initial 'F' in her name?" Buzz said. "Guess what it stands for?"

"I'm gonna take a stab and guess it's Ferro," Maggie said.

"Bingo," Buzz said. "Marge was Angelo's long-suffering sister. She died about two years ago."

"Natural causes?" Maggie asked.

Buzz chuckled. "As far as we know," he said.

"Why would she bail four teenage hookers out of state custody?" Maggie asked.

"The real question is where did the Daddy Cat strip club get four beautiful young hookers to work their back rooms?" Buzz said. "The likely answer is that the Ferro family arranged the deal. They've been suspected of trafficking prostitutes, among other things, for years. Angelo had a lot of contacts with certain organized crime figures, both locally and down in south Florida. He spent the winters down there and apparently made some good friends in the business. The Florida mob recruits disaffected high school girls from Miami, Fort Lauderdale, Palm Beach and sends them up through their networks in the north and midwest. The Ferro family is one of their best contacts."

"So you think Janine Stone is the girl we saw the other day?" Gus said.

"Sounds very plausible," Buzz said, nodding his head. "I can call up to Providence and get her booking photo."

"But why is she still living in the Swamp?" Maggie asked. "Girls like that are worth a lot of money, but only if they keep working, keep hooking. Nobody is making any money off her if she's just sitting around Daniel Ferro's house in her short-shorts."

"You think the other three girls they rounded up that night are living there too?" Gus asked.

Buzz shook his head.

"Nah, Ms. Wells is right," he said. "Once they get their hooks into those girls, they keep 'em working until they drop. If they start at the $100 a handjob level in the back room at the Daddy Cat, the ones who show talent and initiative get moved up to higher class hooking. Somone who looks like this Janine chick would be turning thousand dollar a night tricks up in Boston or down in New York. Eventually, the beauty fades and they join the regular looking girls doing blowjobs for twenty bucks on the back streets of Providence.

That's usually when they get hooked on heroin or other stuff. Meth. Fentanyl. If they don't die of an overdose, their teeth fall out and they forget to wash their hair and most of them are dead by about age forty. Not a fun life."

"So why is our Janine still here in Little Penwick?" Gus said. "Living with an asshole like Danny Ferro?"

"True love?" Maggie suggested.

The two men laughed.

"What?" she said. "No one ever falls in love with gangsters and assholes?"

"I'm sure they do," Gus said. "But not with gangsters and assholes like Danny Ferro. I can't think of anyone with fewer redeeming characteristics than him."

"Me neither," Buzz chimed in.

"Well, this is a good lead, right?" Maggie said. "Former prostitute, Danny Ferro. And what happened to the other three girls? Who were they? Where did they come from? Where did they go? Seems like we have plenty to go on."

Gus held up his hand. "Whoa, Nellie," he said. "Buzz...do we have any outstanding warrants on this woman?"

"None that I'm aware of," he said.

"She turn up on any police reports in the last three years or so?"

"None that I'm aware of," he said.

"Maggie...does the state have any paper on this woman, except for the strip club sweep of a few years ago?"

"Don't think so," she said, shaking her head sadly. "All I found was the Daddy Cat thing."

"Is there anything in the record that shows what happened to her case?" Gus asked. "Did she and her friends ever appear in court to answer the charges of being a minor working in a strip club?"

Maggie shook her head, frowning. "Now that you mention it, no," she said. "Someone must have deep-sixed the paper."

"So," Gus summed up. "We have an adult woman, one past mark on her record, which miraculously disappeared, nothing since, living peacefully and apparently legally in our fair town. Buzz…do we have any grounds to open an investigation?"

"Nah," he said. "Not that that's ever stopped us in the past."

"You ever seen her out and about in the town?" Gus asked. "Trust me, if you had, you'd remember her."

"I'll take your word for it," Buzz said with a wry grin. "No, I haven't."

"You could stake out Danny Ferro's house, see if he's running a prostitution ring out there in the Swamp," Maggie said

Gus and Buzz just looked at her.

"Yeah, I guess that doesn't make any sense, on several levels," she admitted.

"We need probable cause," Gus said, "And we don't even have improbable cause. Far as we know, she's a law abiding citizen who pays her taxes, stops at red lights and crosswalks, adopts stray animals and has a soft spot for Danny Ferro. All of which is legal and legit. Plus, a judge sent her down here and then tossed her case, which seems to indicate that someone at the top might have whispered in his ear."

He saw Maggie frowning. "I know," he said, "We'd all like to believe such a thing could never happen in our fair state. But we all know that it does. It sucks, but it happens."

"We could ask the guys to keep an eye peeled," Buzz said, stroking his chin in thought. "She must leave the Swamp every now and then, even if it's just to go to the grocery store for a loaf of bread. If we can figure out her schedule, find out what kind of car she's driving, well, then we can get creative."

"Creative?" Maggie said.

Buzz Franklin shrugged. "Hey, everyone makes little mistakes. Maybe she glides through a stop sign or doesn't use her turn signal…something like that. We can pull her over, check her license and registration, maybe have cause to sniff her car. We get lucky, we can bring her in and ask her some questions."

"I don't think I heard any of that," Maggie said, shaking her head in disapproval. "Sounds pretty close to entrapment."

"Or creative law enforcement," Gus said. He nodded at Buzz. "Let's do it. We need to make some progress on this case. And the lovely Miss Stone is about the only hook we've got."

"Roger that, Chief," Buzz said.

"I guess I'll head back up the road," Maggie said. She yawned and stretched. "Unless you want to buy me dinner first."

"That can probably be arranged," Gus said.

CHAPTER 11

HE TOOK HER to the Old Stone House, not too far from the harbor at Little Penwick near the mouth of the Sakonnet River. The big rectangular building, faced with round river stones and decked with wrought-iron porches, had originally been built as a private residence for some wealthy resident back before the Civil War. It had operated as an inn for decades, never making much money despite its being placed on the National Register of Historic Places. After World War II, the only people who came to Little Penwick in the summer season were the second homeowners, most of whom owned huge mansions by the sea, and they rarely needed a place to send their spillover guests.

But the Inn did convert its big barn into an event space, and did a pretty good business in hosting weddings and parties for the local wealthy clientele. And the little pub down in the basement of the inn, which had originated during Prohibition as the local speakeasy, still attracted casual diners.

Gus led Maggie in her car a few miles from the center of Little Penwick to the Inn, and they parked and ducked inside the cellar door. Inside, the warm wooden paneling and low beamed ceiling provided some atmosphere, and there was a wood fire burning in the stone hearth against one wall, throwing off some nice warmth against the chill of the night. They took a table near the fire and Gus ordered a beer.

"You drinking anything?" he asked Maggie.

"I'll have some white wine," Maggie told the waitress. "But only one. I gotta drive up to Providence later."

They ordered some chowder and fish and then sat back, sipping their drinks and enjoying the fire.

"I got a question," Maggie said when they had settled in.

Gus took a sip of his beer. "Shoot," he said.

"What's up with your name?"

"Well," Gus said, "Haddock is an old English name. Obviously was given to some ancient fisherman. Like 'Carpenter' was the surname of some old Brit who was good with saws and hammers; and 'Baker' became the name of the guy who made the daily bread. There's an Old English word, *hadduc*—" He spelled it out for her. "That apparently meant someone who worked as a fisherman or fish monger. But some believe that the surname Haddock might have originally referred to people from the town of Haydock, which is near Liverpool. There are some other possibilities, but they've always seemed more obscure to me. Less believable."

Maggie sipped some wine and smiled at him.

"Fascinating, to be sure," she said. "But I meant, what's up with your first name?"

"Augustus?" Gus said. "He was one of the Caesars in ancient Rome."

"I know that," she said. "But your father is named Julius. He was also a Roman emperor. And I've noticed that you both have a middle name that starts with the letter 'C.' What does the initial stand for?"

"Caesar," Gus said, smiling.

"Both of you?"

"Yup."

"That a family name?"

"No," Gus said, with a chuckle. "My grandfather, whose name was John Edward Haddock, by the way, was into all things Roman. He thought naming his son after Julius Caesar would give him a good start in life. My dad decided to inflict the same lifelong pain on me."

She laughed. He liked her laugh. Her face softened and glowed when she smiled like that. Or maybe it was just the soft light of the candles and fire down here in the old speakeasy.

"I would imagine being named Augustus Caesar Haddock would be a burden," she said. "And probably led to some awesome playground fights in school."

"Naw," Gus said. "My Dad was chief of police. Nobody was gonna mess with me."

"What about in the Army?"

Gus shrugged. "My men mostly called me 'Fish,'" he said, "At least out in the field. The only people in the Army who ever knew my full name were back in Washington in the personnel office. And they didn't care."

"Anyone ever call you Caesar?" she said with a mischievous smile.

"No one who lived very long afterward," Gus responded with a grin of his own.

The waitress brought out two bowls of clam chowder, with potatoes and diced clam parts swimming in the rich creamy broth. Gus, suddenly famished, dumped his plastic-wrapped packet of oyster crackers into his bowl and dug in.

"So tell me something about you," he said between spoonfuls. "I don't know anything about your background, except that you were sent to spy on my department."

She frowned at that, but decided to let it pass.

"I grew up in upstate New York," she told Gus. "Not far from Syracuse. My Dad is a lawyer, my Mom a medical records executive. I got into Brown and never left. I guess Providence is just the right size city for me…not too big and not too small. I got my law degree at Roger Williams and then applied for and got an appointment with the AG. That was six years ago."

"No boyfriends? Or girlfriends. Whatever…"

She laughed. "No sex life, period," she said. "Really, my career is too busy for much of a personal life. Every year at New Year's, I go through this horrible few days judging my life and asking all kinds of questions about where I am and where I'm going. But I end up just keeping on with what I'm doing."

"That must mean you like what you do," Gus said.

"Or it means I'm too lazy and unmotivated to do anything to change," she said. Then she laughed again. "See? I've already started my annual emotional reappraisal. And it's not even November yet."

"No sense beating yourself up," Gus said. "You seem like a perfectly capable person to me. If you want to change anything about your life, I think you have that power."

"Yeah, I know," she said, waving her spoon in the air. "And I do love what I do. I guess we're all just trained to keep asking hard questions of ourselves."

"Trained by idiots," Gus said. "Like those liberal assholes at Brown."

"Oh, boy," she said. "Here we go."

This time Gus laughed. Maggie had to laugh with him. She could tell he was trying to wind her up. It was a form of flirting. And she liked it.

"So are you still pissed that I'm here?" she said, as the waitress stopped by and took their empty bowls away.

"Can't think of anyone else I'd rather be having dinner with than you," he said.

"Stop it," she said sternly. "You know what I mean."

He was silent for a few moments, thinking.

"I was never pissed at you, really," he said finally. "I mean, you didn't ask the AG to be sent down here to make my life difficult. At least, I don't think you did. So I was mainly displeased with the reasons why he thought it was necessary."

"And I explained that," she said. "With the situation with your dad and all, plus your lack of experience at the head of the department, I think the AG is right to make sure that everything down here is being run properly."

"Do you think it is?" Gus asked.

This time, Maggie was silent and thinking.

"Yeah," she said. "I haven't seen anything that says red flag to me. The department seems to be very well run, and the personnel seems to be able to handle the work."

"I hear a large 'but' in there," Gus said.

"Only about the Ferro case," she said. "And that's the one the AG is most concerned about."

"What is the deal with him and that family?" Gus asked.

The waitress came back with a tray carrying two broiled scrod dinners, complete with baked potatoes and sides of roasted vegetables. Gus scraped his green stuff onto his bread plate, squirted the lemon wedge onto his fish and began to eat.

"You don't like broccoli?" she asked, smiling at him.

"I don't like vegetables period," he said. "I didn't know this until just a few years ago, but I've been on the Paleo diet my entire life….meat, potatoes, grains and nuts, a little fruit and maybe six approved veggies, three of which are also called salad."

"Geez," she said, shaking her head. "I wonder what your cholesterol levels must be."

"On the high side," he admitted. "But I'm still here. And you've avoided my questions about the AG."

Maggie put some butter and sour cream onto her baked potato. Gus thought about mentioning her cholesterol levels, but decided to keep his mouth shut.

"Well, first of all, this is Rhode Island," she said, adding some salt and pepper to her plate.

"Where everything is political," Gus said. His fish and about half his potato were already gone.

Maggie broke a small sliver of scrod off with her fork, speared it, and brought it up to her mouth, where she chewed it carefully. She nodded approvingly to herself and continued.

"And as I'm sure you know, one of the largest ethnic groups here in Rhode Island, a group that wields rather impressive political weight, is the Cape Verdean community. Ethnic Portuguese, most of them originally fishermen back in the Cape Verde Islands off the coast of north Africa, came here in huge numbers throughout the twentieth century. They settled all over southeast New England, wherever there was a fishing industry. Cape Cod, New Bedford, all around Narragansett Bay. Now in their third or fourth generation, they've learned how to organize and vote."

"The American way," Gus said.

"Indeed," Maggie nodded. "There are Verdean mayors and councilmen everywhere, a bunch of them in our General Assembly, and they come out and vote every election. In numbers."

"And Preston Knox wants them to vote for him," Gus said. "He's running for governor next time, isn't he?"

Maggie nodded. "Yeah, I think so," she said. "We're not allowed to talk about state politics in the office, so nothing has ever been said out loud. But the water cooler talk is that Preston plans to run."

"And he wants our Ferros to support him?"

"I'm sure he does," Maggie said. "But he mostly wants them to contribute money. Of which they seem to have a lot."

"Most of it illegally gained," Gus said. "Which doesn't seem to bother the AG very much."

Maggie shrugged. "If he got his campaign money from the usual suspects down on Wall Street, you gonna get all pissy about morals and ethics from those guys? C'mon, Gus. Spare me the sermon."

He laughed. "Touché," he said. "There are dirtballs everywhere."

When they were finished, Gus ordered coffee for two. "Dessert?" he asked. "They make a bread pudding like your gramma used to make, only better. With bourbon hard sauce, which nobody makes any more."

"I'll pass," she said. "But you go ahead. Sounds like you want some. And since your arteries are already shot to hell, you might as well go for it."

Gus looked longingly at the menu, but decided to stick with coffee.

"Good boy," she cooed at him, patting him on the hand. He smiled at her. He liked her smile. He liked the feeling of her hand touching his. He wanted to reach over and touch her back, but decided that would be inappropriate. She was, after all, his special master. Then he thought about Cranks—real name Charlie Johnson—his old mortar man from the Rangers unit. Cranks, short for Crankie, was the unit's resident misogynist, never at a loss to come out with some kind of sexist, anti-woman comment, even if bullets were flying overhead and RPGs were exploding everywhere. Gus always figured it was just Cranks' way of letting off some steam, and that he was probably as polite and empathetic around women as anyone else. But he knew that had Cranks been sitting at the table with them, and somehow draped in an Invisibility Cloak, he would have said something like "You want to touch her hand? C'mon Fish…think bigger! She's practically beggin' for it!"

That made him grin. And Maggie saw it.

"What's funny?" she asked.

"Nothing," Gus said, his face reddening a little. "Just thinking about an old buddy from the Rangers."

"And?…"

He shook his head. He'd studied enough military strategy to know when to retreat.

So instead, they finished their coffee, he paid the bill, walked her out to her car in the parking lot and watched her taillights disappear in the direction of Providence. Maybe she's not as bad as I thought, he thought as he got into his own car and went home.

CHAPTER 12

A COUPLE OF days later, Buzz Franklin called Gus at home early in the morning. Gus was out of the shower and half dressed.

"What up?" he said, rubbing his wet hair with a towel.

"Thought you'd like to know," Buzz said, "We got Miss Janine Stone in the interview room here at the station."

"You arrested her?"

Buzz chuckled. "Nah," he said, "Not yet anyway. I got a lead on her car and Patrolman Lincoln saw her driving down Main Road earlier this morning. He pulled her over."

"What did she do?" Gus asked.

Buzz's slow chuckle came across the phone again.

"Taillight out," he said. "Patrolman Lincoln thought there was something suspicious and brought her into the station to answer a few questions."

"That doesn't sound bogus at all," Gus said. "How long can we keep her?"

"A couple of hours, I'd guess," he said. "Then we'll either have to let her call a lawyer or let her go."

"I'll be right in," Gus said.

THERE WAS AN electric feeling in the squad room when Gus Haddock arrived ten minutes later. The morning shift officers were delaying leaving for their assignments and the night shift crew were hanging around—all waiting to see what happened next. It was pretty rare for any suspect to be held for questioning at the Little Penwick Police Department. Most of the people arrested in the town were the result of automobile violations: DUIs, driving with suspended licenses or registrations, or more serious moving violations. And those miscreants were rarely questioned much locally. Instead, they were held for a short while before being transported to Newport for arraignment in the Newport District Court, or hauled up to Providence for the staties to handle.

But today they had a live one, and all the cops were interested in that. Especially since the arrestee was Janine Stone, who was pretty easy on the eyes. At least, that's what all the male cops thought. So everyone wanted to see what happened next.

Gus arrived and was met almost at the door by Jessica Martin, the department's sergeant. Her job was personnel and processing, as in paperwork. Martin was in her late forties and had been with the Little Penwick cops for about ten years, which meant she had worked with Gus before he left for the Army. In fact, she had helped train him when he was a probie. Now, she looked worried.

"I hope you know what you're doing, Chief," she said when Gus walked into the station. "From what Buzz has told me, there's not much you can keep her on."

"Don't want to keep her, Jess," Gus said. "Just want to talk to her a little."

"Which is fine, if she wants to cooperate," Martin said. "But if she doesn't want to talk, there's nothing you can do. You gotta let her go."

"I know," Gus said. "We'll see what happens."

"OK," the sergeant said. "But keep it all on the up and up. There are eyes on this place everywhere. Interested eyes."

Gus figured she was talking about Callahan, and he nodded at her. "I know," he said.

He went into his office and hung up his coat. Buzz Franklin came in, holding some file folders under his arm.

"How did you find her car?" Gus asked first.

Buzz Franklin grinned. "I put a little remote camera up on a tree across from the Ferro's private road," he said. "This morning, I watched her little yellow car come out, checked the plate number, and told Carl to bring her in."

"Will any of that stand up in court?"

Buzz just smiled.

"Where is she?" Gus asked.

"In the interview room," Buzz said. "Dottie got her some coffee. She's been quiet and cooperative." He paused and looked at Gus. "You want me to call Maggie Wells? Tell her what we have here?"

Gus thought about that. It was probably the right thing to do. But it would take Maggie at least an hour to drive down from Providence. He knew that Maggie would go bullshit over Franklin's surveillance and intercept. And he didn't want to let Janine loose before he could talk to her.

"Naw," he finally decided. "We don't have time. You and I will go talk to her."

Buzz nodded. He led the way down the hall to the interview room.

The room was twelve feet by eight, windowless, with a row of fluorescent lights on the ceiling. There was a wood-top table in the middle of the room, and six metal side chairs around the edges. Sitting at one end of the table was Janine Stone, dressed in a light gray fuzzy sweater top and black trousers. Her winter overcoat and a knitted cap were draped across another chair along the wall next to her. There was a cup of coffee in a cardboard container in front of her and she was leafing through a magazine that, no doubt, Dottie Adams had given her when she brought in the coffee. Looking at it upside down, Gus thought it was a copy of People.

Janine looked up when the two officers came through the door and frowned. She looked piqued but not the boiling mad kind of angry. I can work with that, Gus thought.

He sat down on one side of the table and Buzz walked around and sat down opposite him. Buzz took out his cell phone, punched and swiped a few times and then put it down on the table top between him and Janine.

He started by giving the date, the time and announcing the names of the three persons in the room. "This interview is being recorded," he added, as if that were not rather obvious.

"Don't you have to read me my rights?" Janine said, a small smile playing at the corners of her lips. Her deep blue eyes were locked on Gus. She knew…or perhaps had been told … that he was the one in charge.

"Ms. Stone, you are not under arrest," Gus said calmly. "This is an informational interview only."

"So I'm free to go?"

"You may leave at any time," Gus told her. "But your car, which is being inspected by our officers, will not be ready for you for another hour or so. And if you choose to be uncooperative, that can be introduced as evidence if, at some time in the future, you are placed under arrest and undergo a court trial. Do you understand?"

She nodded, slowly.

"Please respond verbally," Gus said.

"Yes," she said. "I get it."

"How long have you resided in the town of Little Penwick?" Gus began.

"About three years," she said. "Maybe four. I've lost track."

"Are you currently employed?"

"Is that required by law?" she said. "I gotta have a job to live here?"

"Of course not," Gus said. "I am merely trying to learn a little more about you."

"I…ah…work from home," she said finally.

"And what is it you do?"

She paused again. Finally she smiled. "I'm in personnel," she said. "Like a headhunter."

"How interesting," Gus said. "What kind of people do you recruit?"

"Mostly strippers," she said. "For the clubs up in Providence."

"Is that right?" Gus said.

"Yes," she said. "And I sometimes do job training as well."

"Also for the strip clubs?"

"That's right," she said.

"Is that a good business?" Gus asked.

"It's steady work," she said with a smile. "Thanks to horny men like you."

"How long would you say you've been engaged in this kind of work?"

"Most of the time I've lived here," she said.

"Between Detective Franklin and myself," Gus said, "We've lived in this town for thirty years or more. I don't think either one of us knows a resident of Little Penwick who strips for a living. You do a lot of recruiting here locally?"

She chuckled softly this time.

"No," she said, "No, I don't think any of my girls has ever been to Little Penwick. I get my girls from out of state mostly. A lot of them come from Florida, where I used to live."

"'Your girls,'" Gus repeated her locution. "Do you consider yourself like their den mother, or more like their pimp?"

Janine's face reddened and her eyes narrowed. Gus knew he had landed a shot. But she didn't respond.

"OK," he said after a pause, "Let's move on. What is your current address?"

She gave them the number of the house where Danny Ferro lived, once the home of Angelo. Buzz Franklin wrote it down, his pen scratching on the legal pad.

"Is that the home currently occupied by Daniel G. Ferro?"

"It is," she said.

"Are you and Mr. Ferro in a romantic relationship?"

She laughed out loud. Then she sat up a bit straighter and pointed a finger at Gus.

"Number one, fuck right off," she said. "Number two, none of your damn business. Number three, you've got to be kidding. His wife Catarina would come after me with a butcher's knife."

"So that's a 'No,'" Gus said.

"You're damn right," she said. "Jesus."

"Is Mr. Ferro also involved in the … er … recruiting business?"

"I don't know," she said. "You'll have to ask him. He's got a lot of things going on."

"How many of those things are legal?" Buzz Franklin asked.

Janine shrugged. Then she remembered the tape recorder. "I don't know what Danny Ferro does all day," she said. "Why don't you ask him?"

"Ms. Stone," Gus said, "Is it true that you first came to reside in Little Penwick sometime around …" He riffled through the stack of papers he brought into the room, found the page he was looking for. "…ah, here it is. Sometime around the fifteenth of March, 2017? Two weeks after you had been arrested and charged with solicitation of immoral acts while working at the Daddy Cat Lounge on Allens Avenue in Providence, Rhode Island?"

"If you say so," she said.

"And were you at that time placed in the temporary custodial authority of one Margaret Almeida?"

"Yes," she said. "Just like it says on those papers."

"And what was the relationship between Ms. Almeida and Angelo Ferro, formerly a resident of Little Penwick?"

"They were both old," Janine said.

"Was there a familial relationship that you knew of?"

"I believe they were brother and sister," she said. "Is that illegal in this stupid state?"

"How did Ms. Almeida come to get custody of you and I believe three other girls of similar age who were also arrested and charged following that incident at the Daddy Cat Lounge?"

"A bunch of lawyers huddled with this judge guy," she said. "I couldn't hear what anyone was saying. Then the judge told us we were going to live with Margie. So we did."

"Were those other girls also working at the Daddy Cat?"

"Yes."

"Were those other girls also under the age of 18 years?"

"Yes."

"Did you know them before coming to Rhode Island?"

"I knew a couple of them," she said. "We had known each other in high school down in Fort Lauderdale. The other girl was from West Palm. She was a bitch, though."

"So you and these other girls had come up to Rhode Island from Florida to work at the Daddy Cat Lounge, you all got arrested and then the judge sent you down here to Little Penwick to live with Margaret Almeida."

"That's about right," she said.

"What happened to your case?" Gus said.

"What case?" she asked.

"You were arrested and charged," Gus said. "Did you ever appear in court to answer for those charges?"

"Nope," Janine said. "Margaret told me it had been taken care of."

"Taken care of in what way?"

She shrugged. "I dunno. Margaret just said it was over and not to worry about it."

"Who recruited you?"

"How's that?"

"How did you get recruited to work at the Daddy Cat Lounge in Providence, Rhode Island, a place about a thousand miles from where you lived in Florida?"

"Oh," she said. "I knew this guy from school, and he knew some people and he said I should talk with them and I did. They offered me money to come up here to work. Like I said, I knew a couple other girls who were also offered the same deal. We decided to jump on it."

"What was the name of this guy from Fort Lauderdale?"

She smiled at Gus. "I don't remember."

"Did you parents approve?"

Janine laughed out loud. "My parents haven't approved of a single thing I did after about age thirteen," she said. "Right after I got my period for the first time. They didn't approve of that, either."

"Have you communicated with your parents since you came up here to Rhode Island?" Gus asked.

Janine looked at him with an expression of disgust, but said nothing.

"The witness is refusing to answer, but her expression seems to indicate a negative response to the last question," Gus intoned. He glanced down at his notes and asked another question.

"When you came to Little Penwick, back there in 2017, did you enroll in the local school?"

"Nah," Janine said. "I was pretty much done with school."

"You were under the age of 18, is that right?"

"Yeah," she said.

"We have a law in this stupid state that says all children under the age of 18 must attend school, public, private or parochial," Gus said. "Were you aware that you were breaking this law?"

"Was that me or my legal guardians breaking the law?" Janine asked, smiling sweetly at Gus. "I was just a child, right?"

He pressed on.

"Did you work for Angelo Ferro or his son Daniel at any time over the last three or four years?"

"I always tried to be helpful," she said. "They were nice enough to give me a place to live. Least I could do was try to help around the house as much as I could."

"So you did cleaning?"

"Sometimes."

"Cooking?"

"Well, Margie was in charge of the kitchen, but sometimes I guess."

"Turn any tricks for Angelo's friends?"

Her face reddened again. Gus could see in her eyes that he had landed another shot.

"That's an insulting question," she said.

"So the answer is no, then?"

She remained silent. Gus watched her eyes, which glanced down at her hands, folded neatly on the table in front of her. He watched her jaw twitch slightly and she shook her head, a very slight side to side motion, as if to clear away something she had been thinking about. Then he watched as her eyes rose and locked directly onto his.

"I met your Dad once," she said. Her chin came up. There was an attitude of defiance in her voice.

"Is that right?" Gus said.

"Yeah," she said. "Couple summers ago. Down at the Flume."

The coastline of Little Penwick was mostly bordered by the open Atlantic. There were a few rocky islets off the mouth of the Sakonnet River, but a mile or so east of the river's mouth the rollers came in undeterred by any land masses until you hit Bermuda. East coast surfers knew that the beaches in Little Penwick offered some of the best surfing on the East Coast, especially when a storm motored past the coast just offshore. The place they called the Flume had the perfect configuration—shallow, gradually rising bottom in a single two hundred yard wide section—which resulted in beautiful rollers that broke consistently well twenty yards offshore. During the summer, the beach there was always full of surfers and their friends.

"He on his board?"

She smiled. "Yeah," she said. "The kids got a kick out of this old guy surfin' out there. I remember his wetsuit had this gold badge design on it."

"Yeah, he had that specially made," Gus said with a smile. "He called it the thin blue wave suit."

She smiled back. "So he talked to me a bit that day," she said. "Seemed nice. Everyone liked him. I found out later he was a cop. Chief of police, in fact. Kinda blew my mind."

"Why?" Gus said. "Because he was a cop who surfed, or because he was a cop who was nice?"

Janine shrugged. "I dunno," she said. "Both, probably. I liked him, too."

"Well," Gus said, "That's sweet. I'll tell him. I'm supposed to visit him again at the ACI on Sunday."

"Oh, that's right," Janine said, "He's in jail. Well you can also tell him I know what went down with Angelo."

There was dead silence in the interview room. Neither police officer looked at the other. Both kept their eyes locked onto the face of Janine Stone, who sat back and smiled with a gotcha look of self-satisfaction.

The door to the room flew open and Maggie Wells stood there in her heavy outdoor coat, the strap from her briefcase draped over one shoulder, her car keys jangling from her gloved hands.

"What the absolute hell is going on here?" she said, her voice loud, strained and just this side of being a shout. "Franklin...Haddock...in my office, right now!"

She turned on her heel and left.

CHAPTER 13

"Are you out of your freaking minds?"

Maggie's voice was still in the hysterical, near-shouting mode, even fifteen minutes after she had ended the interview with Janine Stone. Gus and Buzz had picked up their papers and walked silently down the hall and into Gus' office. Maggie had dropped off her coat, returned to the interview room and informed Janine that she was free to leave. Immediately. Janine had smiled, nodded, grabbed her coat and hat and left the station.

Now, Maggie, red faced and angry as a scalded cat, was standing against the wall in Gus' office, arms crossed across her chest.

"I don't know what you two morons were doing," she said, "But I can think of about seven good reasons why bringing that woman in here was a bad idea. A really bad idea. Monu-mentally bad."

"Her tail light was out," Buzz Franklin tried to defend himself. "Sure, that might be weak tea, but we all wanted the chance to talk to her. This was our chance."

Maggie was shaking her head back and forth as he spoke. She wasn't buying a bit of what he was selling.

"Horsefeathers," she said, stomping her foot for good measure. "A goddam first year law student could see the bro-ken tail light excuse as weak as shit. A second year law stu-dent would know enough to ask the judge to have both of you thrown under the jail for contempt. Or misapplication of the law. Or about fifteen other offenses. C'mon, Gus, you should know better than that."

"There is an ongoing and open investigation into the dis-appearance of Angelo Ferro," he said. "We were questioning a witness who might have had some insight into that disappear-ance. That's perfectly legal, ethical and allowed under the law."

"Harassment. False imprisonment. Jesus Christ, stalking comes to mind," Maggie said, ticking her charges off with her fingers. "How did you find her car?"

Gus looked at Buzz, who shifted uncomfortably in his chair.

"We had, um, surveillance that picked up her vehicle," he said.

"Surveillance," Maggie repeated, her voice dripping with sarcasm. "Court ordered? Warrant? Reasonable cause? Any-thing, you know, legal involved?"

"I received a tip that she was driving a yellow Miata," he said. "That automobile was seen this morning on the street.

Officer Lincoln followed the vehicle, noticed the tail light was out and pulled her over."

"Tail light," Maggie said with a sneer. "Lincoln punch it out himself?"

"That would be illegal," Gus said. "My officers are trained to follow the law. He pulled her over and, knowing we had some questions for her concerning the investigation this department is running, asked if she would come into the station. She agreed."

"Agreed or was forced?"

"I believe it was consensual," Gus said. "Ms. Stone did not express any complaints about her treatment or anything else to me. Did you hear anything, Buzz?"

"Not a word," Buzz said.

"I will ask Carl when he gets in off his shift," Gus said. "But I think we're covered."

"Covered." Maggie's voice dripped with venom.

"She said she knew what went down between my Dad and Angelo," Gus said. "We were about to ask her about that when you stormed in and threw a hissy fit. Now I guess we'll never find out what she knows."

Maggie looked at the two men like they had grown horns and tails.

"You're gonna try and turn this around and blame it on me?" she said, her voice rising again into a low-grade shriek. "You've got some fuckin' nerve, let me tell you…"

"I'm trying to run an investigation," Gus said, keeping his voice calm and low. "We're following the leads we have and talking to witnesses that might have something to contribute.

Ms. Stone's interview was part of that process. Frankly, I'm not sure why you're so upset."

"Because you didn't tell me," she said. This time her voice was low in timbre and devoid of emotion. But it was still as effective as if her words were knives, each one stabbing into the men's chests.

"I asked ..." Buzz started to explain. Gus cut him off, thinking to himself that Buzz was trying to cover his own ass, which he didn't appreciate.

"And I made the decision to proceed with the interview," he said. "I didn't know where you were or how long it would take you to get down here, and I didn't want to inconvenience Ms. Stone for longer than was necessary."

Maggie just looked at him. She shook her head, turned, and stalked out of the room.

There was silence for a few moments.

"Well, I think that went well," Buzz said.

CHAPTER 14

GUS WENT UP to the ACI to visit his father again that Sunday. He usually visited every other week, unless Julius got word to him through the grapevine that he needed to see Gus. But the last couple of weeks had been quiet.

"Hey, Junior," his father said when he sat down on his side of the Plexiglas wall and picked up the telephone handset. "How's it going?"

"I think I'm supposed to ask *you* that," Gus said.

Julius shrugged, as if to say different day, same old shit. "It's going the way it goes," he said. "How's things with Miss Maggie?"

Gus frowned. "As bad as it's been yet," he said glumly.

Julius grinned. "Not coming across, is she?" he said. "Too bad. She looks like she'd be a tiger between the sheets."

"Yeah," Gus said. "All teeth and claws and nothing but pain."

"Woo-ee," his father chuckled. "That does sound bad. Tell me."

So Gus related the last few days of interaction between the two. He told his father about his suspicion about Maggie insisting that Gus enroll in counseling. And about the interview with Janine Stone that Maggie had interrupted.

"Do you remember that girl, Janine?" Gus asked his father. "She said she talked to you once a couple years ago when you were surfing the Flume."

"Yeah," his father said, "I know who she is. She recruits new girls for the clubs up on Allen Street. Mostly in Florida, but also in Atlanta and Phoenix. I've heard they think highly of her up in Providence."

"She told Buzz and I that she knew something about what went down between Angelo and you that night," Gus said. "Does she?"

Julius shrugged noncommittally. "I have no idea what she knows or doesn't know," he said. "Too bad you didn't ask her yourself."

"Yeah, well the Tiger Lady came in and put a stop to the interview," he said. "She still hasn't spoken to either one of us. It's been almost a week now."

Julius smiled at his son through the glass. "Women aren't too good at apologizing," he said. "Especially when they're wrong."

"Was she wrong?"

"I believe you'll find that Rhode Island law allows law enforcement to conduct interviews on open matters under investigation," Julius said. "There is absolutely nothing illegal or unethical in asking a member of the public what they know about a case. They can always say 'I don't know' or 'I don't want to talk about that' or even 'I want my lawyer present.' But she did none of the above, right? In fact, from what you tell me, she indicated a willingness to provide further information. Sounds like it was all on the up-and-up to me."

"Then why did Maggie blow it up?" Gus said.

Julius nodded. "That's the right question, sonny boy," he said. "Why does Preston Knox want to throw a blanket over all things Ferro? He's protecting the family. Blatantly. That's what I'd be wondering about, if I were still the chief."

"Maggie gave me the song and dance about the Cape Verdean community and their political clout," Gus said. "Campaign donations and running for governor."

Julius stroked his chin, which was covered with a whitish stubble. Gus wondered about that for a moment. He had never known his father to not shave, religiously, first thing every morning. It was like his ritual for starting the day.

"I don't know what Knox is doing," Julius said finally. "But I'd bet the farm that it's something more important than protecting some campaign donations for his upcoming campaign for governor."

"I don't get it," Gus said. "The Ferro clan are just a bunch of swamp yankees. Northern rednecks. Lowlife bums into a wide variety of scams, cons, petty crime...anything to avoid having to hold down an actual job and earn a living. But they're not rolling in the bucks, not by a longshot. So why is Preston Knox protecting them? What does he get out of the deal?"

"That, my friend, sounds like an excellent avenue for further investigation," his father said. "Danny Ferro is way down on the food chain. Preston Knox, the Attorney General, only deals with the hoi polloi, the ones who have expense accounts for lunch at the Capital Grille, the committee chairs at the State house and those who have the juice to be able to get anyone in Washington on the blower."

"Have the Ferros ever been connected?" Gus asked.

"You mean with the Family?" Julius raised his eyebrows. "Not a chance. Even old Angelo didn't have that kind of juice. These guys are stumblebums…petty criminals…nickel and dime guys. He mighta met Ray Patriarca once upon a time, at some social event or wedding or funeral or something, but there's no way the Family would get involved with a couple of jokers from Little Penwick. Not a chance in the world. Different universes."

"Well, there's something that has Knox's attention," Gus said. "And right now, that means Miss Thing is all up in our grills."

"Well, we all have our crosses to bear, son," Julius said. As if to illustrate his point, a chime rang through the visitor's area. It meant ten minutes until visiting hours were over.

"Janine Stone said she lives in Danny Ferro's house, is not sleeping with him and does recruiting and training for new strippers at the joints along Allens Avenue in Providence," Gus said.

Julius Haddock nodded wisely on his side of the glass.

"Like I said, the boys up in the city seem to like her work," he said. "After all, she looks like a stripper, except more wholesome. And she looks good in a wetsuit, too."

"She's a surfer?" Gus said, somewhat surprised. "She didn't tell me that. My impression was she was just hanging out with the kids at the beach."

"Nope," Julius said. "She's got good stick. I watched her that day. Definitely not a grom."

"Whatever that is," Gus said.

"She can handle her board," his father said. "She's from Florida, right?"

"Fort Lauderdale," Gus said.

Julius nodded. "I've known some guys who grew up surfing south Florida," he said. "They're usually technically proficient. You gotta know how to handle your board when the waves are three feet or less. Lotta those jokers from SoCal wouldn't even go out in the water for waves like that. So if she learned to surf in Lauderdale, she knows how to surf."

Gus blew out a breath. "Yeah, well, that's fascinating and all, but I'm more interested in where she learned how to recruit and train strippers," he said. "There's a learning curve in that business, too, and the teachers are usually goombahs packin' heat."

Julius nodded at his son as the chime sounded again and this time didn't stop. Gus could hear the groans from the fifty or so visitors in the main hall and heard the guards beginning to call for people to pack up and leave.

One of the guards came and stood behind Julius on his side of the Plexiglas window. Gus heard the guard say something and watched Julius nod at him.

"Gotta run, sonny boy," he said. "You're asking the right questions. Good luck with the digging."

Julius Haddock hung up his telephone receiver, winked at his son and turned and walked back to jail.

CHAPTER 15

Since Gus was already in the neighborhood, which is what
he considered all of the western shore of Narragansett Bay to
be, he decided to do a little police work.

He left the ACI facility, got back onto Interstate 95 North
but quickly jumped off at Thurbers Avenue, and after a couple quick turns, found himself on Allens Avenue, down on the
waterfront. The Interstate rumbled by on its elevated concrete
foundations to the west, but down in the shadows, Allens Avenue was a dingy and narrow two-lane road. Looking east, one
could occasionally catch a glimpse of the rotting wharves in
the Providence River, which turned into Narragansett Bay at
Fox Point. The businesses down here were mostly junk yards,
metal processing plants, one of the city's DPW depots with
its tower of sand and salt for winter roadway treatment, a

couple of used car lots, some gas stations, convenience stores and, grouped together within one three-block section, the city of Providence's adult entertainment district.

Providence had always been famous—or infamous—for its strip bars. They had become fixtures in the city when the town was under the control of the Cosa Nostra under its longtime New England capo, Raymond Patriarca. For the Family, the bars and the strippers and the hookers had been a good source of capital. Patriarca made sure that all the necessary Providence politicians, from the mayor on down, were suitably greased, especially around election time, so instead of trying to ban the business, the town fathers zoned it into tightly controlled districts and pretty much left it alone.

As a result, Providence and its freewheeling adult bars attracted customers from all over New England. Over the years, the names of the joints had changed, sometimes frequently and often after law enforcement stepped in to make arrests for gambling rings, prostitution activities and under-age girls stripping in the bars. Usually those offenses would result in a fine or loss of the liquor license for a week or two. More serious transgressions would lead to loss of the business license. But that only meant the old owner would sell the business to a new owner who could pass the background checks and obtain the liquor license. Of course, everyone knew that both the old owner and the new ones were really controlled by The Family. It was just a revolving door where both inside and outside were owned by the same people.

But the same collection of buildings—one of which had recently been painted a particularly garish shade of pink which made it glow when lit up at night for the motorists passing by on I-95—still contained the same activities. And the men who ran the businesses were mostly the same, kept in place by their willingness to siphon off a good percentage of the take to the bent-nose boys who kept their offices in a nicer part of town.

Gus was driving his squad car SUV, so he decided that going in under cover would be a waste of time. He pulled into the Daddy Cat Lounge parking lot, stopped at the V.I.P. valet parking entrance and tossed his keys at the kid dressed neatly in a shirt and tie.

"Good afternoon, officer," the kid said, handing Gus his parking stub. "You want her washed and detailed while you're inside this afternoon?"

"You do anything to this car besides parking it where it won't get scratched or dented, and I'll break every bone in every finger you got," Gus said. "*Capisce?*"

"Yes, sir," the kid said. "Loud and clear."

Gus turned and walked inside.

In the middle of a Sunday afternoon, the lobby was empty and, glancing through the doors to the runway room, Gus could see that business in the Daddy Cat was slow. There was a large blond woman with blue streaked hair sitting in the check-in booth, collecting the $20 cover charge and stamping the backs of the hands of the patrons coming in.

Gus held up his police ID badge and asked the woman "is Benji Stein working today? If not, I wanna see the head guy."

He had met Stein earlier in the summer down at Little Penwick harbor when some kids had egged the man's 50-foot cabin cruiser. Gus had calmed him down, helped him clean up the mess and, in talking with him, found out what he did for a living: Benjamin Stein was the Daddy Cat's business manager. Gus suspected his job title was even broader than that.

"Mr. Stein is not working this afternoon," the blond lady said. "But Mister Giancarlo can probably give you a few minutes."

Gus nodded and the woman snapped her fingers at one of the huge bouncers that had been milling about in the lobby area. The neckless lout with steroidal arm muscles stepped forward.

"Ricardo," was all she said, and the guy nodded.

"This way, please," the guy said and led Gus down a side hallway, and up a flight of stairs to the office level above. He continued down the dark hallway and knocked on the door at the end.

"Come," said a voice from within. The goombah opened the door and motioned Gus to step through.

Inside was an expansive office with plush white carpeting, white leather chairs and a sofa, and a large glass desk. To the right, a large picture window provided a panoramic view of the entire downstairs floor: in front was the central bar and runway area, where a couple of tired looking women were swaying to the heavily amplified rock music. They each wore a spangly G-string and nothing else, save for the garter belt each strapped around her thigh. There were just a few single bills tucked into the garters…it was Sunday afternoon and business was slow.

All around the walls on three sides of the runway room were smaller conversation groupings of chairs and sofas. These were the "private" dance areas, where on a prearranged deal, one of the strippers would perform a lap dance, ten minutes of mostly naked gyrations and whispered suggestion. At the back of the room, a curtained wall hid a doorway which Gus knew led back to the private rooms where more serious activities were going on, far beyond prying eyes.

The man sitting at the glass executive desk, whom Gus assumed was Ricardo or Ricky Giancarlo, was short, heavyset with thick eyebrows and a five o'clock shadow along his jawline. He wore a white dress shirt, black necktie and polyester slacks. When Gus walked in, he stood up.

"Good afternoon, officer," he said, holding out his hand for Gus to shake. "Welcome to the Daddy Cat Lounge. How can I be of service this afternoon?"

Gus ignored the outstretched hand and eventually Giancarlo, with a slight frown, dropped it.

"You the manager?" Gus said.

"Chief executive officer," Giancarlo said.

"You work with someone named Janine Stone?"

Giancarlo sat back down, rearranged some of the papers and pens on his desktop, and looked up at Gus with a smile.

"The lovely Janine," he said. "I hope she's not in any trouble."

"Why would she be?" Gus said. "I'm sure procuring prostitutes for a place like this is perfectly legal."

Giancarlo frowned. "I must protest," he said. "Our employees always follow the laws. There is nothing illegal or unethical going on at the Daddy Cat Lounge. Nothing!"

"Yeah, I'm sure," Gus said. "How long has Janine worked for this place?"

Giancarlo shook his head. "I can't tell you that," he said. "I've only been here two years, and she was under contract when I arrived. If it's important, I'll be happy to ask Human Resources for a print-out of her records."

"Nah," Gus said. "Just tell me what she does."

Giancarlo sat back and spread out his hands. "Janine is one of our main talent recruiters," he said. "She scouts, interviews, tests, and contracts with the talent. And once they arrive, she also provides excellent services in training, orientation and job skill enhancement. She does an excellent job and is quite important to the success of the business."

"Where does she do this recruiting?"

"All over," Giancarlo said. "She herself was originally from Florida, and she maintains contacts down there. But she has also done work for us in Texas, Las Vegas, Phoenix and Atlanta. We have cooperative arrangements with other companies in our industry. We employ several other talent scouts and recruiters, but I'd say she is the top producer. At least she has been for the last few years that I've been working here."

"Does she work with the Ferro family?" Gus said.

Giancarlo looked perplexed. "Who?"

"Angelo Ferro," Gus said. "Danny Ferro. About six other criminals with the last name of Ferro. They part of your organization?"

"I'm sorry," Giancarlo said. "That name rings absolutely no bells with me. Do not know who you're talking about."

Gus studied the man. He looked like he was telling the truth. On the other hand, the guy ran a strip club for the Mob, so honesty was not one of the top qualities Gus would expect of the man.

The door to the office swung open and a cocktail waitress came prancing in. She wore a red sparkly G-string and had a red ostrich feather stuck in her hair: it towered over her head and moved back and forth when she moved. Other than the thong and the feather, she wore nothing. Her firm but pendulous breasts also moved back and forth as she walked. She carried a silver tray with two tall flutes of something bubbly.

"Hi Ricardo," she trilled as she pranced in. "I thought you and your guest might need a little refreshment for your meeting." She held the tray out towards Gus. "A little champers, officer?"

"No thanks," Gus said. He kept his eyes on her feather.

"Put it down, Doris," Giancarlo said.

The woman put the tray down on the corner of the desk, blew both men a kiss, which involved lots of side-to-side action, and pranced out of the room.

Giancarlo reached over and picked up one of the flutes. He tipped it up and took a sip, smacked his lips and replaced it on the tray.

"You sure?" he said, indicating the other glass? "It's Dom Perignon. Only the best."

"That what those guys get when they order a split?" Gus said, indicating the men down in the room below.

Giancarlo laughed. "Only if they pay for it," he said. He paused and looked at Gus. "Is there anything else I can tell you?" he said. "Maybe I can introduce you to one of the girls. Let you two get acquainted in the Den room."

Gus shook his head. "No sale," he said. "Thanks for your time."

He retraced his steps. The bouncer was waiting for him outside the office door and led him back to the lobby and held the door for him as he left. "Have a Daddy Cat nice day," the bouncer said.

Gus looked at him and said nothing. Nor did he speak to the valet kid who brought him his squad car back. He did take a moment to check the car to make sure nothing had been damaged, He had kind of been looking forward to breaking some fingers. Instead, he got in, buckled his seat belt and drove away.

CHAPTER 16

PRESTON HOTCHKISS KNOX stood at the window of his impressive office and looked out at the Woonasquatucket River, today mostly a trashy green stream confined between concrete banks, and the glass-and-steel skyscrapers rising from the blocks beyond. Of course, since this was Providence, Rhode Island, the skyscrapers didn't rise high enough to scrape much of anything and most visitors to the city were more interested in looking at the fine collection of Colonial-era houses that clung to the steep streets of College Hill as it ascended in the general direction of Brown University.

Still, the Rhode Island Attorney General felt a little tingle of pride in his city and all that it had accomplished through the centuries. The founder of the Rhode Island, Roger Williams, had been something of an odd duck, at least in comparison to the other Puritan fathers of his era. Williams seemed to actually believe some of the things written down in the Scriptures that those holy men preached, especially the admonition to love one another, and that didn't sit well with the Cotton Mathers and John Bradfords who eventually kicked Roger Williams out of the Massachusetts Bay Colony, whereupon he came to the head of Narragansett Bay and started his own colony.

Not only did the iconoclastic preacher (he founded the first Baptist Church in America) rub his neighbors the wrong way with his more liberal interpretation of the Word, he also made the effort to get along and work cooperatively with the indigenous native tribes that lived in the area. That kind of tolerance and brotherhood was also considered blasphemous.

Knox watched as a police car, blue lights flashing but without siren, sped rapidly down South Main, along the path of the dirty river. That was then and this is now, he thought to himself. These days, most Rhode Islanders considered themselves the very best of tolerant citizens who extended the hand of friendship and acceptance to all, except for most of the blacks, the wrong kind of Hispanics and, of course, all Republicans.

"General K?" The squawk from Knox's office intercom was irritating. "Staff meeting in five minutes. Conference Room A."

"OK," Knox called out from his spot at the window. He took in one last view of the cityscape and turned back to his desk. His staff had prepared a meeting agenda for him, and it was neatly contained in a file folder on his desk. Knox picked it up and glanced at the first page. It was the usual: a long list of pending cases about which Knox expected one of his assistant AGs to recite the latest developments. Knox didn't really care about any of the cases. They were all the usual stuff and nonsense of state government. Inevitably, people got their noses out of joint about any action the Rhode Island government took and somebody usually filed a lawsuit. It was Knox's job to answer and defend those matters. More accurately, it was Knox's job to delegate work on those matters to one of his staff of attorneys; today's meeting was the weekly opportunity for him to get updated on where things stood by that staff.

He smiled to himself when he thought about "his" staff. Knox had announced before he had been elected AG three years earlier, that he intended to hire a staff in the Attorney General's office that "looked like Rhode Island." Had he done that, he would have hired twenty people who were overweight, angry, bad drivers, dressed sloppily, wanted stuff for free or suspected that everyone else in the state was getting stuff for free that they weren't, and who seemed to be personally offended by everything that was new and modern in the world.

Instead, he had hired fifteen of the best looking women he could find, of all colors and nationalities and religious backgrounds. Knox didn't care about the diversity of his staff, he wanted the hottest women lawyers he could find. It made him feel good, and important, and powerful. Naturally, the press wrote about "the Knox Harem" amid other derisive comments, but he didn't care. As long as they handled the cases without disaster, Knox was happy. He was even happier when

he could attend staff meetings or get photographed surrounded by his bevy of brainy beauties. He liked that. A lot.

He picked up the folder with the meeting agenda and
walked out of his office, down the hall and into the expansive
Conference Room A. A long mahogany table surround by
twelve upholstered chairs dominated the room. On one side,
three latticed windows looked out on the city; on the other
wall, gilt framed portraits of former attorneys general hung
on the wall. Most of the chairs were occupied. Knox went to
the head of the table, nodded at several of the women and sat
down.

"Morning, everyone," he said. "Abigail?" He turned to his
chief of staff, a beautiful black woman with elaborately braid-
ed hair who liked to wear long flowing outfits with robes and
shawls and scarfs in primary colors and African-influenced
designs. Abigail was a native of Massachusetts who had never
been further from Rhode Island than a high school field trip
to Washington D.C. to see the sites.

Like always, Abigail took over and began running down
the list of cases. One of the assistant attorneys around the
table responded to her questions about the first case on the
list and began reading the case status to the group. Like Knox
himself, most listened with half an ear, and almost nobody,
except Abigail herself, took any notes.

The cases were the usual assortment of bureaucratic boil-
erplate. A snowplow from the town of Johnston had acci-
dentally struck a state-owned bridge abutment and dislodged
a guardrail and the town had sued the state to recoup the
damages. Two ferry companies were competing for the con-

tract to run passengers and their cars over to Block Island and neither company was happy about the bidding process from the state's Ferry and Conveyance Board and lawsuits were flying back and forth. A wealthy homeowner in Westerly who could afford high-priced attorneys from New York was upset about some state easement that had been conveyed against his beachfront property and was demanding restitution.

They continued down the long list of these and other cases. To keep himself awake and to try and look like he was concentrating, Knox checked off each case on his meeting agenda once it had been discussed. He saw that there were just four or five more items to go, and he began to think about lunch. He knew he would probably go to the Capital Grille overlooking Kennedy Plaza downtown. He was trying to decide if he would invite some of his staff to join him. He liked the picture it made in his mind's eye: the powerful Attorney General ushering a group of lovely and intelligent women into the unofficial lunch spot of the state government, where state senators and representatives and the lawyers and lobbyists who suck up to them went every day to see and be seen. And there would be Preston Knox and his beauties, sitting around one of the round tables draped in white linens and elegant china, talking animatedly amongst themselves about the hottest legal issues of the day. That mental picture made Preston Knox feel happy.

"Little Penwick," Abigail was getting down near the bottom of the list. "Maggie? What's going on with the police department down there? Any news on the former chief?"

Preston Knox came back from his daydream and sat up a little straighter. He looked down the table and found the curly hair of Maggie Wells, one of his beauties.

"Nothing much new," Maggie said, looking down at her yellow legal pad. "The department is running along fine. Chief Haddock the son seems to have the department in control. His father continues to refuse to testify and Judge O'Rourke still has him locked up at the ACI."

She paused for a moment, thinking, then apparently decided to go ahead.

"The police last week interviewed someone they thought might be connected to the disappearance of Angelo Ferro about a year ago," she said. "A young woman named Janine Stone. But no new information was obtained from the interview. So that case continues to go nowhere."

"Maggie?" That Preston Knox actually spoke during the case rehash was unusual. That he seemed to be about to ask a question was even more so. All eyes in the room swung to look at the boss at the head of the table.

"Please see me after the meeting," Knox said.

All the eyes swung back and looked at Maggie Wells, who, although she tried mightily not to, had turned a shade of red. The boss almost never addressed one of the assistants during a staff meeting, and to be summoned to the inner sanctum was ... troubling. She wondered if she was in hot water, and tried to think of what she might have done wrong so she could conjure up a quick defense.

Momentarily unable to speak, Maggie simply nodded. Abigail moved on to the next item. Knox checked off the Little Penwick item on his agenda. The meeting continued.

About half an hour later, the meeting concluded, Preston Knox retreated to his sanctum. Maggie took a minute to visit the restroom, which gave her more time to think. She really couldn't think what the boss wanted, so she finally decided to just find out. She freshened up her lipstick in the mirror, fluffed out her hair, straightened her cuffs and nodded at her image.

Knox's gatekeeper outside his office motioned for her to enter. Maggie knocked softly and went inside.

The attorney general was on the phone, but waved for her to come in. She took a seat in one of the chairs arrayed in front of his huge desk.

"So, Bobby…we still on for squash tonight?" the A.G. was saying. "You kicked my ass last week and I'm looking forward to returning the favor." He paused, listening, a big grin breaking out on his face. "In your dreams, Roberto," he said. "I'll see you at the club."

He hung up the phone and looked across the desk at his assistant.

"Who brought Janine Stone into this matter?" he asked. Maggie Wells noted that he didn't beat around the bush, start with any disarming preliminaries. He went straight for the jugular.

"Chief Haddock and his chief of detectives brought her in for questioning," she said.

"Why?"

"I—I don't really know, chief," she said. Knox liked to be called chief. It made him sound important. The women on his staff thought it made him sound ridiculous, but none of them would ever say that out loud. So they went along. "Two weeks ago, we went out to the Ferro place. I wanted to re-interview the witnesses from the night Angelo disappeared. She came out on the porch while we were there. Haddock and Franklin wanted to find out who she was."

"None of their goddam business," Preston Knox said. "She has nothing to do with Angelo Ferro's disappearance. Nothing."

"Um…chief…" Maggie knew she was wandering out onto the thinnest of ice. But she went anyway. "This Stone woman told Chief Haddock she did know something about the disappearance," she said. "But I arrived and dismissed her and so …"

"Janine Stone has nothing to do with Angelo Ferro and Julius Haddock," Knox repeated. "She knows nothing about that matter. Is that clear, Maggie?"

"Yes, chief," she said.

"I sent you down there to ride herd on those yokels," Knox said, sitting back in his executive swivel chair and crossing his legs. "You let them get a head of steam up and there's no telling what dark alley they'll go charging down. Your job is to control that department. Don't let them go nuts. Manage, Maggie…manage the personnel. Are we clear?"

Well, no Maggie thought to herself. But she couldn't say that out loud. Not only did she not feel she could confront her boss, she had no idea why he was telling her this. So she had no reason to ask him to explain.

"Got it, chief," she said.

"Good," he said. "Listen…I'm taking a few of the ladies over to the Capital Grille for lunch. You wanna come along?"

He gave her the full wattage politician's smile with the invitation. She knew he expected her knees to weaken at the chance to see and be seen with the Big Boys. For some reason, her knees stayed strong.

"That's very nice, Chief," she said, "But I really need to get down to Little Penwick. Got some personnel that needs managing this afternoon."

"Good," he said. "Good girl." He waved her away with his hand and she left his office.

'Good girl' this, she thought as she walked out.

CHAPTER 17

GUS HAD BEEN asked to attend the November meeting of the Town Council, held in the town hall on Tuesday night. Bob Murtha had told Gus that the status of the police department had been put on the official agenda and he wanted the chief of police there to answer any questions.

Little Penwick's town hall had been constructed in the 1880s utilizing the architectural genre known as "New England barn." The big drafty wooden building housed the warren of town offices in the front section. Every time he went over there to talk with someone from the town, Gus had noted the creaky floors, the walls stained with rain water that often leaked from the century-old roof and the scary-looking nests of electric and computer wiring that ran over, under and beside the desks and offices.

But the council chambers, occupying most of the rear section of the town hall, was an exercise in wishful thinking. At the front of the room was a dais, raised six inches above the floor in the rest of the space, on which the council sat at a long table. Murtha, the council president, sat in the middle of the table and was flanked on both sides by two more councilors. Louise Cox, the town clerk, had her own desk just in front of the dais.

The rest of the room was filled with old wooden pews, like in a church. Row after row of them, so that the space could easily hold 150 citizens or more. That was the wishful thinking part: in a town of around 5,000 citizens, the most contentious issue, say a proposed property tax increase or a change in the local schools, would attract an audience of maybe 20. Most months, the attendance at the council meetings was a dozen or less. The local newspaper sent a reporter, two or three old people showed up for every meeting because they had nothing better to do, and the rest were lawyers whose clients had some kind of issue before the council.

So on this Tuesday night, Gus counted seven onlookers, grouped together in the first two rows of pews. There was no ceiling in the council chambers, just rafters and beams underneath the roof, with a few ceiling fans to move the air and cobwebs around a bit. Gus went and stood against the wall to wait for his department to come up on the agenda. He carried a three-ring binder full of the latest crime statistics for the town.

The meeting began promptly at seven o'clock. The minister from the Congregational church on the village green read an invocation and the council all stood and pledged allegiance to the flag which stood at the end of the dais. Murtha then banged his wooden hammer down and called the meeting to order.

After dispensing with the reading of the minutes from the last meeting. Murtha led the council through a discussion about the proposal to add a traffic light to the town at the intersection of Easterly Road and the Long Highway. The neighbors in the area were against it, but one of the council members claimed that intersection was dangerous, having seen three auto accidents in the last two years. For Little Penwick, that was a lot. But after 30 minutes of debate, the council voted to table the proposal for further study.

"Item two," Murtha read from his agenda sheet. "Status of the town's police department. As you all know, the state attorney general has appointed a Special Master from his office to oversee the operations of our police department. The council thought that it should hear from the chief of police to get updated on operations in the department. Chief Haddock?"

All eyes on the council table turned to look at Gus. He walked forward and put his notebook down on the edge of their long table.

"Thank you, Bob," Gus said. "Approximately four weeks ago, I was informed that the attorney general of Rhode Island had appointed a Special Master for the department," he said. "The reasons given to me at the time of this action was that the state was concerned about ongoing operations in the town, due to the fact that our former chief, my father, had been sent to jail in a dispute over an investigation into a missing person of this town, and that I, the newly appointed acting chief of police, might not have the requisite experience and ability to oversee and manage the police department in this town."

Gus paused and looked up and down the table. All the councilors were staring back, rapt in attention.

"I, of course, strongly disagreed with the state's reasoning," he continued, "The incident that led to the former chief of police's resignation was grossly exaggerated, and my father is appealing his case to the fullest extent. And, as you know, I myself have extensive experience with this department and its operations. Still, my department has fully cooperated with the Special Master. Her name is Margaret Wells and she is an assistant attorney general for the state. She is physically present in our station house quite often and I am in daily contact with her to keep her apprised of all ongoing investigations and other matters. I can assure the council that our police operations are unaffected by this new regime and we continue to serve and protect the citizens of Little Penwick every day to the best of our ability. I would be happy to answer any questions."

Freddy Bull, an older man who had been serving on the council for more than ten years, raised his hand.

"How much are we paying for this master woman?" he said.

Gus smiled. How much anything cost was always the first issue with the town council. Unlike other governments, like on the state and federal level, the town of Little Penwick had to make do with whatever money it could raise through taxation, or from what it received from the state or federal government programs and grants. The town couldn't print money, it was not allowed by law to go into debt, so the annual budget was the cap.

"The town is not paying Ms. Well's salary," Gus said. "That comes from the state. Nor is the town on the hook for any perks and benefits. Even her mileage expense for driving down here from Providence several times a week is picked up by the attorney general. She drinks our coffee, but like every other employee of the police department, she is expected to drop some dollars into the kitty from time to time to pay for it."

Jillian Montague, who represented the ward that encompassed the beachfront mansion part of the town, had a question.

"Is this about you, Gus?" she asked. "Does the AG want someone else to be police chief? Do we need to start a national search for a replacement?"

Gus smiled at her. "I don't think so, councilor," he said. "You'll have to ask Preston Knox if he has a problem with me being acting chief. I've never met the man, so I can't imagine why he would. It was explained to me that the state is just concerned that our former chief is in prison and that I may not have the experience to run the department. I think that the special master will report back to the AG that neither concern is valid, and the state will let us get back to normal operations."

"When?" Jillian asked.

Gus shrugged. "I don't know that, councilor," he said. "But I'm hoping it's soon."

Out of the corner of his eye, Gus saw Louise Cox, the town clerk, write something on a Post-It note and reach over to pass it up onto the dais to Bill Christy. Christy was a new member of the council, elected just a year ago, and was one of the few members of the council who were politically partisan. In federal elections, like the rest of the state, Little Penwick usually supported Democrat candidates, although the margins were always much closer than in other, more urban areas. Bob Murtha, for instance, was known as a local leader of the Republicans. But on the town council, open partisanship was rare. Council elections were non-partisan: the first five candidates past the post were elected.

But Christy had been encouraged to run by an active group of locals who staged regular prayer vigils against war, held fund raisers for Democrat candidates and sponsored community meetings on racial equity, abortion rights and an end to capital punishment. Gus had only greeted the man in passing at previous council meetings, but suspected if there was a defund the police movement in Little Penwick, Bill Christy would be in favor.

Christy now raised a finger for recognition to ask a question.

"Chief Haddock," he said, "It has come to our attention that you make regular visits to the ACI to see the former chief. I am wondering if that is appropriate behavior on your part?"

Gus felt a ringing in his ears, which he understood to be a rising of his blood pressure. He told himself to remain calm.

"Thank you, councilor," he said. "You do understand, don't you, that the former chief of police is my father. I would visit him on a regular basis even if I were not the acting chief."

"That's not my question," Christy shot back. "I'm asking if that is appropriate."

"Why wouldn't it be?" Gus said.

"Well," Christy sat back. He seemed happy to have engaged with Gus, as if this was fun. "The former chief was removed from his position for mishandling government funds. As his son, he could easily be using you and your current position in the department to cover up these and other crimes he might have committed. He could even have enlisted you in his scheme to defraud the town and drain other monies for his...and your...personal use ...Why—"

Bob Murtha slammed his hammer down on the table. The report made everyone in the cavernous chamber jump.

"Councilor Christy is out of order," Murtha practically yelled. "He is making insinuations of unethical and illegal behavior that are not supported by evidence. Gus Haddock has lived in this town his entire life and has been a valued member of our police force for more than five years, after which he served his country honorably and bravely as a Ranger in the U.S. Army. In all that time, there has never been the slightest hint of dishonesty in the man. Your insinuations, Councilor Christy, are unfounded and out of order. You may proceed if you have further questions."

Christy's face darkened for a moment, but a small smile began to play on his face. He had succeeded in goading the bull into action. Next, he thought, was the cape work, followed by the sword to the heart. He liked this game.

"I insinuated nothing of the kind," he said in protest. "I was just asking hypothetical questions. Chief Haddock...what do you and your father talk about when you visit him at the ACI?"

Gus stood there silently for a moment, waiting for the sound in his ears to decrease.

"I ask him how he's doing and ask him if there's anything he needs that I can do for him," Gus said.

"Like destroying evidence?" Christy shot back. "Covering his tracks? Hiding his ill-gotten gains?"

Murtha began banging his hammer again. Gus just stood there glaring at the councilor down the table. Some of the other councilors began to speak, protesting Christy's line of questions.

"That's about enough of that," Murtha said when order had been restored. "Chief Haddock, you do not have to answer that question or any others. The council appreciates your coming here tonight to brief us, and as soon as the state withdraws the Special Master, I hope you'll come back and update the council on the department's operations."

Gus nodded and picked up his notebook. Council president Murtha called the next agenda item and Gus left the chambers.

CHAPTER 18

5:45 p.m. Hazel Cushing of a Blankenship Drive address called the police to report that someone had posted a Friend request on her Facebook page, and since Mrs. Cushing did not know who the person was, she wanted to report it as a possible scam against old people in the community. The dispatcher explained to Mrs. Cushing how she could hit the "Decline" button on her Facebook page.

"I DO HAVE a dream," Gus said. "Pretty regular. Once or twice a week."

Dr. Mahoney nodded and jotted something down in her notebook. Gus kept his November appointment with the shrink. They had chatted for a few minutes. Nothing significant. Then the words came out, almost by themselves.

"Tell me about it," she said.

He told her about that day in the mountains near Talaqan, when his squad had been pinned down and then the two Afghan children had approached on the road before the boy had detonated his explosive vest and died, right in front of Gus' eyes.

"I don't know why that episode is the one that's stuck in my head," he said. "I saw lots of bad things when I was over there. Saw men shot. Saw IED explosions hit our trucks. Saw people die. Ours and theirs. None of that was fun. None of it was normal. None of it was routine, as far as I was concerned. But I can't seem to forget those two kids in Talaqan. They wanted candy. All kids want candy, right? But the boy, especially, he knew what he was wearing. He knew what was going to happen. And he asked for candy. The girl tried to get away. I think she knew, too."

"I read something recently which stuck with me," Dr. Mahoney said. "The line was 'the reactions are right, the environment is wrong."

"I hope you plan to explain that," Gus said.

"What they are saying," she said, "And these are experts in treating veterans with PTSD, is that patients like you are reacting to the stimuli they experienced in the war zones. Those reactions—all the dreams, the anxiety, the lack of sleep, the hitting out at those you love—all that stuff is a perfectly logical response to what you experienced and witnessed. Any human being would experience what you saw that day and react with shock and horror. And be unable to forget about it. So what you are going through right now is the right reaction a human being should have."

"But—?"

"But their theory is that your reaction to a horrible wartime experience is being expressed here and now, in a non-wartime environment. Nobody around you here experienced what you did, but your reactions affect them. It's not your reactions that are wrong…they're clearly not. It's just this environment is the wrong place to react to them."

"So I should go back to Afghanistan, and then the dream will go away?" Gus said. "I dunno, Doc, but that sounds a little whacked. Whether I think about those two kids in Talaqan or Little Penwick, they're still dead. Ain't coming back anytime soon."

"We can rationalize war and its atrocities, when it comes to adults," Dr. Mahoney said. "Men have been killing each other in wars, well, ever since there were men. Unfortunately, it's considered part of the human condition. But you are right… when children are involved with war and with death, it strikes a very discordant note in our psyche. Children are supposed to be protected from war, not used to foment it. So seeing… experiencing…an episode like that can be deeply troubling. The memories are like repercussions, blowback, echoes that never leave."

"So I'm going to wake up with the sweats and the night-mares for the rest of my life?" Gus said. "I thought as the doctor you would have a cure."

She smiled at him across her desk. "I wish," she said. "But this branch of medical practice doesn't have a magic wand. I guess none of them really do. But there's no scientific formula I can give you to banish your memories. All I can do is talk them through with you and assure you that eventually those memories will lose their grip on you. The literature of cases like yours is clear—the memories eventually fade. They may never disappear entirely. Certain stimuli may bring them back, all of a sudden, when you least expect it. A car backfiring. The sound of a baseball hitting the bat. But those kinds of memories do not have to dominate your life. You still have some measure of control."

"How?" Gus asked. "I can't control what I dream, can I? And the dreams come when I'm asleep."

"We will explore some therapies in the weeks ahead," she said. "I'm sure you will see some improvement. It's a good sign that your memory is intermittent. I have some patients who have their bad dream every single night, no matter what. Those patients require some harder work."

"Great," Gus said, "I'm only part crazy."

Mahoney smiled. "And maintaining your balance and sense of humor is also a good sign, Gus," she said. "I think you'll be OK, and soon."

He sat there silently for a while and thought about that.

"How is the rest of your life going?" she asked. "Work OK?"

"The actual work of policing Little Penwick is fine," he said. "The department is running well. No problems. Crime is down, which is good."

"But?"

"Well, some of the ancillary stuff is still troubling," he admitted. "The town council is concerned about the Special Master business, and one guy on the council thinks that because my father is in jail that I'm probably conspiring with him to either continue or cover up his criminal activity."

She jotted down some more notes, her pen scratching across the paper.

"When do you think your father will be released?"

Gus shrugged. "I don't know for certain," he said. "Judge O'Rourke gave him 12 months, so with time off for good behavior, he could get out after the first of the year. Even sooner if the judge has a pang of conscience."

"Or if someone applies political pressure," she said.

"Yeah," he said, "That too. But that well seems to be dry. Dad got along with the other chiefs in the state. God knows he knew them all after 24 years on the job. The chiefs of police are usually pretty tight and together when it comes to political interference in their towns. But none of them have gone to bat for him. Not one. Either the judge or the AG or the two of them together are hiding something about this case. And until I can figure out what it is, I'm afraid he's stuck where he is."

"Unless you can determine what happened that night with Angelo Ferro," she said.

"Yeah," Gus said. "And so far, we haven't gotten very far. Lotta questions, not very many answers."

"What do police departments do, when they have lots of questions about a matter?"

Gus thought for a minute.

"They open an investigation," he said. "Collect evidence. Interview witnesses. Follow leads. Pull on a thread and see where it goes."

Dr. Mahoney was nodding. "Yes," she said. "That sounds about right."

He stared across her desk at her. The HVAC made that soft whooshing sound in the background.

There is an investigation already, he thought. Maybe it's time to kick it into gear..

CHAPTER 19

Gus called Buzz Franklin into his office the next morning.

"OK," he said, "It's time we started acting like a police department on this case. We need to start running down some facts and take a look at what's right in front of us."

"Agreed," Franklin said, nodding, "And way past time."

"First," Gus held up his index finger. "I want a complete sheet on Janine Stone. From the day she was born until today. Where she's from, who her parents are, what they remember about her, is it true they don't communicate." He was on a roll and Buzz Franklin was furiously writing down Gus' instructions.

"I want interviews with friends and family in Florida. School records. Guidance counselor reports. Interviews with her high school friends. Interviews with the parents of her school friends."

"Sounds like a field trip to Fort Lauderdale is in order," Buzz said. "Town going to pay for that?"

"Hold that question for a minute," Gus said. "We'll get back to it. Two." He held up two fingers. "I want to know if the feds are looking at the Daddy Cat Lounge or any of the other clubs up there for prostitution rings, child abuse cases, anything along those lines. We don't want to step on anyone's toes, and we also don't want them swatting us down before we get going. So talk to your contacts with the FBI or whichever alphabet agency is currently handling the Family business. Tell 'em the truth—we've started a local investigation into a possible interstate ring that flows young girls up from various southern cities into our local clubs. See if you can find out if the feds are tracking what happens to the girls once they get up here. Where do they live? With who? Can they leave when they want or are they locked in? I want to know what's going on and how deep Janine Stone is involved. Right?"

Buzz nodded as he wrote notes.

"Three. Let's draw up some warrants, see if we can get approved for taps on the phones over there in Ferro land. We're investigating possible child prostitution, child endangerment, child exploitation. I think we've got a good case for a judge. Let's get it done and see what we can find about what Janine and Danny Ferro do all day long."

"Got it," Buzz said.

"Four. I noticed a fairly new building out back of Danny's house," Gus said. "It's one of those metal-clad garage buildings, one story, no windows, big garage door in the front. Let's pull the permits on that and see what they said it was for. I wanna know what they're doing in that building."

"Could be they're just fixing up their cars and stuff," Buzz said, tapping the end of his pen on his front teeth."

"Or it could be something else entirely," Gus said. "I want to know."

"Got it," Buzz said and wrote it down on his pad.

"But here's the problem with that," Gus said. "To pull the construction permits and zoning variances and all that stuff, you've gotta go through the town offices. That could be a problem."

"You mean Louise?" Buzz was referring to the town clerk, Louise Cox.

"Yeah," Gus said. "Until further notice, we don't trust anyone outside of this room. And Louise Cox is the first person we don't trust. She could be working for the AG, she could be working with the Democrat party, she could be working with the feds. Or all three at once. So we've gotta figure out a way to get the town records without the town knowing about it."

"Always tricky," Buzz said, "But not beyond the realm of possibility. I've got some contacts over at city hall."

"You're sure they're good?"

Buzz smiled. "I've been dating Frannie Holmsted," he said. "Nothing too serious yet. Just some dinners, some concerts, a movie or two. I like her, I think she likes me. And I know she doesn't like Louise, because half of our dates is her complaining about what a conniving bitch Louise is. So she might be in a position to help."

"Excellent," Gus said. "And congrats, you sly devil. Frannie's good people. I know she had some trouble when she was married to that salesman asshole, but she seems to have straightened her life out. She'd be a good catch."

Buzz nodded and looked pleased with himself.

"Okay. That'll get us started," Gus continued. "Now, we've just got two big problems left."

"I'm guessing Maggie Wells is one of those," Franklin said. "How much of this are we sharing with our oh-so-special master?"

"If it was up to me, I'd say none," Gus said. "But clearly she has to be read in. Otherwise, the department is in deep shit. Let me handle Maggie. I'll figure out how much to tell her and when. That way, if it all goes south...and it might... then I'm the only one with exposure. The rest of the department will be in the clear."

Buzz nodded. "Okay," he said. "But don't get too cute. You're right. This one feels like it's backed up all the way to Providence. They play hardball up there. So watch your step."

Gus nodded. He didn't say it, but he was gratified that Buzz had his back on this. One lesson he had learned from his father was that ambitious police officers working their way up the career ladder could be as dangerous and backstabbing as the worst felon in the world. It's only human nature, his father had often explained. Humans are greedy, ambitious and can be vicious in getting what they want, at grabbing for that brass ring. Even those you think would be loyal often aren't when a good career advancement is on the table. Buzz Franklin seemed to be a dedicated employee, but Gus was under no illusions that Buzz hadn't thought of himself occupying the chief's office. Human nature dictated that he had. Gus could only hope he hadn't acted on it. Yet.

"And that leaves money," Gus continued. "Again, everything we're doing here is completely legal and well within the bounds of our investigatory mission. But if I start sending big expense vouchers over to town hall for reimbursement, Louise is gonna hear about it. And then she is going to tell whoever she tells things to. And that will put you and me in the soup. So we gotta find an alternative way to finance your trip to Florida."

Buzz was silent for a few moments. Then he nodded, to himself.

"Let me make some calls," he said. "I can get a good fare on Southwest down to Fort Lauderdale. They fly direct out of Providence. Rental car for a few days? Not too bad. Food? I can live with McDonald's three times a day. Hotel rooms are pricey, even though it's not the high season down there yet. But I know a bunch of people who've moved down there, including a few guys who used to work here. I'm pretty sure I can find a place to crash for a few days on the east coast, and the people I have in mind will be glad to keep it on the Q.T."

"That's great, Buzz," Gus said, and he meant it. "I appreciate that. I've got the department's civil forfeiture account at my disposal. Haven't checked the balance in a while, but if I remember correctly, there was around five grand in there a while back. So I can front you some cash, reimburse some other stuff after the fact and nobody else will know about it until I file the paperwork. Which I will, but not right now."

Buzz nodded. "Sounds perfect," he said. "I'll get on the horn, make some appointments and maybe head down there in a week or so. Just before Thanksgiving, it ought to be quiet. And people will be home, getting ready. This might just work out."

The two cops nodded at each other. They had a plan.

CHAPTER 20

GUS CALLED MAGGIE Wells in Providence and said he needed to talk to her.

"Okay," she said, "Shoot. I got a few minutes before my next meeting."

"No," he said, "I mean face to face. Got a few things to go over with you."

"Fine," she said. "I was going to come down tomorrow morning. I've been going over your budget for next year and I have some questions. You going to be in the office around eleven?"

"Yep," Gus said. "See you then." He hung up.

He was smiling when he did so. Partly because he liked the feeling of hanging up on her. Of course, he realized that was a bit juvenile on his part, fighting back against her position in the hierarchy above his own. But he was also smiling because his ruse was working. Gus had told Maggie that he had to present a complete budget for the police department to the town's Budget Committee in December, so that committee could incorporate his figures into the town's annual budget for the next year, which had to be approved by the Town Council in March. All of that was true, but Gus knew the police department budget was pretty much static from year to year. Everybody in the town knew how much money the council would allot to the police department—it was the same number plus a little more or a little less here and there. But basically the same, year over year.

But Gus had given Maggie three thick budget files filled with spreadsheets and financials, knowing that she'd pour over every last line item. He knew that she did not want to miss a thing, and would question the expenditure of every stray dime she saw. That's what Special Masters are supposed to do. So he had loaded her up and sent her off to act like a Special Master, which would get her out of his hair for a week or two. So far, his plan had been working: Maggie had not physically been in the station house for five days now. Everyone in Little Penwick seemed to enjoy the respite, and people were acting more relaxed than Gus had noticed in a while.

Bob Murtha stuck his round bald head in the doorway of Gus' office. "Knock knock," he said and strolled in. He handed Gus the agenda for the next council meeting and a few other town council documents that were cc'd to the chief of police.

"Where's the ole ball and chain?" Murtha asked with a smile. "Not coming down today?"

"I thought that term referred to one's wife," Gus said. "Maggie Wells ain't that."

"Not yet, anyway," Murtha said, chuckling to himself.

"Not ever," Gus replied. "Listen…I have a question."

"Not guilty," Murtha said. "Didn't do it, nobody saw me do it, you can't prove anything." Then he laughed out loud at his own Bart Simpson impression.

"Okay, Bart," Gus said. "Give me the background, if there is any, on that new building out behind Danny Ferro's place."

"The garage?" Murtha looked a little surprised. "Not much to it, really. They applied for a building permit. They had to adjust the footprint a little bit from the original plans because it got too close to one of the property boundaries out there. The Ferro place looks like it's a hundred acres of vacant land, and it mostly is, but it's been divided and subdivided over the years so on a plat map the place looks like a spider's web. Anyway, when Angelo wanted to build that garage, it ran up against one of the property lines and he had to move it about sixteen feet to the west. He acted all pissed off about it and threatened to file a suit against the town. But Shecky Grant on the Planning board showed him the plats and read him the zoning regulation and explained how easements worked, and he eventually moved his garage sixteen feet west, just like he was supposed to."

"When was this?" Gus asked.

"Two, two and a half years ago, I think," Bob said. "You want me to go dig out the records?"

"Nah, not necessary," Gus said quickly. "I'm just asking for background. I saw that building when Maggie and I went out there a week or so ago and wondered what it was."

"Danny and his brothers like to work on cars," Murtha said, shrugging. "They wanted a place to do that inside, warm, out of the rain and snow. Can't say I blame them."

"Does the town ever physically inspect a place like that?"

Murtha frowned and shook his head. "Not unless there's a reason," he said. "You heard of any reason why we should?"

Gus shook his head. He didn't want to get ahead of himself yet. Let the investigation proceed. "Nope," he said, "Like I said, I was just curious. That new building just seemed out of place on the Ferro land."

"Yeah," Murtha said, "I know what you mean. Lot of those houses and trailers have seen better days. Now, if you wanted us to do an inspection on the houses and trailers to make sure they're up to code, that might be something we could arrange. Lot of dilapidated buildings in that property. But the Ferros like it that way. They get to protest about every attempt to raise their valuations for property tax purposes. Point out the leaky roofs and weathered clapboards and all the rest. Just another scam from the best scamsters in town."

"Indeed," Gus said. "Well, thanks for the info."

Murtha gave Gus a two-finger salute and left the office.

But Gus thought about what he had said, long after he had left. Snap zoning inspection, he thought. Hit 'em before they know we're coming. Do it in force. Full-court press. It might be a way to get into the garage, see what they had in there. He played with the idea for the rest of the afternoon.

CHAPTER 21

By the time Maggie Wells arrived at the police station for the scheduled 11 a.m. meeting, Gus Haddock was flying on caffeine. He had been drinking coffee all morning, ever since he arrived at around eight, and he could feel his face was flushed and his body had that edgy feeling he remembered from preparing to go into combat in unknown locations. He used to think of that feeling as the screaming heebee jeebees.

So when she walked in the door of his office, he stood up rather quickly and knocked his desk chair backwards into the wall behind him with a crash.

Maggie took a look at him and shook her head.

"Have you thought of changing to decaf?" she said.

"No need," Gus replied. "After our meeting, I'll go out and run five miles. That'll help."

"Hoo-rah," she said, "Don't forget the fifty-pound back-pack," and took her overcoat off, unpacked a thick stack of documents from her briefcase and sat down across from Gus. He pulled his chair back into place and sank into it.

"Before we get into the financials, there's something I need to go over with you," Gus said. He tossed a file folder across the desk and watched as she picked it up, opened it and scanned the contents.

"You've opened a new investigation into Janine Stone?" she said, almost to herself.

"Yep."

"Without telling me?"

"That's what I'm doing right now," he said.

"That's not how this works," she said hotly. "You are supposed to get approval from me before launching any new investigations, especially ones that affect the Ferro family."

"I'm not investigating the Ferro family," Gus said. "I'm investigating Janine Stone to see if her ongoing recruitment of strippers and hookers might transgress any state or local laws."

"See? That's a problem right there," Maggie said. "Ms. Stone would claim she's recruiting dancers and entertainers. Which is perfectly legal."

Gus chuckled. "'Dancers and entertainers?'" he said. "Who do stripping and hooking? I didn't know Special Masters were supposed to believe and agree with whatever a defense counsel could claim in court. My job, as chief of police, is to investigate any crimes that may or may not be taking place in my town. That's exactly what I'm doing here."

Maggie continued to read the file, which listed the possible violations that the Little Penwick police department was looking into.

"And how do you intend to pursue this matter?" she asked next.

That was the question that Gus had been dreading, the one that had kept him running back to the coffee pot all morning for fresh fuel. He didn't want Maggie to quash his investigation before it got off the ground. Buzz Franklin had made some calls, arranged a place to stay for a few days near Ft. Lauderdale and had booked an airline ticket for early the next week. If Maggie found out about that, Gus was certain she would make him cancel.

"We're talking to some people locally who might know something about Ms. Stone's activities, and following leads from elsewhere," he said, hoping that sounded generic enough.

"Leads?" She picked up on that word, as he knew she would.

"My investigator knows some people in Providence who are connected to the strip club industry," Gus said. That part was true: Buzz Franklin knew most of the vice cops in Providence, and they would be the first ones he would talk to in such an investigation. "He's planning to talk to them, as well as some others with knowledge of the business."

"What others?" Like a good attorney, Maggie was paying attention to the details.

Gus shrugged. "Buzz Franklin has contacts. He's been around a long time in this state. He is pursuing some leads. I can't tell you who they are yet, nor what they might or might not say. But that's why we're investigating. There's a lot of unknowns and I'm trying to eliminate those, one at a time."

Maggie nodded to herself, then closed the file and handed it back to Gus.

"The AG is gonna go ballistic," she said. "He told me specifically that Janine Stone was off limits."

"Did he now?" Gus said, sitting up a little straighter. "And why is that?"

He didn't tell me," Maggie said. "Which I found a little troubling."

"Troubling," Gus echoed. "Whatever that means."

"It means I wondered why the attorney general of the state of Rhode Island didn't want any police to go looking into this young woman and her activities," Maggie said. "So I did a little research to see if I could find out why."

"Did you now?" Gus said, a smile playing on his face. "And does the Big Dawg know that his pretty young assistant has been digging into his background?"

Maggie frowned. "I hate that," she said. "I mean, I really *hate* that."

"What?"

"Being referred to as a pretty young anything," she said. "I'm the goddam assistant attorney general for the state of Rhode Island and Providence Plantations. I have a law degree and several years of experience. I have put a bunch of bad guys away for long spells in the ACI. To take all that and boil it down into a 'pretty young thing' phrase just makes my blood boil."

"As well it should, Madame AAG," Gus said. "So what have you discovered about the great Preston Knox?"

As it turned out, she had learned quite a bit. She began to talk.

Preston H. Knox was the oldest of three sons of Franklin Delano Knox, who had been a well-known member of the Rhode Island bar. The senior Knox was a partner in one of the bigger Providence law firms and personally handled the legal work for some of the biggest corporations in the state. Those corporations included Cross pens, Hasbro toys, the Textron conglomerate and a large handful of jewelry making companies which had once been headquartered in Providence. F.D. Knox was also an important cog in the Democratic political machine, but only as a backroom guy and money raiser. He had never run for office himself. No doubt, the Knox family credo was to make enough money in the private sector to be able to buy and influence those in the public sector to do their bidding.

In any case, Preston Knox was groomed from childhood to follow in his father's size-thirteen footprints. He had attended Dartmouth as an undergrad, because he wanted to spend his winter semesters skiing at the nearby resorts in New Hampshire and Vermont. Then, at his father's insistence, he had enrolled at Yale Law graduating not at the top of his class, but comfortably in the second quintile. Strictures against nepotism prevented his joining his father's firm, at least at the outset of his career, so Preston Knox had signed on with a medium sized Boston law firm, and spent fifteen years in the corporate law trenches, making many good contacts and expanding his network of friends along the way. He had married a well-connected Boston girl, sired two kids of his own and joined the Charles River Country Club, like all the legal hotshots in Beantown.

He could have continued down that comfortable career path as long as he wanted, piling up wealth and influence along the way until he retired with an enviable nest egg and spent the last twenty or thirty years of his life traveling the world, spending his winters skiing in Chamonix or Kitzbühel.

Instead, Preston Knox came back to Rhode Island when he was around 50 and ran for Attorney General. That news must have upset old F.D. Knox greatly, since he died of a sudden stroke three months before Preston Knox was elected. And maybe those two events were in fact connected, since Knox' candidacy was heavily bankrolled by about a half dozen of the most powerful attorneys and politicians in the state. They were buying a friendly face—F.D.'s son—to occupy the attorney general's office and make sure their particular oxen were not gored by the state of Rhode Island. In return, Preston Knox got the nice office on South Main Street, got to hire his bevy of legal beauties and got the benefit of lots of great stock tips from the movers and shakers which enabled Knox to increase his net worth tenfold in less than five years. Win-win for everybody, save for poor old F.D. Knox, who died, perhaps, of shame.

"So ole Preston is in place to move the levers of power in whatever way the big money boys want," Gus said, recapping the scenario that Maggie had just described. "And he can do pretty much anything he wants as long as he takes care of the big boys first."

"That's pretty much it," Maggie agreed, nodding.

"So where does the lovely Miz Stone fit into this story?"

"Ah," she said, "That's where it gets really interesting."

"I like interesting," Gus said. He felt a strong need for more coffee, but decided that maybe enough was enough. He could wait until lunch, which was imminent.

"If the Chief has a weak spot, it is with the ladies," Maggie said. "That much is pretty obvious. He gets lots of publicity for having an all-female staff."

"Publicity or derision?" Gus asked.

Maggie shrugged. "Either or," she said. "Hard core feminists praise him to the skies for helping break the glass ceiling in the state. Others just think he's an old horn dog."

"What do you think?" Gus asked. "You work for the guy."

"I would have to recuse myself," Maggie said. "I can see both sides. Personally, he's never acted inappropriately with me; nor have any of my colleagues reported anything untoward. At the same time, he does like to parade us out in public, all to make him look like the alpha dog. We all see that, and it irritates all of us to one degree or another. But it's more of a personal peccadillo than a major character flaw. At least that's what I thought..."

"You did some digging, didn't you?" Gus said with a smile. "You found something."

Maggie sighed. And frowned. And cast a questioning look across the desk.

"You gotta promise me that nothing you hear will go beyond this office," she said.

"As long as nothing you tell me constitutes evidence of laws being broken, I can keep my mouth shut," he said. "But if this guy is a criminal, I'm under an obligation to do something about it."

She nodded. "He almost got expelled from Dartmouth," she said. "He was accused of a sexual assault against a fellow student, a woman he was dating. The college wanted him gone, but Daddy Knox stepped in and pulled some strings and he just got suspended for a semester. His record shows that he did a semester abroad in England, but he wasn't doing any school work. When he came back to Dartmouth, he had to take make-up classes for two summers in a row in order to graduate with his class."

"What kind of sexual assault we talking about?" Gus wanted to know.

"Date rape," Maggie said. "Reputed to have roofied her cocktail at a party, dragged her into a nearby room and had most of her clothes off when her friends found them and interceded. It was the witnesses...several of them...that made his case serious for the university. Most of the time, it's he-said, she-said and the college just tells them both to go forth and sin no more. But when there were three young women who saw what he was trying to do, well, they couldn't sweep that under the rug."

"Which is why Daddy Knox had to get involved," Gus said.

"Exactly," Maggie nodded. "But there's more."

"There usually is," Gus said.

"Preston was also involved in an incident at Yale," she said. "A study group turned into a drinking party where some of the scholars got naked. One of the women involved report-ed it and everyone at the party got a demerit or something."

"College hijinks?" Gus said.

"Yeah. Apparently, they're used to such behavior at Yale Law," she said, shaking her head. "You know, if they would just cut the balls off one asshole like that, one time, I think that shit would stop. But no, they gotta protect the elite class, no matter what."

"But you're not bitter," Gus said.

"The hell I'm not," she said. "Then, at Cabot and Calla-han, the Boston firm where he worked, I tracked down some women who used to work with Preston. Sure enough, there were several reports of harassment. None of the secretarial pool would work after hours if they had to work alone with Preston Knox, I was told. Guy had wandering hands and believed that he was God's gift to womenkind. Total asshole. And, of course, back in that day and age, he could get away with it. His partners covered up for him. There was no Me-Too stuff back then. If Preston Knox liked to pat your bottom or squeeze your boob or expect you to touch his hoohah… well, you had to deal with it. Nobody from the firm was going to do anything about it."

Gus could see she looked furious just talking about it. He didn't blame her. Preston Knox sounded like a Grade-A ass-hole.

"Well," he said, "That's all interesting, and discouraging to hear. Shit like that shouldn't happen, but it does, and we all know it. Men…well, lots of men can be pigs. Sounds like your boss is a prime example. It also sounds like his all-female staff nonsense is designed to be a pro-active defense in case any of his deep dark past rises up to smite him. Which is smart in a way, but also cynical and manipulative as hell. But when do we get around to Janine Stone?"

"Ah, yes," Maggie said. "The glitter girl. As it turns out, Preston was in the courthouse the day the Daddy Cat Lounge case was heard. He was there on another matter, totally unrelated, but just happened to be there when the case was called and young Miss Stone walked into the courtroom, in handcuffs, with three other young women from south Florida. He took one look at her and ..."

"Oh, my God," Gus said, exhaling loudly. "He fell in love with her?"

"I wouldn't call what he felt towards her as 'love,'" she said. "But he was smitten, for sure. He stayed in the back of the courtroom that day and listened to the disposition of the case, and thus found out where she and the other girls had been sent. Which is right down here to Little Penwick and the custody of the Ferro clan."

"And he followed her down here."

"Eventually, yes," Maggie said. "I got all this info from one of the bailiff's in the courthouse. A female bailiff, by the way. Who has been hit on by the Chief more than once. So she watched him watching her and knew that something evil was going on."

"Geezus," Gus said. "Weirder and weirder. What, did Knox come down here with candy and flowers and ask Marge Almeida if he could take Janine out to the movies? Have her home by eleven all in one piece?"

"Don't know," Maggie said. "I don't know what happened after that. But what I suspect happened is that Attorney General Knox arranged a meeting with Janine Stone and they made a deal. He'd keep her out of trouble with the law as long as she favored him with …"

"Her favors," Gus finished. Maggie nodded and looked pained.

"There is no other reasonable explanation for his telling me to tell you to back off on Janine," she said. "She's banging the attorney general and he's protecting her. Win-win for both of them."

"And big-time lose for law and order in my town and the state," Gus said.

"That's about it," Maggie said. She looked across the desk, locked eyes with Gus. "So," she said, "It appears my boss, in addition to being a sexist pig, may also be involved in obstruction of justice and maybe three or four other illegal things. Which begs the question: What are we gonna do?"

CHAPTER 22

Buzz Franklin could not believe how humid it was in south Florida in the middle of November. Back in Little Penwick, people were watching the news with dread, waiting for the day that would certainly come soon when the smiling weatherman would look out from the screen, frown and say "Looks like a big one's coming folks. Get those snow shovels ready."

But the wall of hot humid air smacked Franklin right in the kisser the moment he walked off the plane, and, now even a few days later, he still wasn't used to it. He felt like he had not sweated this much in his entire life. Armpits, crotch, down his chest, behind his knees…hell, he felt like his face was melting it was so sweaty from the time he awoke until the sun dropped below the horizon late in the afternoon.

He had compensated by drinking bottled water almost constantly during the day, and that had helped, although it also meant he spent a lot of time in restrooms, draining away the water that had filtered through his system. All that time standing at one urinal after another gave him time to think of things, like what percentage of sweat could be found in the average liter of pee.

Still, Buzz Franklin never felt more alive than when he was on the chase. This time, he was only chasing information, which wasn't as much fun as chasing an actual bad guy, but it still energized him. He loved following leads, building a story brick by brick until the facts pointed overwhelmingly in one direction, at one person. And that was his assignment this week: follow the leads, if any, left behind by Janine Stone and see where they might take the case next.

He was staying with Johnny Dublin and his wife Bette. Johnny D had started his career as an officer trainee in Little Penwick, then ten years later switched over to the state police. He had finished his thirty-five years in, pulled the pin, sold everything and moved down to Fort Lauderdale, where he had bought his little three bedroom, two bath house out on the western side of town, out near Tamarac and Sunrise, where the endless march of concrete and asphalt gave way, for the time being, to the sugar cane fields, the swamps and eventually the Big Cypress Preserve. Johnny D's house looked exactly like his neighbors', on both sides, and the perfectly rectangular neighborhood layout gave way, every six or seven blocks, to a strip commercial block, with a grocery store, liquor store, taco restaurant and a bar or two. Everything looked just like everything else, from the swaying palms to the green swards of grass, and Buzz had gotten lost a couple times trying to find his way back to Johnny D's place. Luckily, he had the address and his smart phone had Google maps installed.

Franklin had spent a couple days tracking down Janine Stone's family. Her parents were now divorced, which had added some complexity, but eventually Buzz had found them. The Stone family had lived in the Browderdale section of town, block after block of residential neighborhoods contained in the two or three miles between the Florida Turnpike and I-95. Comfortable, middle class, uniform, conventional, totally boring.

Janine's father, who owned an auto parts franchise near the Lauderhill Mall, didn't want to talk about his daughter very much. "She OK?" he had asked when Buzz had sat down with him in his tiny office in the back of the shop. Assured that she was, he nodded. "Girl's gonna do things her own way," he had said next. "Always has, since maybe fifth grade. I couldn't reach her. I don't think her mother could either." He had shrugged. "We did the best we could. But Janine always wanted something different than this…" He waved his hand around, meaning the neighborhood, the area, the whole south Florida thing.

Janine's mother, Nancy, was a bit more pointed in her comments. "That girl pretty much screwed up my life," Nancy Stone said to Buzz. She was now living in a two-bedroom condo down near Port Everglades. The building itself was concrete block with a steeply inclined metal roof and the views from the windows in her small unit were mostly of the blacktop in the parking lot. At least the lines in the parking lot were freshly painted in bright yellow.

"When she left, Jeremy and I went nuts," she said. "We did everything we could think of to try and find her, get her back home. The local cops down here tried, but she was way gone. About a year after she disappeared, we got a postcard from New York City. It said "Not coming back," and it was signed 'J.' She didn't even sign her entire name." Nancy Stone shook her head at the memory.

"Her leaving killed the marriage," she continued. "Without Janine, Jeremy and I had nothing left in common. He still had his business, selling motor oil and spark plugs. I had to find something else to fill my time."

"What do you do now?" Buzz had asked.

"Multi-level marketing," she said. "Hey…would you be interested in looking at my Amway catalog? Might be something in there you've always wanted."

He had thanked her, but declined. She gave him a handful of colorful product brochures to take with him. After a few more questions, he realized that both of Janine's parents had moved on. Janine had left without a trace, told them she wasn't coming back, and that was that. Each of them had decided to just continue with life as if their daughter had never happened.

Franklin had a little more success at the Broward Estates Elementary school. The principal at the school was new and didn't remember the girl, but the head of guidance and counseling, a large black woman named Beverly DeAngelo, did recall Janine Stone. She even pulled the girl's records up on her computer screen after Buzz flashed his badge at her.

"Oh dear yes," Beverly said, shaking her head sadly as she reviewed the information on the screen. "Janine Stone was quite a handful for her teachers here. Always questioning authority. Deliberate misbehavior. Acting out. Even a little precocious sexuality."

"How's that?" Buzz had asked.

"We don't get many twelve year old girls who flaunt their bodies," Beverly said. "This one did. A lot. I mean, girls at that age will act out some. Try to model whichever rock star or singer they admire. Brittany Spears, Beyonce, people like that. But this girl took it further. Rubbing against male teachers, making suggestive remarks. It says here that we recommended to her parents that she get some counseling."

"Did she?"

Beverly looked at her screen some more, then shrugged. "It doesn't say anything here, so my guess is no," she said. "Maybe the parents were against that. Maybe they couldn't afford it. Even though we give them all the resources, including public counseling, that's available."

"What about when she went to high school," Franklin asked. "Same thing?"

Beverly DeAngelo smiled. "Can't say," she said. "That's someone else's problem. Once she left here, her problems belonged to someone else."

"You got the name of your counterpart over at the high school?"

"Sure," she said, and scribbled down a name and telephone number. "But don't get your hopes up. The high schools don't usually keep the same kinds of records that we do. I guess they believe that once a kid is in high school, he or she is on their own. Behavioral problems get swept under the rug. Now if she wanted to go to college, there'd be someone up there who would've taken her under their wing."

"She left school at age 16 or 17," Buzz said.

"Then you'll be lucky to be able to pull her GPA," Beverly said. "If they leave the system before they're supposed to, the system purges them and their records. They only keep statistics on the ones who do what they're supposed to do and ride it out to the bitter end."

Buzz was starting to get a picture of what life had been like for the young Janine Stone, and it didn't look like a nice picture. But he wanted more information. So he called Nancy Stone back and asked who some of Janine's best friends in school had been. Especially in high school. She had given him three names. "Those three girls and my Janine were the posse," she told him. "They did everything together. Had an almost unhealthy devotion to one another. Never did anything unless they could all do it together. I think a lot of high school girls are like that, but this group was pretty tight. Jeremy and I used to laugh about it." She sounded wistful. Maybe it was the laughing with her husband part.

With the names in hand, Franklin spent a half day back at Johnny D's using his telephone and laptop to track them down. He finally found the parents of one of the posse, the Curtiss family, still living in their cookie cutter Browderdale house.

Buzz called and made an appointment to come talk to them, after dinner, after the sun had set and the air had cooled off a few degrees. The humidity was still the same, but it felt a little less sweaty in the cool of the evening. He let the Google voice guide him turn by turn to find their house, and Carl and Jan Curtiss welcomed him inside. They offered him a beer and they all sat down in the air-conditioned comfort of their living room. There was a TV playing in the corner, but they muted the sound.

"So what can we do for you, officer?" Carl Curtiss asked. Buzz had learned that Carl was a CPA, and Jan taught Pilates at a local spin club. They both exuded south Florida healthfulness, with deeply tanned skin and lithe, well-toned arms.

"I'm investigating a young woman who used to live around here and, I am told, was close to your daughter Megan," he said. "Her name is Janine Stone."

"What has she done?" Jan Curtiss said at once. "I told you Carl…I told you that one was no good."

"No good in what way?" Buzz asked.

Jan blew out a breath of air and shook her head sadly. "In every way, you ask me," she said. "Megan knew Janine since fourth grade, I think. They were close friends for years. So I watched them growing up together. And Janine Stone was like that movie…what's it called, Carl?"

"The Bad Seed," he said.

"That's the one!" Jan said, nodding. "Just something about that girl was off, right from the start. Always trying to get Megan and the other girls to get into trouble, do bad things. Smoke cigarettes. Smoke weed. Sneak a bottle of booze out of someone's home and go drink it in the park. God only knows what she tried to get them to do sexually. In fact, I don't want to know."

"So she was the ringleader of this little posse they had?"

"Oh, Christ, yes," Jan said. "Ringleader, CEO, chief strategist, attorney for the defense. You name it, Janine Stone was doing it. And she was just a girl! With the mind of a hardcore criminal."

"Where is Megan today?" Franklin asked.

"She's doing very well," Carl said, a touch of pride evident in his voice. "She graduated from high school, then went to Broward Community College for a couple of years. Moved up to Orlando and got a good job with Universal Studios. They're helping her get her degree at UCF, and she tells us they'll also pay for her to get a master's after."

"That sounds great," Buzz said.

"And she's got a steady boyfriend," Jan chimed in. "Nobody's said anything yet, but we're kinda hoping that with Christmas coming, there might be an announcement."

"Sounds like she has her act together," Buzz said, and the woman nodded and smiled.

"Do you remember when Janine left school?" Buzz asked. "Left Florida, in fact."

"Oh, yes," Jan said. "That was a big crisis."

"How so?"

"Well, first, Janine tried to recruit our Megan to go with her," Jan said. "Told her there was nothing interesting about Florida and that Megs should come with her up North. Said she was going to make a ton of money and have a ton of fun."

"But she didn't go?"

"Naw," Carl said. "Megan has always been pretty ground-ed and sensible. She did some crazy things from time to time, but all kids do. But this was a pretty big deal, and Megan spent a couple weeks agonizing about it. She finally confided in her mother, and we were able to put a stop to it."

"Did you tell her parents what Janine was planning to do?"

Carl and Jan looked at each other. Buzz thought they exchanged a guilty look.

"Not really," Jan said finally. "We never got along all that well with the Stones. We weren't sure if it was our place to warn them what the girl was planning to do. Not really our problem, you know? So we let it lie."

"And then she left?"

"Yeah, about a month later," Carl said. "She took Jennifer Roscoe with her and two other girls from up near Pompano. I heard that Jennifer came back home a year or so later, but none of the others ever did."

And did Megan ever stay in touch with her? After she left town?"

"Not that we know of," Jan said. "But we never super-vised our daughter's communications or her friends. Megan is a good girl. We trust her."

Franklin nodded, made a few notes in his notebook.

"So tell us," Jan said, leaning forward conspiratorially, "What did she do? Up north, after she left here? That brings a detective all the way down from Rhode Island to ask us a bunch of questions?"

Buzz smiled. "I'm not at liberty to divulge that information," he said. "But she got involved with a pretty rough crowd. A crowd into some criminal things. Like prostitution and things of that kind."

"I told you, Carl Curtiss," Jan said, sitting back in her chair, "I told you that one was no good, right from the get-go."

CHAPTER 23

Buzz was out of town, pursuing leads down in Florida. Gus ordered all his patrolmen to keep an eye out for a yellow Miata. He wanted to talk to Janine Stone again. This time, he believed that Maggie Wells would not object to an interview. She might even have some questions of her own.

But none of his men reported any sightings. Gus wondered if she had changed autos. After all, a sporty bright yellow Miata was not exactly the car to use if you were trying to stay incognito.

He was pondering all this when there was a knock on his office door. Gus looked up and saw a bright red head of hair atop a youthful looking man who still had a spray of freckles across his nose.

"Hey chief," the man said. He came into the office and unfolded his badge, holding it out for Gus to look at. It was gold, with an official insignia in the center showing an eagle with wings spread. There were two navy banners across the badge: the big one at the top read "I C E" while a narrower one at the bottom told Gus he was looking at a Special Agent.

"Dick Riordan," the man said, holding his hand out for Gus to shake. "ICE in Providence. I got a shout-out last week from Buzz Franklin. Wanted to know if we were working on any trafficking cases in these parts."

"Welcome to Little Penwick," Gus said, indicating that Riordan should take a seat. "Yeah, we're working a case down here. We don't have any hard evidence yet, but we suspect a local family may be working with someone who's bringing in workers for the strip clubs, both here and across New England. I asked Buzzy to let you guys know so we didn't bump into each other."

"Appreciate that, Chief," Riordan said. "In fact, we've got a bunch of investigations going on that involve bringing in women for the sex trade. As you might expect, that's one of those jobs that Americans no longer want. So they leave it for the immigrants."

Gus smiled and nodded in appreciation of the man's joke. If he was joking, that is.

"Any of those cases go through Little Penwick?" Gus asked.

"Not that we're specifically aware of," Riordan said. "We track the usual groups and entry points. Most of the trafficking cases are made up in the city. The nail-painting businesses and the massage parlors are mostly Asian-run, and they bring in victims they claim are relatives, and put 'em to work on the side doing tricks and performing other services. Lot of Hispanics come in allegedly to work in restaurants or in cleaning companies. Same thing…they get put to work doing tricks in the back or running drugs in and out."

Riordan shook his head.

"It's the age-old story," he said. "The victims are recruited and told they'll have good jobs and be able to send money back to the families, eventually to have them join them here in the states. Instead, they work twenty hours a day. And if they try to leave?" He looked at Gus and shook his head sadly. "Best case is they get beat up bad. Worst case? Well, you can figure that out. We had three women brutalized just last week. Asian girls. Really awful."

"What about young girls from the States?" Gus asked. "Like maybe from Florida?"

Riordan's eyebrows went up and down. "Not unheard of," he said, "But on the rare side. American girls are sought-after in the sex trade, of course, but much harder to get into the program. They're a little smarter and they all have a rough idea of their rights." He shook his head. "No, most of the victims we see are from overseas."

"How do they get into the country?" Gus asked. "They can't all be coming from the southwest border."

Riordan chuckled. "Any way they can get here, that's how they do it," he said. "Lotta Caribbean and South American victims come in via Miami. But even over on Long Island, they've got those MS-13 gangs and other criminals working full time on moving women into the country. Planes, trains, boats, on foot…you name it, they get here."

"Sounds like you guys have a full time job," Gus said.

"We do," Riordan nodded. "When we can get the assholes in Washington to leave us alone and let us do our jobs."

"I hear ya," Gus said.

"So what do you have cooking down here in bucolic Little Penwick?" he asked.

"You ever hear of the Ferro family?" Gus asked first.

Riordan frowned and shook his head. "Can't say that I have," he said.

"How about a young woman named Janine Stone?"

Riordan shook his head again. "Rings no bells," he said. "And I'm in charge of supervising all the cases we develop in this state. Who is this chick?"

"Florida native," Gus said. "Recruited to work in the clubs about four years ago, immediately got popped. But for whatever reason, she was sent down here, put under the care of a woman connected to our local scofflaws. We haven't found out why that happened … yet … but there may be some connection higher up the food chain."

"Hey," Riordan said, "I'm a native Rhode Islander. Lived here all my life. You don't need to explain to me how corrupt this state can be."

Gus nodded. "Again, we haven't yet connected all the dots, but it appears that this young woman went from being a victim to actually running a program to recruit young girls from various U.S. cities. She brings them in, trains them and they send they all over New England to work at the strip clubs."

"That's Mob territory," the ICE agent said. "One of the few things left the Mob controls anymore."

"I know," Gus said. "But she seems to be connected to a local family here that has trouble remembering how to tie their own shoes," he said. "I can't figure out how that works. Or why. But from what we've learned, the guys up in Providence seem to love her work and want her to continue. As does whoever it is that's the angel on her shoulder."

"So she's protected?"

"Very."

"That's not good," he said. "What do you want from me?"

"Just let us know if you hear of anything about to happen down here," Gus said. "We will try to find out more about our suspect and see if we can discover who is playing the role of her guardian angel."

"You got any ideas?"

Gus pursed his lips. He wasn't ready to let that out of the bag. At least not yet.

"I got my suspicions," he said.

Riordan looked at him across the desk, then nodded. "I hear ya," he said. "Okay, I'll keep my eyes and ears peeled for any action on the Sakonnet River. Meantime, you let me know which public official you think is involved. We always like to know about our local corrupt officials. If we can't bust them, at least we can try to make their lives difficult."

"Thanks for coming down," Gus said, standing up and shaking the man's hand.

"No problem," Riordan said. "They still got that seafood store over by the harbor?"

"The Freshery?" Gus said, "Yeah, he's still there. Pretty good prices most of the time."

"That's what a guy in the office told me," he said. "Thought I'd stop by over there and see what they got."

"Lobsters and clams all the time," Gus said. "And whatever fish they have came off the boat this morning."

"All over that," Riordan said. And with a last wink, he was gone.

CHAPTER 24

Nov. 16:   High winds from the cold front last week toppled a tree on East Road, near the Weetamoo Swamp, taking down a power line in the area.

Little Penwick police were called to the scene around 3 in the afternoon and secured the scene until the power company could clear the tree and restore service.

Police said about fifty homes were affected. Power was restored by six p.m.

CHIEF HADDOCK HAD spent the better part of three hours sitting in his patrol car on the side of Easterly Road, blue lights flashing, to keep traffic away from the downed line. He had taken that duty since all the other officers on the day shift were needed elsewhere. The storm had roared in off the ocean before noon bringing gusty winds and heavy rain, and traffic in town was a mess. There had been three accidents report-ed, none with injuries, thank goodness, but Little Penwick's thin blue line had been stretched out more than usual, so Gus had assigned himself to the incident on Easterly. Lt. Callah-an and Sgt. Martin had been sent down to the harbor, where one of the larger trawlers had broken loose from its mooring and been blown onto the rocky shore. They were checking to make sure no fuel was leaking into the harbor, which would have meant calling out the state Environmental Management Police as well as the Coastal Commission, resulting in hours of paperwork and forms to be filled out. The crews from the electric company were stretched as thin as the police, as the storm had wreaked havoc everywhere in the area, but the cen-tral switching station had cut the power to the downed line and the trucks were reportedly notified of the problem and on the way to deal with it.

Gus had used the down time to return some phone calls. Buzz Franklin had called from the Ft. Lauderdale airport to tell Gus he was on the way back home. They agreed to meet in the morning so Buzz could report on what he had learned. Gus had talked to Dottie the dispatcher several times, keeping up to date on where his men were and what they were doing. It was all the usual drill for bad weather. When the wind blew, the rains poured down or the snow piled up, people did crazy things, and it was up to the police department to pick up the pieces and try to get life back to normal as soon as possible.

Maggie Wells had called to report in from Providence. She told Gus that Preston Knox had not been happy when told that Little Penwick was officially investigating Janine Stone. He had started in on a rant that blamed Maggie for disloyalty, but she had stopped him cold, telling him that the police had more than reasonable cause to think that Janine was involved in some illegal behaviors and that she, Maggie, had personally approved the investigation. That had shut him up, but he was not happy.

"I haven't been invited to one of his lunchtime babe parades to the Capital Grille for at least a week now," she told Gus. "I kinda miss the grilled scallops in a citrus cream reduction, though. Much better than the cold tuna sandwich I brought in from home today."

"Well, speaking as one of the taxpayers who doesn't have to pay the $40 for your scallops, I'm not sorry," he said. "You got anything else?"

"Still doing some digging," she said. "Nothing to report yet."

Gus looked out his squad car's rain-streaked window. The downed tree had fallen almost exactly between two power-line poles, causing the thick black wires to bend absurdly out of shape. It looked like one of the lines had snapped with the tension. Easterly Road was a long and mostly straight connector between the main north-south routes in Little Penwick. Main Road followed the route of the Sakonnet River as it ran between Mount Hope Bay and the Atlantic. Easterly Road cut across to the Long Highway, which ran north-northeast into Westport, Mass., and on to Fall River and east to New Bedford.

The entrance to the Ferro land lay about a mile further east. Gus looked out at the old stone wall that bordered the road, built probably two centuries ago when the farmers cleared the land of New England's main agricultural crop: a never-ending supply of stones and boulders: granite, schist and sandstone. Left behind when the glaciers receded, and covered by a millenia or ten of dirt and deposits, the stones slowly worked their way to the surface, pushed by rain and frost, where farmers had to dig them out, pick them up and, in back-breaking work, carry them away with the help of exhausted horses, mules and oxen to the sides of the fields and stack them in endless rough stone walls. Tourists liked to take pictures of the quaint walls. Chipmunks made condos out of them. Farmers would have preferred blowing them up with dynamite.

But as Gus sat there looking at the walls and the empty fields they contained, he started thinking. Thinking like an old Army Ranger not as the chief of police. What if, he thought, he had a reconnaissance mission? Proceed overland and undercover to the target location. Observe all incoming and outgoing transportation. If conditions allowed, maybe some close recon work on the target building itself.

He was thinking about the Ferro garage and what might be inside. As chief of police, he'd need a search warrant to get a look inside. As an Army Ranger, he could proceed with stealth and gather the intel he needed. Then, of course, he would call in the flyboys, give them the coordinates and stand back to watch as they destroyed the target.

He shook his head, bringing his thoughts back to reality. As satisfying as it would be to watch the Ferro garage go up in a bright orange explosion followed by a billowing cloud of black smoke, he couldn't do that as chief of police. But the recon part … maybe that was possible.

He reached into the back seat pocket of his squad car and found the multi-page street directory map of Little Penwick he kept back there. He opened the book to the page that showed Easterly Road and quickly found his current location. Then, he found the Ferro private road, followed it into the interior of their land and saw where the big white house was situated. The garage was behind that. He moved his finger slowly back towards his current location, this time through the woods and fields. The back way. He noted three or four ponds or wetlands, which told him that the terrain was low and wet, but decided it wouldn't be that difficult to navigate his way around them. With this map, a compass and his training in stealth overland movement, he realized that he could probably pull it off.

He thumbed the button on his mic and called Dottie.

"Hey chief," she said. "Electric boys out there yet?"

"Not yet," Gus said.

"They called me half hour ago," she said. "Said they were on the way. So sit tight."

"I'm sitting," he said. "Listen, what's the weather forecast for tonight?"

"Bad," Dottie said. "More rain coming after dark. Wind should ease a little. But it's looking like a good night to be indoors."

"Right," Gus said. "Thanks."

Dark night. Bad, if not horrific weather. Fit for neither man nor beast.

"Just about perfect for a Ranger," he said to himself.

CHAPTER 25

After the electric company truck had come and gone, Gus drove back to the station and spent an hour or so supervising the post-storm clean-up. Little Penwick had come out pretty well in the storm which had ravaged other parts of the New England coastline. A few fender benders, some fallen trees and a couple of neighborhoods without power for two hours was a reasonable, and small, price to pay for a major Nor'easter.

Once things were calm again and the night shift sent out on duty, Gus went home. He made some coffee and then rummaged around in his fridge for something to eat. Then he went into his closet, way in the back, and dug out some of his old Ranger gear. He had kept most of his uniforms after he pulled the pin and left the Army, hanging them neatly on hangers, pressed and ready for service. Part of that was just force of habit. But maybe he had hoped for…wanted even… another chance to don his gear and set out on a mission. That had given his life some meaning and purpose for several years, and it had been a hard thing to have to set it aside. Being chief of police helped fill the need he felt, a great chasm of desire, to do something to serve. But he missed his Ranger days, and the rush of excitement that he had felt back then. Missed it all probably more than he was willing to admit. Even to Dr. Mahoney.

He found and dressed in the black Army Physical Fitness Uniform he still had. The long black nylon pants were scratch- and water-resistant. He put on one of his own long sleeved T-shirts before adding the long-sleeve APFU sweatshirt. Black socks and his black trainers. He added a black woolen skull cap for warmth. Going into the bathroom, he found the old dop kit with his operational stuff and pulled out the stick of the Bobby Weiner brand face paint. He daubed some on his forehead and cheeks and rubbed it in to cover. Looking in the mirror, he realized that if anyone took his picture and put it online, he'd likely get canceled for donning blackface. But all the troops in the war zones of the Middle East knew that white Western faces reflected light off their white skin, and any missions undertaken at night required the soldiers to use the camo face paint to blend in to the dark surroundings.

In his pantry in the kitchen, he found the bag of doggie treats he had bought to make friends with Mrs. P's Irish setter. He put a small handful of those in one of his pockets, think- ing he might run into one of the Ferro's German shepherds during his reconnoiter mission. In Afghanistan, he might have sprinkled the treats with powdered drugs that would ensure the mutts would fall asleep almost instantly, but he decided he didn't need to get that serious here in Little Penwick. Then again, in Afghanistan, he and his fellow Rangers would probably just shoot any enemy dogs they encountered during a night mission. That was definitely not on order here.

Finally, he rummaged around on the top shelf of the hall closet and found his night vision goggles. Indispensable tools for conducting night operations, the goggles allowed him to use whatever ambient light existed in the location to see pretty clearly what was going on. He replaced the batteries, and put the goggles into a small black shoulder pack, along with a seven-inch flashlight, bottle of water and a couple of protein bars. He wasn't planning to be outside that long, but had long ago learned to plan for contingencies.

Then he waited. He sat in his warm garage apartment and listened to the last of the gusty storm pass by. He wanted to go late, after everyone in town had bedded down for the night. He especially wanted his landlady, Mrs. P, to be asleep. He didn't know what kind of explanation he could come up with for being sighted in his black clothes and black face, so he waited until almost midnight before setting out on his mission. He checked his map again, mentally running the route, planning for whatever surprises might occur. There were always surprises on a night recon. Experience taught him that. With the route memorized, he tore the page out of the map book, folded it a couple times and slipped it into a front pocket.

Finally, at about 11:30, he figured it was time. Most people would be in bed, snoozing, canoodling or watching The Tonight Show. With the last of the gusty winds and spattering rain squalls passing by, nobody would be outdoors, especially deep in the woods or wandering around the swampy land where the Ferros lived.

The last thing Gus did before he left his apartment was to check his arms. Like many cops, Gus carried the SIG Sauer P229 with 9 mm Lugar rounds in a 10-round clip. He had used a Glock in the Rangers and liked that weapon, but the SIG had a nice hefty feel and enough stopping power for any conceivable law enforcement use. He checked the magazine, jacked a round into the chamber and slipped the gun into its black leather holster on his left hip. He wasn't planning to shoot anyone tonight, but on the other hand, he was sneaking onto the Ferro property. And that was always dangerous.

He also strapped his knife sheath to his upper thigh. Gus had carried the Cold Steel SRK in combat for many years. The Cold Steel was pretty basic: eight-inch black steel straight blade that came out of its sheath quickly and the heavy handle fit his hand perfectly.

He drove his squad car back to where the electrical crew had untangled the downed tree from the power lines, and parked it off the road and out of sight. He waited in the dark, engine and lights off, for about fifteen minutes. No cars went past, which made him feel like his plan was working—everyone in Little Penwick seemed to be safely home and in bed, right where he wanted them.

Making sure that the interior lights were off, Gus slipped out of the car, threw his backpack over one shoulder, pulled the woolen hat down low and felt in his pocket for the round compass he always carried there. Standing there on the familiar road, he knew where the four compass points were. But he knew that out in the woods, especially if he had to detour around some swamps, and in the dark of night, it would be easy to get turned around and confused.

After one last mental check, Gus crossed the empty road, climbed over the stone wall and set off across what had been a cornfield full of bushy green plants just a few months earlier. Now there were just yellowed stalks, cut off about six inches above the dark earth. Even though there was no one about, he took care to walk between the stalks and avoided brushing up against them. Stealthy and silent. The Ranger way.

Once across the field, he climbed over the stone wall again and entered the woods. He quickly realized he needed his night vision goggles—there were low branches and thick stands of thorny pucker brush, and it was so dark that he ran the danger of running right into them. So he pulled the goggles on over his woolen hat, flipped the switch and saw the implacable and black woods turn into a greenish haze. But he could now see the low hanging limbs and the thickest stands of the pucker brush, so he was able to avoid them and make pretty good time.

He got deeper into the woods, heading roughly east by southeast. The map told him that he would encounter a swampy area, and in about ten minutes, he came up on it. He saw a large eight-point buck drinking at the side of the swamp, and managed to get within about ten feet before the beast saw, heard or smelled him and took off in a leaping crash through the woods.

Better pay better attention than that, Gus sent thought-waves as the deer ran away. *I was almost close enough to jump on your back.*

He skirted around the swamp, keeping it on his left, and found an old footpath on the other side. He had seen the curving dotted line on the map and thought it might have been an old farmer's road. Human beings had been trying to grow crops on this land for almost four hundred years now. Most of what today was thick woods had been open farmland in the Colonial era and long afterwards. Those early settlers had chopped down all the trees they had encountered, for fuel and timber and to clear the land for growing crops. It was only after World War I, when motorized farming took hold and people switched over from raising their own food to buying it in a store that farming began to decline and huge swaths of the land were left fallow and unused. The result, a hundred years later, was the thick second-growth forest that Gus was now navigating in the dark.

Gus had seen on the map that the dotted line footpath led him almost all the way around to the back of Danny Ferro's house, and the garage behind it that was Gus' target. It was about fifteen minutes before Gus caught the first glimpse of the compound of buildings circled around that large open plain. That was the Ferro place.

He stopped to rest and listen. He stood there for about ten minutes, listening hard, looking all around at the green neon world he saw through his goggles. He could hear nothing but the gusts of wind rattling through the woods. No dogs came growling at him out of the dark. He hadn't expected the Ferros to have posted sentries or guards but was glad to discover that they hadn't.

But now that he was close to the target, he slowed down even more. He kept one eye on the ground, to look for trip wires. In Afghanistan, those were usually connected to some kind of IED that would take off an arm or a leg, if not one's entire head. Here, Gus imagined the Ferros might have installed warning alarms. But he also knew that if they had, they probably spent a lot of nights chasing deer, possum, coyotes and other animals that would set them off.

At the same time, Gus kept scouting high up in the trees, looking for a motion-detector and floodlight set-up. That's the first line of defense he would have set up, if he lived out here, but he didn't see anything, and was glad that the cover of darkness was left undisturbed.

Now that he could see the main house, the one with the wraparound porch, he knew where he was, and where he was going. He crept silently around behind the house, still in the cover of the woods, and approached the metallic structure of the new garage. It sat there, dark, silent and quiet as the grave. Again, the dogs all seemed to have been taken inside, out of the rain. Gus uttered a silent prayer of thanks for that.

With the aid of his night vision, Gus could see the dual floodlight on the roofline above the big roll-up door in the front. He wanted no part of that, so he made his way in a wide circle around to the back of the garage. There were no windows on the side or the rear of the structure. He came up close, close enough to touch the metallic cladding, and stood there listening hard for a minute or two. Nothing. Silence.

He continued around the back and was about to turn the corner and walk up the far side of the garage when he spotted the red glow of a cigarette. He quickly pulled back out of sight, and at the same time, caught the scent of the smoke. Somebody was not in bed on this cold rainy night, and they were outside having a smoke.

He stood up tightly, back against the wall of the garage at the back, standing still and listening hard. He thought he heard a metallic squeak of some kind that sounded like a door opening and closing. Then he heard a soft female voice.

"You got another one of those?" the voice said.

Gus heard some rustling paper, then there was a pause, then there was the distinctive scratch of a match being struck against the striker strip on the matchbook. The female voice spoke again.

"Thanks," she said.

"Can't sleep?" The first smoker was a man.

Gus heard a whoosh of breath being expelled, and imagined the cloud of smoke drifting up against the wind and vanishing into the rainy night.

"Nah," the female voice said. "I've never been a good sleeper."

"Exercise," the male voice said. "You gotta work out during the day, run a few miles, lift some weights. Then, a couple of drinks after dinner. If that don't work, then some sex will. Puts me right to sleep, every time."

The female didn't answer.

Gus heard the male chuckle. "Nothin' to say to that?" he said. "Why am I not surprised?"

"You know what the boss says," the female said. "No freebies."

"Well, fuck her," the male answered. "I'm just trying to help you get some sleep."

"Yeah, I'm sure you are," the female answered. Her tone of voice was sarcastic.

"Well, I'm going to bed," the male answered. "And I've got no problems at all falling asleep. Suit yourself."

Gus heard the metallic scraping of the door opening again, and then there was silence. The smokers had apparently gone inside. He took a deep breath, then stuck his head quickly around the corner of the building. There was no one outside. He walked up along the side of the garage until he reached the door. He paused outside and listened hard. He couldn't hear anything from inside. He thought about pulling his gun, throwing the door wide open and charging in, but decided that such gung-ho tactics, which might have worked against the Taliban, probably wouldn't here. And would leave him with lots of questions to answer.

So instead, he took a quick look around the area near the door, where the smokers had been standing. There were several crushed cigarette butts in the dirt. An old 50 gallon metal drum stood next to a tree trunk a few steps away. Gus went over and felt the side: it was warm. He could smell the smoke from inside the drum. Somebody had been burning something. Gus reached in with his gloved hand and grabbed what he could. He came out with a handful of half-burned papers, black with ash around the edges, but still somewhat legible in the centers. He folded them and tucked them away in one of his pant pockets and retraced his steps towards the back of the garage.

He had taken maybe three strides when the squeaky hinges on the door made their sound again. Gus felt the door swinging open and then he heard someone say "Hey!" in a protesting voice.

His reaction was almost automatic. He reached down and grabbed the knife off his thigh, reversed it so an inch or two of the handle was sticking out of his fist, planted his right foot and made a sweeping pivot, bringing his hand up to shoulder level and driving it into the side of the head of the man who had come out the door. The whole sequence took less than two seconds, and Gus heard the thunk of the solid metal handle meeting cranium. The man went down as if switched off, falling heavily against the metallic wall and slumping to the ground.

Looking back at the door, Gus saw a female head peer through the door opening.

"Go back inside," he growled. "And keep your mouth shut."

The head disappeared.

Gus turned and walked quickly and quietly back behind the garage, and then plunged ahead into the woods. He walked about a hundred yards straight ahead and then began circling back to the right, where the old foot path had been. He kept his ears open, but could hear no alarms going up behind him. No barking dogs. His luck seemed to be holding. He knew the one he had hit would be out cold for several minutes, if not longer, and just hoped the female would obey his command to keep silent. But he kept moving as fast as conditions would allow.

Ten minutes later, he found the path and was able to make better time, knowing roughly where he was going. He stopped at one point to listen again, checking for pursuit, but heard nothing. So he kept going. Twenty minutes later, he was crossing the field adjacent to the road, scaled the stone wall and was back inside his car. He peeled off some of his gear, removed the night vision goggles and sat there for another ten minutes, waiting and watching. But there was nothing but darkness and silence in the night around him, and after convincing himself that no one was following, he started his car and drove back home.

CHAPTER 26

Gus was already in his office the next morning when Buzz Franklin came in. Gus had a sheet of newspaper spread out on his desk, and he had laid out the charred pieces of paper he had recovered from the metal drum the night before. Most of the papers were too scorched and blackened to read, but there were a few pieces that were still legible, and Gus was peering at them carefully.

"Morning, chief," Buzz said as he came in, carrying a briefcase and a cup of coffee.

"How was your trip back?" Gus said, still studying the paper on his desk.

"I made it, so I guess it was successful," Buzz said. "What do we have here?"

"Paperwork," Gus said. "From the Ferro place. They have a burn barrel and tried to use it, but I managed to rescue some of it."

Franklin bent over the desk and tried to read some of the charred pieces.

"Rescued, huh?" he said. "And when did we do this?"

"Last night," Gus said. "I authorized an operation. Then I carried it out. A little off-the-books night raid. I wanted to see what was going on inside that garage."

"Ah," Buzz said, "The ole night-time raid gambit. I'm sure that was totally legal and everything." Gus was silent. "Anybody get hurt?"

Gus smiled. "Somebody over there probably has a bad headache this morning," he said. "But no casualties."

"So what have we learned?" Buzz said.

Gus pointed to one of the larger segments of readable paper on the desk. "This looks like a print-out from an airline, listing the names and arrival times of six passengers, all women," he said. "Three arrived from Orlando and three from New Orleans. All landed in Providence last Tuesday."

He pointed to another stack. "And here are some store receipts, all dated Wednesday, the day after these six arrived in town. There's one from Target, one from CVS, one from WalMart. They show purchases of sweaters, heavy coats, and cosmetics and toiletries from the drug store. Everything purchased with cash."

Buzz looked at the stack, nodding to himself. "They flew in a fresh supply of strippers, fixed them up with winter clothes and other stuff they might need. You think they're keeping them out in that garage?"

"Yeah," Gus said. "I think it's a way station. They hold the girls out here in the boonies until they get them placed and delivered to one of the clubs. Maybe here in Providence, maybe in whatever other city they send them to … Worcester, Hartford, Manchester. I'm sure the clubs in those places all have apartments booked for their talent to use. It looks like a pretty big operation, planned and executed right here on the Ferro property. Janine brings them in, the Ferro boys deliver them."

"Any of this stuff admissible?"

"I do not like the sound of that," said a voice from the doorway, and the two men turned to look at Maggie Wells, who had just walked in. "To ask that question is to answer it."

"We're building a wall here," Gus said. "One brick at a time. This stuff is just a small part of the whole. We've got probable cause. Once we're ready, we can start popping some of these people, and then the fun will start. They'll start throwing each other under the bus to avoid getting locked up, and that's when we'll have our case. Signed, sealed, delivered."

"What is this stuff?" Maggie asked as she shucked her overcoat and began studying the pieces of charred paper arrayed across Gus' desk. "Where did it come from?"

"There's a fifty-five gallon metal drum outside the garage at the rear of the Ferro property," Gus said. "They tried to burn a bunch of documents, but yesterday's rain storm put out the fire before they were done. I managed to save these remnants."

"Great!" Maggie said. "You got a warrant for this search?"

"Well, no," Gus said. "I conducted a reconnaissance operation last night. Or maybe this morning. Didn't check my watch a lot. Went out there to see what's what."

Maggie looked up at Gus, frowning. "Recon—? Oh my God, you actually went out there without a warrant? And still seized their property? Are you actively trying to get this case thrown out before we've even started?"

"This stuff was recovered from a trash receptacle," Gus said. "I need a warrant to snoop through their trash?"

Maggie paused, thinking. "I remember we talked about this in law school," she said. "The question is, if you leave trash outside on the curb to be picked up, can the cops look through it without a warrant? Case law is divided. But generally, the law holds that if you abandoned the trash, or put it out for collection, then the cops don't need a court to approve a search."

"And if they burned a bunch of paper in a metal drum, that kinda indicates abandonment, right?" Gus said. "Turning documents into ashes is the same as giving them up for good. So I think I'm justified to recover what I can from the ashes and look at it."

Maggie shook her head. "Maybe so, but any good defense attorney is going to challenge you on that point," she said. "Especially if you were trespassing illegally on their land at the time."

Gus shrugged. "No one saw me," he said. "Except some guy with a headache and maybe one of the victims." The other two looked at him questioningly, so he explained how he had defended himself against whoever it was who came out of the door, and then told what looked like a woman to go back inside."

"Yeah, I think we're inadmissible here," Maggie said.

"But we can use this to seek more information, right?" Buzz said.

"We've got the names of six girls who are being held out there," Gus said, pointing to the travel agency document. "Can't we ask a judge to let us go out and interview them, make sure they're not being held against their will?"

Maggie thought about that. "Maybe," she said. "If we can tell the judge that somebody asked us to check on their welfare. Like a parent. Or a relative. Or if we somehow came up independently with this list of names. But I think using this list here would be illegal."

"OK," Gus said. "We just need to get another source."

"I might be able to help," Buzz Franklin said. "Before I got on the plane to come home yesterday, I had a phoner with Megan Curtiss. She was one of Janine Stone's besties in high school in Broward. Janine tried to recruit her to come up to Rhode Island with her four years ago, but Megan turned her down. But she told me the whole story."

Gus carefully moved the newspaper page to one side of his desk keeping the charred pieces of evidence secure.

"Is anybody else hungry?" he said. "I've been up all night and could use some coffee. Let's go over to the Commons Cup."

FIFTEEN MINUTES LATER, they were seated at one of the tables at the Commons Cup, hot mugs of freshly brewed coffee in front of them along with a plate of cinnamon buns that Betty Billingsly had baked earlier that morning. It was around eleven and the place was empty except for the three of them. The lunch crowd wouldn't start filing in for another forty minutes or so.

"OK," Gus said, "What did you learn from Megan?"

Buzz Franklin took a bite of his cinnamon bun and had to stop and wipe some of the frosting off his chin. He washed it down with a sip of coffee and wiped his face with a napkin.

"Dang," he said, "I hope this doesn't interfere with lunch." The other two just stared at him.

"OK," he said, flipping open his notebook to read what he had jotted down the day before. "Megan Curtiss is now 22 years old, gainfully employed by one of the amusement park companies in Orlando and is on the management track. But she told me that in her junior year of high school, in the spring, Janine Stone told her she was planning to run away from home, come up East and pursue a career in stripping."

"She called it that?" Maggie Wells asked. "Stripping?"

"She used several euphemisms," Franklin answered. "Private performance, entertainment business, adult business. But Megan knew what she was proposing."

"What was the sell?" Gus asked. "Why did Janine think Megan would buy in?"

"Money," Buzz said. He flipped through the pages of his notebook. "Here...she told Megan that she could make two thousand dollars a month. She, Janine, had been told this by someone at the clubs."

"That would sound like a lot of money to a teenager," Maggie said. "Hell, it sounds like a lot of money to me."

"And it did, Megan said," Franklin continued, nodding. "Janine also pitched it as a great opportunity to get out of south Florida and Broward County and find a way to spread her wings and do something important. From what Janine's parents told me, that was what motivated Janine. She hated her life down there and was ready to get out and see the world."

"I take it Megan was not so excited about that part," Gus said.

"Yeah," Buzz nodded. "Megan told me that at first, she was excited about the idea. She wanted to buy a car, and thought this was the way to get it. One of their other friends..." He flipped through his notebook again ... "Ah, here it is. Kayley Cramer was part of the clique. She agreed to go with Janine. But Megan began to have second thoughts, almost right away. Didn't tell the other girls, but she began to wonder if she really wanted to get into stripping and whatever else that entailed. She said Janine was always a bit cloudy on some of those details, like 'Am I going to have to get naked?' and 'Will I have to screw anyone?'"

"So she didn't go," Maggie said.

"Nope." Buzz nodded. "Janine and Kayley, along with another girl from Palm Beach that Janine knew, came up to Rhode Island in May, just a couple weeks before the end of their junior year in high school. Megan was supposed to meet them someplace, but didn't go. By then, she had confided in her mother, and her parents were aware of what was going on."

"Do we know how they got up here?" Maggie asked. "The girls who left?"

"Megan didn't know," Buzz said. "She thought she heard something about a car waiting to drive them north."

"What do you want to bet it was Danny Ferro and maybe his cousin Emilio?" Gus said. "Making the booty run."

"And now they're flying the prospects up on Southwest?" Maggie was angry. "That indicates a larger investment by whomever is paying for this. They must be making a lot of money."

"It does sound like the operation has grown," Gus said. He thought about that for a moment, frowning. Maggie noticed.

"What?" she asked.

Gus shrugged. "I don't know. My general impression is that the Ferro bunch barely have enough smarts to know when to tie their shoes, and have a hard time baiting the hooks on their fishing trawler.. And now they're doing all kinds of cross-country coordination and scheduling and logistics? Color me skeptical."

"So you think someone else is doing all the thinking and the Ferros just provide the garage?" Buzz said.

"Well, I think someone else is in charge," Gus said. "But I have no idea who. Danny Ferro can drive a truck, maybe operate a fishing boat, and probably has enough smarts to figure out how to use his TV remote control. But to be in charge of a multi-state trafficking operation? Don't think so."

He looked across the desk at Maggie, who was staring out the window. But she wasn't looking at the scenic view of the town triangle. She was thinking about something.

"What?" he asked.

She blinked, twice, then focused again on their conversation.

"I just thought of someone who could be running the operation," she said. "But I really don't like who I thought of."

"Who?" Buzz asked.

Maggie just shook her head. "I don't know," she said. "It fits. But it can't be. Really cannot be possible."

"Oh my God," Gus said, slapping the table. The other two jumped at the sound. "You think it might be Preston Knox."

Maggie didn't answer, but just stared at Gus. Then, almost imperceptibly, she nodded.

CHAPTER 27

Fifty miles away, at that same moment, Preston Knox was slipping into the back door of Gianni's Italian bistro on Atwells Avenue. The restaurant was in the Federal Hill neighborhood west of downtown Providence, the part of town noted for its Italian heritage. Not only was there a pizza joint, grappa house or Italian restaurant located in every other building along the avenue, Atwells was also the location of the National Cigarette Service Company and Coin-o-Matic Distributors, a dingy, run-down, one-story building that had once housed the main hangout of Raymond Patriarca, known as "The Man," who ran New England organized crime for four decades. Patriarca broke into the crime business, back in the 1950s, by smuggling untaxed cigarettes into Rhode Island and selling them on the street at cut-rate prices.

Patriarca was long deceased and control of New England's crime businesses had long since passed on to other crooks and killers, but Federal Hill was still Italian and still had that reputation as a slightly shady part of town. Where you could still find some authentic *cucina* from whatever region of the old country you preferred. Or purchase something from some guy off the back of his truck. With cash. No questions asked.

Gianni's bistro was one such place, renowned for its veal scallopini, cacciucco--a rich Tuscan seafood stew with prawns, clams, mussels and shrimp--and linguine con le Vongole. In the front, with windows looking out on the scene on Atwells Avenue, the restaurant had a dozen private booths with high wooden backs upholstered in dark red leather, candles in woven straw holders and a purplish red house wine said to be made from Gianni's own backyard grape arbor. That might have been true back in the day, but today the owner of Gianni's lived in a glass-walled condo high above the Providence River, with views out to Narragansett Bay, and the only thing he grew was a ficus tree in a planter stuck by the window.

Normally, Preston Knox would have strolled in the front door of Gianni's stopping to shake hands and chat with customers, servers and the owners alike. There were still a lot of Italian voters in Rhode Island. And he would have been happy to stay for lunch, tucking into a plate of the clams linguine while he held court with the locals and the tourists alike. But today, he was here on business, so he had his driver take him down the alley behind the row of storefronts, and he quickly stepped inside the back door, dodging past the big blue metallic dumpsters fragrant with the leftover smells of yesterday's menu. They were waiting for him: the door opened as he approached and a heavy-set man in a black suit showed him down a dingy and dark hallway and into a wood-paneled office. Three other men were waiting there, small white cups of espresso in front of them.

"*Buon giorno*," Knox said, nodding at the men as he doffed his overcoat and sat down in a chair. The others, all dressed in identical black suits and white dress shirts, nodded back, but said nothing, their small dark eyes watching every move he made. Knox took their silence as a message that they wanted to get down to business.

"We might have a problem down in Little Penwick," he said. "The police are asking questions about our Janine."

One of the men, a rotund man in his sixties stirred, sitting forward in his chair. He was balding, heavy jowled and thick lipped. His voice, when he spoke, was a deep gravelly baritone, with just the slightest hint of an Italian accent.

"The police are supposed to be your concern, General," the man said. "If there is a problem there, it is your problem."

"All that is true," Knox said, "And I have done everything I can to control the situation. I moved the old chief of police out and installed one of my best people to oversee the department under the new chief. But I can't keep them from doing what police do, which is investigate things and pull on strings. And they may be getting close to pulling on Janine's strings, which would not be good for any of us."

The three men exchanged glances. Preston Knox was not sure what those looks meant, but he knew they could communicate with each other in that way: with glances, nods, raised eyebrows and cleared throats. And he knew that he had no idea what they were saying to each other in these ways…he was not fluent in that particular language, which put him at a disadvantage.

The man behind the desk leaned forward again.

"What is it you want us to do, General?" he said.

Preston Knox held up his hand like a stop sign. "I don't want you to do anything," he said hurriedly. "I just wanted to keep you informed about what is going on down there."

The three men exchanged another glance. The same man spoke again.

"We do not wish to be kept informed," he said. "We expect you to handle whatever problems arise. Janine is doing a good job, is that not correct?"

"Yes, she is," Knox said.

"We agree," he said. "We want her to continue in her work. You promised that you could ensure she would not be bothered by the police. Now you come to see us and tell us that she may be bothered. That is a problem. But it seems to be *your* problem, General. How do you intend to ensure that she will not be bothered?"

Knox let out the air in his lungs with a rush. "See," he said, "That's what I'm trying to tell you. I can't stop the police from investigating if they think there's a crime."

"Do you wish us to eliminate the problem?" the man asked. "We can remove the new chief of police."

"Dear God, no!" Knox almost leaped out of his chair. "If you do anything like that, the FBI will be down there crawling all over everything! As will the state police. And the media. No, that is the worst possible thing you can do."

"Then, my friend, it is our strong recommendation that you find a way to stop the local police from looking any further into the matter," the man said, sitting back in his chair.

"And how—"

The man in the black suit held up a hand, a thick-fingered hand decked with several gold rings.

"It is not our job to tell you what to do, General," he said. "You are the attorney general for the state of Rhode Island. You are in charge of law enforcement and the courts. You promised us that you could control the situation in Little Penwick and let our little enterprise continue without problem. We expect you to keep that promise."

He paused. The air in the room suddenly seemed heavy and hard to breathe to Knox. *We expect you to keep that promise* sounded like a not very veiled threat.

"OK," Preston said, "Got it. My problem. Right. I'll take care of it."

"Buono," the man said. He waved his hand at a man who had been standing behind Preston Knox during the meeting, standing against the wall silently. "Would you like a nice glass of grappa or an espresso before you leave?"

Knox stood up. He felt his knees were a little wobbly. He shook his head.

"No, thank you," he said. "I have to get back to the office. I've got a meeting with the governor this afternoon."

"Ah, our good governor," the man said. "You will please tell her that everyone at Gianni's Bistro sends their regards and very best wishes, yes?"

"Sure," Preston Knox said. "I'll do that." He knew he wouldn't do any such thing. The mere mention of Gianni's Bistro and the men who ran it spoke of things best not spoken. At all.

He turned and walked out. The silent man opened the door to the hallway and Knox retraced his steps back out into the alley. His official car was still parked next to the dumpster. He got in the back seat and his driver pulled away.

Preston Knox saw his driver's inquisitive glance in the rear view mirror as they drove away. As usual, he ignored it. The man was not on his social level, and he felt no need to explain his actions. But as he was carried back up to Capitol Hill, Knox allowed himself some fleeting moments of reflection. He knew he was in deep with some pretty rough clientele. But they had cash to burn, and Knox well knew that he would need as much cash as he could find to run for governor. There were others in government, a mayor or two and one of the state's two Congressmen, who had their eyes on running. Knox was not a lock. He had enemies, plenty of them. So he decided he didn't need to worry about who some of his friends were. *Let the others worry about them,* he thought.

Back at Gianni's, the three men looked at each other again. One shrugged, one scratched behind his ear, the other smiled to himself as if he knew something the others didn't.

CHAPTER 28

Emilio Ferro had a bad headache. He sat, head in hands, on one of the unused bunks in the garage and tried to ignore his cousin Daniel, who was pacing back and forth.

"What the hell, Meels?" Danny said. "You were supposed to watch the inventory, that's all. Make sure nobody gets out, and sure as hell make sure nobody gets in. No touchies, no feelies, no talking, no nothing! And somebody just walks right up without you seeing or hearing a goddam thing and conks you on the head."

Emilio tried to defend himself. "Look," he said, "None of the girls ..."

"Inventory," his cousin snapped. "We call them inventory."

"Right," Emilio said, "None of the inventory got away. Everyone's present and accounted for. I don't see what the big deal ..."

"Somebody walks up to this place in the middle of the night—we have no idea who—and   you don't see what's the big deal?" Danny said, stopping his pacing and throwing his arms out in exasperation. "What kind of idiot are you? Now, tell me again what happened."

Emilio took his aching head out of his hands and looked at his cousin with weary eyes. "I told you a dozen times already," he said, his voice a thin whine.

"Tell me again."

Emilio sighed. "OK, OK," he said. "I was here with the lad—, I mean inventory. It was raining and windy all night long. One of them said she wanted a smoke. It was late…after midnight. So I took her outside, so we wouldn't set off the smoke alarm and wake everyone up, and we had a smoke. It was dark, it was raining, it was quiet. We smoked and I sent her back inside, turned around and something hit me in the side of my head. Knocked me out cold. When I come to, the chickie is tossing water in my face, standing over me. Soon as I could think straight, I called you. That's all that happened."

"When she threw the water in your face to wake you up… where were you?"

"Outside," Emilio said. "Lying against the wall just next to the door."

"So she was outside," Danny said accusingly.

"We had just had a smoke," Emilio responded. "I just told you that. Yeah, we were outside smoking. So what?"

"So how long were you out cold?"

"I dunno," Emilio said, "I …"

"Exactly," his cousin said, and began pacing again. "You were out like a light and one of the inventory was outside, unsupervised, footloose and fancy free. Did she talk with the guy who cold-cocked you? Give him any information? Share a phone number? Set up a plan to be rescued?"

Emilio put his head back into his hands again. It felt better that way. "No," he mumbled. "I don't know. I don't think ..."

"No, you don't think," Danny snapped. "For all we know, it coulda been someone from Providence. Coulda been the staties. Coulda been the FBI."

"The FBI?" Emilio looked up in surprise. "What the hell would they be doing out here?"

"Looking for something that would send you to prison for the rest of your life, you idiot," Danny said. "What do you think?"

"It wasn't the FBI," said a female voice. Emilio and Danny looked up. Janine Stone was standing there, wearing a down parka, jeans and boots. "It was the local guy, the new chief. What's his name? Some kinda fish?"

"Haddock," the Ferro men said in unison. "Gus Haddock," Danny said. "How do you know it was him?"

"I just spoke with Katrina, the one who you let go outside and smoke, Emilio," Janine said. "She told me what he was wearing. She described him as a ninja."

"A ninja?" Emilio said.

"Dressed in black, head to toe," Janine said. "Wearing big goggles on his face. Probably night vision glasses. You know who uses those?"

Danny and Emilio just looked at her.

"Special forces," Janine said. "Navy Seals. Army Rangers. Marine Raiders and ReCons. They're all trained and set up to do night raids. With night vision goggles. Chief Fishie here just got out of the Rangers. It was him, no question."

"What's our move?" Danny Ferro asked. "Are they coming?"

"Of course they are," Janine said. "But not right away. They gotta get a search warrant from a judge. That'll take some time. Plus, the police chief is not in total control of the department at the moment. He's got someone from the attorney general's office supervising him. He's gotta get her approval before he can make a move. That'll take more time to negotiate. So we've got at least twenty-four hours, maybe forty-eight. Should be enough time."

She paused, thinking. Danny and Emilio knew enough to keep quiet while she was thinking.

"Okay, first thing, we move the current inventory out of here. Right now." Janine was in control, throwing out orders. "Use the truck, not the vans. They'll be looking for white panel vans, expecting to find them full of smuggled girls. They're not gonna look inside the oil truck."

She looked at Danny Ferro, who nodded. A year ago, he had spent an entire summer constructing an inner chamber to replace the oil tank in an old delivery truck, creating a small but comfortable space where upwards of ten girls could sit. From the outside, the truck looked like it was making the rounds of customers, filling their homes' tanks with heating oil. No one would ever suspect the truck instead held humans sitting comfortably on benches.

"Second, we gotta break down this garage. Make it look like a garage again," she continued. "Emilio…you know the drill. Break down the beds, get the mattresses outta here, then bring in the work benches, tools, equipment. Make it look and smell like a garage again. You got an old heap you can drag in, open the hood, spread some parts around like it's being fixed?"

"Yeah," Emilio nodded. "We got a few old cars out in the yard. I'll bring one inside."

"Don't forget the bathroom," Janine warned him. "Empty and burn the trash. If they find a tampon or a toothbrush, they'll be all over it looking for DNA. All trace of the inventory has to go, and right now," she continued.

The Ferros looked at each other and nodded.

"OK, once the truck is gone and the garage is back to normal, then Danny, you get ready for the police. You act normal, like nothing is different than any other day of the year. You can put up some fuss when they get here, but eventually, you let them look inside the garage. The house too, if that's what their warrant says. They'll expect you to resist, and are probably hoping you get physical so they can pound on you. So you gotta find that sweet spot, where you put up a fight, but not one that gets your head caved in. Got it?"

"I do," Danny said. "But where are you gonna be?"

"Ah," Janine said, standing up and smiling grimly. "I gotta go up to Providence and see a guy. We were supposed to be protected down here. I'm gonna find out why we're not."

CHAPTER 29

The Murray Judicial Complex, which houses the District and Superior courts for Newport County, Rhode Island, was located in a lovely Colonial Revival-style three-story brick building, built in 1927 to echo the much older Colony House just next door. The impressive front entrance of the building is framed by one of the last remaining large elm trees in the eastern United States, two massive round columns, a triangular pediment and, on the roof, a glass-and-frame tower. Government power at its best, even if the building was named, just a decade or so ago, after Florence K. Murray, a Newport native who was the state's first female judge appointed to the state Supreme Court.

Maggie Wells and Gus Haddock had taken the longish drive over from Little Penwick—north up to the Sakonnet River bridge and then westward towards Newport on one of the Main Roads, East and West, that traversed Aquidneck Island. They parked on Washington Square and Maggie led the way up to the second floor of the courthouse, where Judge Maryann F. Parker of the Second District Superior court, had agreed to give them fifteen minutes before she resumed a criminal trial that had recessed for lunch. They checked in with the judge's clerk who ushered them inside her chambers.

Like everything else in the building, the judge's paneled offices reeked of history. Her windows looked down on the Square and Gus could see the round expanse of Newport harbor just a block or so away. Judge Parker was likely one of those who kept a sailboat on a mooring in the summertime there, as her office decor was heavily into the nautical theme, with paintings of clipper ships at sail, brass and varnished knobby helm wheels and framed burgees from famous yacht clubs hanging all over the walls.

The judge herself was a small woman in her sixties, with graying hair pulled back into a bun at the rear of her head. Her judicial robes hung on a rack next to the door. She was wearing a navy blue dress with long sleeves and a smallish collar. She waved them inside and pointed to the guest chairs in front of her desk.

"Whattya got?" she said, grabbing her eyeglasses, dangling from a chain around her neck and popping them onto her nose.

Maggie introduced herself and handed the judge the file containing her motion for a warrant to search the premises of the Ferro place, specifically the garage area. Gus, who had donned an official uniform shirt for the trip into town, sat silently and watched.

"Suspicion of trafficking," the judge said, almost to herself as she read Maggie's brief. "Abetting prostitution. Use of property for interstate transportation of girls for illicit purposes." She paused and looked up at Maggie.

"Sounds terrible," she said. "I assume you have probable cause for all this?"

"Chief Haddock and his department have been investigating this matter for several weeks, your Honor," Maggie said. "They have reason to suspect that the garage facility on the property in question is being used to temporarily house girls brought in from other states, and possibly other countries, for employment in the strip clubs on Allen Street in Providence, and elsewhere in New England."

"And I've got reason to suspect the Patriots need a good quarterback," Judge Parker said. "But that's not probable cause, is it? What have you got, Chief Haddock, which points to this particular piece of property? A property that you want me to give you the authority to search?"

"One of my investigators has been to Florida, to interview friends and family members of a local woman who is the chief suspect in this case," Gus said. "Testimony from these witnesses indicates that this woman, who lives at this property in Little Penwick, has been actively recruiting young girls to come north and work in the adult entertainment business.

We believe these girls, some of whom may be under age, are housed, at least temporarily, at the subject address, and we want to take a look."

Judge Parker took her spectacles off and chewed on the end of one of the frames.

"Have you asked the owner of this property if you, the police, can take a look inside the garage?" the judge asked.

"No, your Honor," Gus said. "We, and I mean the Little Penwick Police Department, have something of a history with this family and this property. I would say there is little or no spirit of cooperation at work."

The Judge looked at Gus and nodded. "Ah," she said, "I remember now. Your father, the former police chief, is said to have something to do with the disappearance of the elder Mr. Ferro a year or so ago, isn't that correct?"

"Yes, your Honor," Gus said. "Although he denies any involvement, and none has been proved in a court of law."

Judge Parker nodded again. "OK," she said, scribbling her name on the bottom of Maggie's brief. "I'll approve this warrant, since it is limited in scope to the garage building. I don't want to hear anything about a search of the Ferro home as well. Understood?" She raised an eyebrow at Gus, who nodded.

"Thank you, your honor," Maggie said. She collected the signed brief and she and Gus got up and left the judge's chambers.

Judge Parker sat there for a minute or two after they left, thinking. Then she picked up the phone and dialed a number. She waited while the call went through. Someone answered.

"Preston?" she said, "Maryann Parker here. Yes, yes, I'm fine. Listen, I thought you might want to know that I just signed a search warrant for a garage on the Ferro property in Little Penwick. I know you're keeping track of the new chief there, young Mister Haddock, and his interactions with the Ferro clan. Your assistant, Ms. Wells, drew up the brief I just signed. I just thought you'd like to be informed."

She paused, listening to his response. "That's fine, Preston," she said. "No worries. Next time you're down in Newport, let's get together. Have a drink. It's been far too long."

She smiled as he said something back. "I'd like that, too," she said. "I've got a courtroom waiting for me. Talk soon." She hung up.

CHAPTER 30

When Janine Stone found him, Preston Knox was sitting in a booth at the back of a Subway franchise in East Providence, getting ready to dig into a foot-long hero. She had to do a double-take to make sure it was him—he was wearing a stained old sweatshirt and a ball cap. Trying to fit in with the workaday types, she figured.

Indeed, Knox had shucked his suitcoat in the back seat of his limo on the ride over from his Providence office, pulling on the old sweatshirt and Paw Sox cap he kept in his official car. Preston tried to ignore the strange looks he got from his driver, whose name he always had trouble remembering. Charles? No…Chuck? Not it. Oh, Chas! That was it. Whatever. Man's job was to drive the car and keep his mouth shut. Knox thought it best that no one recognized him during this meeting with Janine. And it was amazing how by just eliminating the official uniform of a state official, most people looking at him would not see the Attorney General of the State of Rhode Island and Providence Plantations, but just a guy stopping for a sandwich in the middle of an otherwise busy day.

"Mind if I join you?" Janine said as she slipped onto the hard plastic bench opposite Knox. He nodded at her and tried to smile, but his mouth was full of his three-meat sandwich, with cheese, tomato, onions, oil and vinegar and ranch sauce. Totally unhealthy, but Knox didn't care…he only got to eat a Subway sandwich once or twice a year.

He swallowed and finished smiling. "You want something?" he asked her. "They make a good veggie sandwich."

"No thanks," Janine said, her stomach turning a little. "I ate already."

"Thought you said you wanted to talk over lunch," Knox said.

"It was metaphorical," Janine said.

Knox nodded wisely. But he wasn't sure what she meant.

"So what's up?" Knox said, reaching into his bag of chips. It was part of the package price for a Subway lunch, along with the large soft drink.

"Our local police are getting active," Janine said. "Somebody—and I think it was Ranger Rick our chief of police—dropped by the facility in the early hours of the morning. My guess is they're in some judge's office right now asking for a search warrant."

Knox nodded. "Got a call from the judge half hour ago," he said. "She approved the warrant to search the garage. You got the boys ready?"

Janine nodded. "Yeah," she said. "Place will be back to a garage in another hour. I figure the cops will be out in the morning. They'll find nothing but grease, tools and auto parts lying around."

Knox took a long sip of his cola. "Good," he said.

"The reason I wanted to meet for lunch, Preston, is that you said you could keep the law out of our way," she continued. "Based on the fact that the cops were able to obtain a search warrant, it appears you're doing a world-class crappy job, so I just wondered, what the absolute fuck?"

She spoke in low tones, mono-tonally, smiling at the older man. She reached over and plucked a potato chip from his bag and plopped it into her mouth. Anyone looking at the two of them from the next booth over would see two people having a regular lunchtime conversation. Nothing special. Ho-hum.

Knox's face darkened as he fought the urge to strike back at her impertinence. But he didn't. That would ruin the nice image they had created. Instead, he took another long sip of cola and let his anger subside.

"This whole thing started going south when you got hauled in on a fake traffic count the other day," Knox said. "I don't know what you told them, but since that interview, Haddock and his department have been actively investigating. So don't come blaming me for the increased heat. It all started with you."

Janine sat back and looked at Knox, shaking her head sadly.

"I figured you'd try to pass the buck," she said. "It's what you politicians are best at. Blame the other guy for your own faults. Lucky for me, I knew you were a worthless fuck-up from day one. I knew you would be worthless as protection. So I made other plans."

Knox took another huge bite out of his sandwich, and Janine watched as he took his time chewing it. It was sickening to watch, but she made herself keep looking at him. Now was not the time to show weakness.

"Other plans?" he finally said. "What might that mean?"

She laughed. "You think I'm going to tell you what I'm going to do?" she said with a smirk. "You'll find out when the rest of the world does."

Knox took a deep pull of cola, looking at Janine while he did.

"You realize who it is you're working for, right?" he said finally. "These are people that do not take kindly to smartass little Florida bitches who think they know better than anyone else. And when they don't take kindly to something, they generally act on it. You might want to keep that in mind, honey."

"You honey me one more time, Knox and I'll cut your balls off myself," Janine said, smiling sweetly as she spoke. "I work for one person and one person only—myself. And our partners know that, because I told them that on day one. And I'm doing exactly what I promised I would do. I'm finding the talent they need, I'm bringing that talent here, training it, preparing it and inserting it where it is needed. Faultlessly. So I'm not worried about what they might do, because when it comes to me, I'm putting money in their pockets. Now you, on the other hand …"

She let her voice trail off. Knox ate the last part of his sandwich. She looked in his potato chip bag and saw there was just one left. She wanted to grab it, but didn't. Discipline, she thought. Some of us have it, most do not.

Knox took his time chewing the last bit of sandwich. He washed it down with more cola, then wiped his hands with one of the Subway napkins. It gave him time to think. This one is quite a piece of work he thought. He had thought that since the moment he first met her, three years ago, at the Daddy Cat Lounge, in the office of Ricky Giancarlo. Well, that had been his second thought. His first thoughts had all been sexual in nature. Just looking at Janine Stone, young, blond, lissome and drop-dead gorgeous, a man thought of sex, thought of what it would be like to have that slender body writhing uncontrollably beneath him. He had wanted her, badly. And since she was barely into her twenties at the time, he figured it would not be that hard to get her under his spell. She was a nobody from nowhere, Florida, after all, and he was attorney general. How hard could it be?

But it had turned out that she really was different. Eventually, Knox had arranged to meet her, face-to-face. That had been in Ricky Giancarlo's office at the Daddy Cat Lounge, some months after she had been sent to Little Penwick. He had thought she'd be a pushover, a young thing from out-of-state meeting a big, powerful politician like himself. But then they had started talking, there in Giancarlo's office. Talking about business, about increasing the supply of talent, getting them trained and prepared to hit the floor running. And, Knox had to admit, this beautiful young blond had had some damn good ideas. About recruitment. About transportation. About other places from which to find workers for the clubs. And she had laid out a plan to accomplish all that, with her as the head of operations. She had specified the costs to be expected, and the revenue benefits of having a ready supply of talent so the clubs never missed a beat, no matter the season, no matter the location.

Giancarlo and his friends, including the three gnomes Knox had met with just a few days ago up on Atwells Avenue, had listened and nodded in agreement with almost everything Janine said. And in fact, Knox had to agree that her operational plan had been extremely well conceived and covered all the bases. She knew what the weaknesses of the clubs' business plan were, and she outlined a sensible plan to overcome those weaknesses and instead help the clubs make more money. And in the three years or so that she had been given the assignment, the clubs had been very happy and had made a lot more money. Knox knew that the Family was happy with Janine's services, and they had paid her very well.

So his initial plan to use his own power and position to quickly seduce the girl had fallen through. In truth, once she got the Family's approval, it was Janine who held all the power. She had promised. She had delivered. Knox, whose job was to provide legal protection and warning, had not. Oh, he had been able to head off certain investigations from time to time, and to use his political pull to find out when one of the city departments was planning some kind of regulatory foray against the strip clubs. Knox controlled the state police, and under his direction, that institution had completely washed its hands on all things organized crime in the state, leaving only the local police departments to take any actions against The Family. And the local departments didn't have either the manpower or the resources to mount any kind of serious attacks against them. But he had completely failed at his assignment of keeping the Little Penwick police department off the back of the Ferro family, which was at the center of Janine's operation. But Knox wasn't that worried. He was still attorney general, and the people he was working with needed him more than he needed them. At least, that was what he believed.

"So what's your play, Knox?" Janine had grown tired of sitting there watching Knox eating.

He finished wiping his mouth and tucked the napkin away in the clear plastic bag, along with the bag of chips. Janine watched the bag, still with the last chip inside, get tossed away with regret. She was, actually, hungry.

"I can't do much to stop the Little Penwick PD from executing their search warrant," he said. "My friends in the judiciary will keep me apprised of what they want to do next. But I still have Julius Haddock tucked away in a jail cell. He's my ace-in-the-hole when it comes to making Chief Haddock dance. He wants his dad out of jail. That'll cost him. And he'll pay. They always do."

Janine nodded. That made sense to her.

"OK," she said, nodding. "That will help. Just keep him off my back. We've got an important shipment coming in about two weeks from now. International. This represents a significant upgrade in our services and there's a lot of money at stake. Plus, this time it involves a certain, umm, organization from south of the border which is expecting the operation to go as planned. So if we're all keeping in mind what might happen if someone gets mad … well, the group I'm dealing with is a helluva lot scarier than the guys over at the Daddy Cat. Understand?"

Knox nodded. "Got you," he said.

She looked back at him. Her face could not hide her derision.

"No, you don't, and you never will," she said.

CHAPTER 31

IT WAS THURSDAY, the day after the judge had approved the search warrant on the Ferro garage, that the Little Penwick police moved in.

Gus had called in all his men, save the four patrolmen who had worked the night shift on Wednesday night/Thursday morning. After returning from Newport, Gus had called his counterparts in Tiverton and Portsmouth and those chiefs had agreed to lend Little Penwick a few patrol officers for about six hours so that the local officers could assist in the execution of the search warrant.

They went in at eight a.m. with blue lights blazing. Four cars blasted up the crushed shell drive and surrounded Danny Ferro's house and driveway, two cars continuing on to the garage out back. Another car blocked off the drive where it turned off Easterly Road. Gus drove his own squad SUV and Lt. Callahan and Sgt. Martin rode with him. He stopped in front of the Ferro house and went and knocked on the front door. Danny Ferro opened it almost immediately, as if he had been waiting, and Gus handed him the signed search warrant papers. Ferro glanced at them, nodded to himself, and led Gus around to the back to the garage.

There, Danny unlocked the rolling front door and hoisted it up and open. Inside, there was an old gray Dodge Ram pickup, its front hood open showing the dusty insides of its Hemi engine. There were car parts and tools everywhere...on the ground in front of the Dodge, and on the workbench along the side of the garage. A big rectangular piece of metal, what looked like the pickup's radiator, was leaning against the near wall.

Gus waved his men inside, and four patrolmen began looking through the garage. Gus noticed that about five feet behind the pickup, there was a wall running across the width of the garage. He looked on the left side of the garage and did not see the side door from which the two smokers had emerged two nights earlier. He went back and pushed against this back wall. It felt flimsy, not solid.

"This is a fake wall," Gus said. "Look behind it."

One of the patrolmen had some with a three-foot metal crowbar and he raised it as if to smash into the temporary wall.

"Hang on," Danny Ferro said. "Take a chill pill, fellas. There's a door." He went to the back of the garage and pulled on a small handle. There was indeed a door, which opened. Gus nodded and two of the officers went on through, into the back.

Gus turned to Sgt. Martin. "Photographs of everything," he said. "And I want a full listing of everything they find inside. She nodded and pulled out her notebook and pen.

For the next hour, they scoured the garage, taking pictures and making an inventory of everything in the garage . Behind the false wall, there was nothing but empty space. The garage had a concrete floor and it contained several greasy spots here and there, as one might expect of a place where cars were worked on. But other than that, nothing.

"Looks like you guys were waiting for us," Gus said to Danny as they watched the officers carefully cataloging the tools and car parts.

"How so?" Danny said, smiling. "This place is our garage. As you can see, we work on cars back here."

"Why the fake wall?" Gus asked.

"We usually don't need the entire space," Danny said. "So we came up with a way to close it down some. Saves on heating. Money doesn't grow on trees, y'know."

"Why'd you build it this big if you didn't need to?" Gus said.

Danny shrugged. "We might use the whole thing one day," he said. "I got a business to run. You never know."

"Whose truck is this?" Gus asked, indicating the Ram pickup.

"That was Angelo's," Danny said. "Don't look like he's coming back, so Emilio said he'd fix it up, getting it running again, so he could use it around town."

Gus nodded and peered into the engine compartment. Without the radiator in front, the engine looked more open and roomy than normal. You could see all the way down to the concrete floor, save for a few wires and hoses.

"Janine Stone on the premises?" Gus asked.

Danny Ferro shook his head. "She left here couple, three days ago," he said. "Haven't seen or heard from her since."

"Where'd she go?"

Danny shrugged. "Away on business," he said. "She's a busy lady."

"Don't suppose you'd mind if we look through the house while we're here?" Gus said. "Just to make sure?"

Danny began leafing through the search warrant papers. "I dunno, Chief," he said. "This search warrant seems to be limited to the garage, not the house. I'd be happy to let you look in the house. If you bring me an authorized search warrant." He smiled at Gus. Checkmate, he thought.

Gus didn't answer, but turned on his heel and walked away. He went into the back of the garage and looked at the empty space. He went out the side door and saw the metal drum next to the tree. He looked over the side: it was empty. Not a thing in it, including ashes. They knew we were coming, he thought.

He went back inside. Jerry Hanlon, one of his officers, was looking at the walls in the empty space behind the false wall, running his hands along the back wall.

"Whaddya got, Jerry?" Gus asked.

"Dunno, Chief," Jerry said, cocking his head to the side. "There's some markings on the wall here—" he pointed to a four-foot section. "Looks like something scraped against the paint."

"What do you think it was?"

"Don't know," the officer said. "But it is at just the right height for a kitchen counter. If they did have women in here, they'd have to feed them. Counter, microwave, coffee maker … and it's right next to these twin outlets, set at counter height. I'll bag some samples from the sheetrock and maybe the lab can figure out what might have caused the scrapes."

On the far wall, just behind the false wall, there was a small bathroom. Gus stuck his head in the door and looked at the toilet and the small sink, which rested on a rectangular wooden stand, with a small mirror hung on the wall. Toilet and sink were both clean and shiny, and the small plastic wastebasket was empty except for a new white plastic liner, which struck Gus as something you normally wouldn't expect in a typical garage. He looked down at the concrete floor and then waved Carl Lincoln over.

Gus pointed at a four-inch square drain set flush to the concrete floor, just in front of the sink.

"Strange place for a drain," he said. "Unless they had the ladies taking quick showers in here. They could have attached a hose to the sink faucet and used a hand-held shower device to hose themselves off. Let's get that drain cover off and take some samples from inside. Might find some hair samples, or something else. And while you're at it, take apart the sink trap and see if there are any hairs or fibers in there."

"Got it, chief," Lincoln said, and went back out to his squad car for some tools and evidence bags.

The other two officers stayed in the front portion of the garage and painstakingly cataloged and photographed everything there. They looked under and inside the pickup and bagged anything they found that could possibly be considered evidence. Outside, Lt. Callahan engaged Danny Ferro in conversation, mainly to keep him out of the way. Sgt. Martin was making lists of everything they found and bagged for further investigation.

Gus leaned against the wall and watched his men at work for a while. He was disappointed, but not surprised. He hadn't expected to find a garage full of kidnapped women held against their will. That would have been too easy. But he hadn't expected to find a sanitized scene, which is what he was looking at. That indicated that the Ferros had received advanced word that the Little Penwick police were coming, warrant in hand. That disturbed Gus. Who tipped them off? It was pretty clear someone had.

He began to ponder his next steps. Maybe Jerry Hanlon's theory of a kitchen counter would bear out, and they could find some wood fibers from a countertop that would prove one had marked the wall. Or maybe they'd find several kinds of hair, women's hair, trapped in the bathroom sink or floor drain. Both were long shots, but possible. Then, Gus could call in the Building Inspector and come back for another visit, and maybe that time they could catch the Ferros unaware.

He sighed. He knew the chances were slim. So all he had was Angelo Ferro's old pickup, left in a hundred pieces. He looked at the old gray beast, hood yawning open, engine dissembled.

And that's when the light bulb went off, in his head.

"Geezus," Gus said, mostly to himself.

CHAPTER 32

MAGGIE WELLS WAS shown into the windowless, eight-foot by eight-foot room and told to wait. She was someplace deep in the bowels of the Adult Correctional Institution in Cranston, far away from the public visiting area of the jail. The row of meeting rooms on this floor were designed for conferences between inmates and their attorneys. Or, in this case, between an inmate and his prosecutor.

About five minutes after she sat down at the metal table anchored in the middle of the room, and removed some files and legal pads from her briefcase, she heard footsteps from the hall outside—footsteps enhanced by the unmistakable sound of ankle chains dragging on the floor like Marley's ghost—and then the door was unlocked and opened and Julius Haddock was escorted in by a uniformed prison guard.

The guard unlocked Julius' handcuffs and was about to affix them to the metal ring on the top of the table when Maggie spoke.

"You don't need to cuff him on my account," she said to the guard.

"It's procedure, ma'am," the guard said.

"I think you can leave that part out," she said, giving him a winning smile.

The guard shrugged—*it's your funeral, lady*—and put his keys away. "I'll be right outside," he told her. "Knock when you're done."

"Thank you," Maggie said.

Julius rubbed his wrists while he looked across the table at Maggie, waiting until the guard had shuffled his way out the door, which closed behind him with a heavy clicking sound. Then he smiled at her.

"You must be the lovely Maggie Wells," he said. "Thanks for this—" he held up his hands. "How's Junior doing? Taking care of business to the satisfaction of the attorney general?"

"Chief Haddock is extremely competent," Maggie said carefully.

"He likes to do things his own way," Julius said. "That can drive you a little nuts, I'm sure. He's always been an independent sort like that. I thought the Army would beat that out of him, but instead they seem to have let him do his thing. I guess it worked out better for them that way."

"I will admit that working with Gus has not been entirely easy," Maggie said. "But he knows the job and does it pretty well."

"Your boss agree with that opinion?" Julius said, cocking his head to the side.

Maggie decided to let that pass without comment. "I want to go back to the events of last January," she said, flipping open a file folder. "I've been interviewing all the principals involved in Angelo Ferro's disappearance that night. I wanted to get your input as well."

"I'm betting you haven't interviewed Angelo Ferro," Julius said. "Be kinda hard if he's sleeping down there at 3,000 feet below sea level somewhere."

"Is that where he is?" she said.

Julius shrugged. "No idea," he said. "I went home and went to bed."

"Why did you go to the Roadhouse that night?" she asked, since he had brought the subject up. "Did you know that Angelo was going to be there, having dinner?"

"Yes," Julius said.

"How did you know that?"

"Someone told me," he said. "They were right."

"Who told you?"

Julius smiled. "I don't think I'm ready to answer that question yet," he said.

"Why not?"

"Might impede the investigation," Julius said.

"Who's investigation?"

"Junior's, of course," he said.

"You won't tell me who tipped you off about the whereabouts of Angelo Ferro on the night of January 5th because you think that might interfere in some way with the investigation being run by the Little Penwick Police Department? Is that your statement?" she said.

"No," he said. "Because Junior is looking into it, and anything I say might get in his way."

"Gus Haddock is the chief of police, isn't that right?" she shot at him.

"Last I heard," he said.

"Isn't one investigation the same as the other?"

"Not always, no," Julius said.

Maggie shook her head in frustration, her ringlets bouncing around her forehead.

"What did you say to Angelo Ferro in the restaurant that night?"

"I told him to watch his back," Julius said. "I told him someone was gunning for him."

"Who?"

Julius smiled. "Funny thing," he said, "That was exactly what Angelo asked me."

"What did you tell him?"

"I told him I wasn't entirely sure, but that I had been informed by a usually impeccable source that someone in a high position wanted Angelo out of the picture," Julius said. "I told him he needed to step up security and watch his six."

"What did he say?"

Julius laughed, softly. "The usual," he said. "He accused me of trying to scare him, of providing false information, of wanting to do the job myself, and I think one or two other insults. I got the strong impression that he didn't believe me." Julius spread his hands out wide. "Guess he was wrong and I was right, huh?"

"What did you do?"

Julius shrugged. "What could I do?" he said. "I had done my duty as chief of police by warning a resident of my town of an impending threat. He chose to ignore my warning. He died, apparently. Too bad."

"So you left and went home to bed?"

"Yup."

"When did you hear about his disappearance on the *Lizzie B*?

Julius thought for a moment or two, stroking his chin and looking up at the ceiling tiles.

"I don't think anyone knew anything had happened until a couple days later, when the Ferro kids came in and said they hadn't heard anything from Angelo, who'd gone out on his fishing boat. So we put out a missing persons alert, notified the Coast Guard about the *Lizzie B.* and opened up the MP file. My guys went out and started talking to people, asking questions. It's all in the book."

Maggie paused for a moment.

"So you had heard from someone that organized crime had put out a contract on Angelo Ferro and you went to warn him about that," she said, recapping. "He didn't believe you and went on about his business. He and his fishing boat disappeared that same night. Is that your story?"

"I never said anything about organized crime, but generally, yes that's what happened," Julius said.

"And you won't tell me who told you that Angelo was in danger?"

"Again," he said, "I was not told and did not tell Angelo that he was in danger. I told him I had heard that someone wanted him out of the way. In the end, it was the same thing. But I had no foreknowledge that Angelo's life was in imminent danger."

"You're playing semantics with me," Maggie complained.

"You're a goddam lawyer," Julius retorted. "'Playing with semantics' is actually an accurate description of your profession."

"I don't get what you're telling me," she said hotly. "You go to the Roadhouse on a frigid January night to tell Angelo Ferro that someone was gunning for him."

"That's right," Julius nodded.

"Why would you do that?" she asked. "You hated Angelo Ferro and his entire family. They were the bad seeds in Little Penwick. The entire police department is locked and loaded to watch out for every one of them. I just don't understand."

"Two out of your three assertions are correct," Julius said. "One is not."

Maggie stared at the old man across the table. He wore a half smile but otherwise was expressionless. She sat for a minute, thinking.

"You're telling me you didn't hate Angelo Ferro?" she said finally.

"I don't hate anybody," Julius Haddock said. "I may not like some people a lot, and Angelo fell into that category for sure, but I never hated him. In fact, I always kinda respected the guy. He was a hard working dude, even if most of the work he did was against the law. He took care of his family. Tried to raise them right. Didn't succeed, but most of that is on them, not him."

"You grew up with Angelo Ferro," Maggie said, as the idea finally entered her head.

"We went to school together," Julius said, nodding. "He was a year older than me. We played football for Portsmouth High together. Enlisted in the Army together. I knew his Mom and Dad and all the uncles and aunts. Good people. Well, most of them. A few were kinda off, if you know what I mean."

"Good people?" Maggie was amazed. "They were almost constant law breakers."

Julius shrugged. "Yeah, and I arrested Angelo myself probably six times over the years. Doesn't mean I hated him. Just means I applied the law as written to someone in my jurisdiction."

"Hate the sin, love the sinner," she said, shaking her head.

"A little simplistic, but yeah, that's the basic idea," he said.

"Did you know Janine Stone?" she asked, changing the subject.

"Met her once," he said. "Didn't really know her."

"Where did you meet her?"

"Down at the Flume, couple summers ago," he said. "She was hanging with some of the surfer dudes from town."

"You surfed with her?"

He shook his head. "Nah," he said. "I had just finished a set out on the water. Waves weren't bad that morning. Tide was starting to come in. When I came in to the beach, she was there with five or six guys I know. They were just hangin', drinking beer and smoking some weed. I stopped, dropped my board, talked a little trash with them, like I always do. I know most of the surfers from Little Penwick. Heck, I've known most of them since they were in kindergarten. They're good kids, mostly."

"And Janine was surfing with them?"

"She was sitting around shootin' the shit and waiting for high tide, when the waves crest," Julius said. "But she and Billy Groats were getting ready to go out. She was pulling on her suit."

"Her suit?"

"I take it you've never surfed," Julius said, cocking an eyebrow at Maggie. She shook her head. "Well, the water around here is always pretty cold, even in midsummer, so if you want to stay out on the water without suffering almost instant hypothermia, you need a wet suit. That neoprene stuff. Does the trick, but it's a bitch to take on and off. Fits like a second skin, but you gotta pull and tug and strain to get it on. And off. I've always said the only thing sexier than watching a woman get undressed is watching one struggle herself into a wet suit."

"So you thought she was sexy?" Maggie said.

"You've seen her in person, right?" Julius said with a laugh. Maggie nodded her assent. "Then you already know that Janine Stone is a stone-cold babe, no matter what gender or sexual orientation you might have."

"Did you two talk?"

Julius chuckled to himself again. "Yes we did," he said. "I stuck out my hand and said 'Hello, I'm Julius Haddock.' She shook my hand and said 'Janine Stone.' Then I asked her where she was from, and she said 'Fort Lauderdale.' And I said, 'Well then, you're used to our size-small East Coast waves,' and she said 'The ones I'm used to are a little warmer.'

She finished shimmying into her suit, zipped it up, grabbed her board and she and Billy went into the water."

"That's it?" Maggie sounded dubious.

"Yeah, sorry," Julius said with a smirk. "I didn't know her background, I didn't know she was staying at the Ferro compound, I didn't know she would end up in this investigation you and Junior are doing. I guess my time travel machine was broken. She was just a girl I met at the beach."

"You never talked to her after that?" Maggie pressed. "Never saw her around town? Didn't know she was living at the Ferro place?"

"Never had the pleasure of speaking with her again," he said. "I saw her driving around town now and then in her little yellow Miata. Didn't know or hear about her place of residence or what she does for a living until Junior told me that a couple of weeks ago." He shrugged. "I was chief of police, not head of the morals squad. I never saw her break a law. But you and Junior and Detective Franklin did some good work on her back story. Hopefully, you can find enough evidence to put her out of business."

Maggie studied her notes for a moment or two.

"You and the attorney general are not close," she said.

"Well, no, of course not," he said. "That asshole drummed up some charges to get me out of office and into a cell in this hellhole. But we worked together with no problems until that happened. His job is different from mine."

"How so?" Maggie asked.

"As attorney general, Preston Knox is a politician first and always," Haddock said. "His main job is to get re-elected, or lay the groundwork for a run at a higher office. My job is to keep my town safe and secure, arrest miscreants and protect the general order. He did his thing and I did mine and our paths and our jobs rarely intersected with each other. So I'd say we got along fine. Until he moved to get rid of me."

"Why do you think he did that?"

Julius Haddock looked across the table at the young attorney. He smiled. "Interesting that you didn't protest my assertion," he said. "Which means you probably think he did try to get rid of me. And maybe you've found out the reasons why. Maybe you haven't. But I think I'll just say 'no comment' and leave it at that."

She looked at Julius and realized he wasn't going to say much more. She got up and pounded on the door. "Ready!" she called.

The corrections officer came and unlocked the door and slipped the cuffs back on Julius' wrists. Julius stood up. "Nice talking with you," he said, nodding at her. "Let's do it again soon."

He walked out of the room, followed by the officer. Maggie sat thinking by herself for a minute or two, then gathered up her notes and papers, stuffed them back into her briefcase and left.

CHAPTER 33

Friday morning, the week before Thanksgiving, Gus Haddock called a meeting of the investigation team for 9 o'clock. Maggie Wells drove down from Providence. Lt. Callahan, Sgt. Martin and Detective Franklin crowded into the conference/interview room at the back of the Little Penwick station. Gus had stopped off at the Commons Cup and bought a dozen cranberry muffins from Betty Billingsly, and had them piled on a plate in the center of the table.

At the stroke of nine, Gus walked into the room clutching his mug of coffee and sat down at the head of the table. Maggie sat opposite at the other end and the others pulled up chairs on the side. The muffins quickly began disappearing.

"OK," Gus said, "Let's start by reviewing what we learned from yesterday's search at the Ferro garage. Jess? Anything important?"

Sgt. Martin sighed as she flipped through her inventory of items taken away and her notes. "Not a whole lot of anything, Chief," she said. "We're still waiting for the state crime lab to get back to us on the contents of the floor and sink drains. We recovered a lot of hair. Clumps of it. Pretty disgusting, actually,. It will probably take them some time before they can sort out what belongs to who. Same deal with the scrapings from the wallboard. Right now, all inconclusive."

"OK," Gus said. "Stay on top of the lab. We need to know as soon as possible."

"Will do, chief," she said.

Gus turned to Lt. Callahan. "Callahan?" he asked, "Anything?"

"Not really, chief," the lieutenant said. "We found the space was being used as a garage and didn't see anything lying around that said otherwise."

"Place was clean as a whistle," Gus said. "Which means one of two things. That space has never been used for anything other than working on cars, or someone tipped off the Ferros that we were coming, and they cleaned it up basically overnight. I'm leaning towards the second option, since I've never seen a garage used for fixing up cars that was as clean as that one was, even with the rags and oil they scattered around before we got there."

"The lab should be able to tell us something about all those hairs," Jessica Martin said. "At least if they came from men or women. And if we're lucky, we may get a profile on nationality and maybe even some DNA we can run through the databases."

"Which is why you need to ride herd on the lab boys and keep a fire going under their butts," Gus said.

"The way the place was sanitized, I think they got tipped," Lt. Callahan said.

"Who by?" Gus asked. "I'm ruling out anyone in this room." As he said that, he was looking directly at Callahan, since he was the one person in the room with the best reason to undermine the investigation.

Callahan's face reddened slightly. He knew that as the longest serving officer in the room and the one who would benefit the most if Gus Haddock was removed as chief, he was probably the prime suspect. It was the classic case of loyalty to the force versus personal advancement. And like most cops, Callahan understood that greed was a powerful motivator of human behavior.

"If it's true that the AG is somehow connected to Janine Stone," he began, casting a quick sideways look at Maggie Wells, "Well, he's got a lot of connections in a lot of places. Could be someone at city hall, or anyplace else for that matter. This is Rhode Island, the 'I know a guy' state."

Everyone chuckled at that.

"Okay," Gus said, "We'll table that discussion for now. Let's wait and see what the crime lab comes back with. In the meantime, I had an a-ha moment yesterday. When I saw Angelo's truck. Made me think of something. So I came back here last night and looked in the book again."

He reached out and tapped the thick file folder containing all the notes on the Angelo Ferro disappearance. He had brought the file in to the conference room earlier.

"There's no mention of the truck in here," he said. "It wasn't recovered down at the harbor when we were looking for Angelo. Which leads to the question: 'How did Angelo get down to his boat that night?' All of his relatives were interviewed and none of them said they drove the guy down to the harbor. They all said they remember him leaving for the docks that night, but no one said how he got there. He didn't drive himself, or his truck would have been found in the parking lot. Nobody said they gave him a ride. So how did he get there?"

"Someone gave him a ride," Maggie Wells said. "It's the only explanation that fits."

"Exactly," Gus said. "And whoever drove him is our prime suspect in his disappearance. Or at the very least, the last one to see him alive."

Maggie grabbed the thick notebook, spun it around and began leafing through it, looking for the index at the back.

"We never interviewed Janine Stone," she said. "Not about anything having to do with Angelo's disappearance."

"Of course not," Gus said. "We didn't even know about her, or that she was living among the Ferros, until a couple of weeks ago."

"We were about to talk to her about what she knew of Angelo's disappearance when we had her in this room about three weeks ago," Buzz Franklin said. He avoided looking at Maggie Wells. "But she, um, left before we could get answers."

"So maybe it was Janine who drove the old man to the *Lizzie B.*," Maggie said. She glanced at Gus with what seemed to him to be an apologetic look.

"That's my guess," Gus said. "There's nobody else who makes sense."

"And that was right after your father warned Angelo that someone was coming for him," she said.

"What?" Gus stood up, his chair clattering back into the wall. "Where did you hear that?"

"From Julius himself," she said. "I went over to the ACI yesterday and had a little chat with him."

"You never told me that —" Gus started to protest, his face red and angry.

"I'm telling you now," Maggie said. "Julius said he had heard—from some mysterious source he wouldn't divulge—that someone was gunning for Angelo and told him to watch his back. Then, an hour or two later, Janine—or somebody—drove him to the dock and he and his boat disappeared forever."

"Wait a minute," Callahan said, holding up a hand like a stop signal. "Not so fast. How do we know Janine was the driver? And how did she pull off the murder? What was her motive? And how did she get the boat to sail away into the deep blue sea with Angelo on board, to disappear without a trace? There are more than a few holes in this theory."

"Good questions, Barry," Gus said. "Let's take them one at a time. We don't know that Janine was the driver. But it shouldn't be hard to re-interview some of the Ferro boys and see if anyone specifically remembers how the old man left that night. Two: if it was her, that puts her alone with Angelo on his fishing boat. No witnesses, late on a frigid January night, no one around. Perfect opportunity for killing him. Gunshot, knife in the back, pills or drugs to put him asleep, conk him on the head with a wrench… a thousand different possible scenarios, right?"

"What's her motive?" Callahan asked. He was frowning, like he wasn't convinced.

"Janine seems to be a most ambitious woman, trying to climb the corporate ladder," Gus said. "First, she talked her way into a job as chief recruiter for the Family's business in the strip clubs. That alone took some level of gumption on her part. Then, she's spent most of the last three years performing that job to the satisfaction of all. She's been busy adding new sources for bringing in strippers and sex workers, including some foreign ones. Maybe Angelo wasn't totally on board. Maybe he didn't want to get in too deep with the goombahs up in Providence. Maybe he didn't like watching her impress the bosses and build her influence with them, maybe at his expense. She was being well-paid by the boys at the Daddy Cat…maybe Angelo didn't like that, or wanted some of her remuneration for himself. He could probably see some of the risks to himself and his family if her little human trafficking business got bigger and bigger. Risks that he and the Ferro clan could be rendered obsolete. Risks that her operation got so big that it might attract the attention of the feds. However you slice it, he might not have liked what was going on. So maybe Janine thought getting rid of the old guy was good for business … *her* business. And maybe Danny Ferro was on board with her. They lived in close proximity. Maybe he was smitten with her. We really don't know what that relationship is all about, do we? Maybe Danny saw the potential for making lots of money through her. Maybe she thought Danny and the others would come around once she got Angelo out of the way and started growing the business big time. Hell, maybe Danny himself came up with the idea to get rid of the biggest stumbling block in the plan ... Angelo himself."

There was silence in the room as everyone digested this and thought about it. Buzzy Franklin shifted in his chair. There was a pile of muffin crumbs on the table in front of him.

"But how did she pull off the disappearing act?" he asked. "She'd have to steer the *Lizzie B.* out of the harbor with a dead or disabled Angelo on board, point it towards the horizon and somehow get back onto terra firma. We didn't find her car at the harbor, either."

"Not sure," Gus said, "But I have a theory. Janine, remember, is a surfer. Down in Lauderdale, according to the people who knew her down there who talked to Buzzy, she surfed a lot. And she's been seen surfing here as well. Which tells us that she's a good swimmer. At the very least, she's comfortable in the water."

"Neoprene," Maggie said. Everyone turned to look at her. "Your father mentioned that yesterday. When he met Janine, a couple summers ago, it was down at the beach where they were surfing. He watched her pull on a neoprene wetsuit and jump into the ocean. He said most of the surfers up here wear a wet suit against the cold water. She could have worn one that night, or, even better, gotten hold of a dry suit, which is even thicker and warmer. Some of the hardcore surfers wear those around here to surf in the winter, which is totally crazy. After she killed Angelo, she could have driven the boat out of the harbor, driven it close to the beach just past the jetty, pointed the bow dead south, hit the auto pilot and jumped overboard. She would have had to swim maybe a hundred yards. Yeah, it would have been shockingly cold and in the dark, but a strong swimmer like her could have done it easily. Maybe she even put on a life jacket or flotation device. She makes it to shore, walks back down the jetty to the docks, gets in her car or Angelo's truck, whatever vehicle she used, and drives home. Meantime, the *Lizzie B.* just kept steaming due south. Nothing between Little Penwick and Antarctica except maybe Bermuda, and past that, one of the outer Caribbean islands. She turned off the GPS signals and all the running lights. And it would be easy for her to open some of the scupper drains in the bilge so that water would begin coming in. The boat would skate along at speed without too much water coming in, but eventually it would run out of gas and stop. Then the water would come in and the boat would founder and go down. Never to be seen again."

There was silence in the room again as they all thought about the possibilities.

"You think she could do all that?" Buzzy Franklin asked.

"You think she couldn't?" Gus responded.

"Be nice if we could find her and ask," Maggie said.

CHAPTER 34

GUS AND MAGGIE were in his office at the police station late that afternoon. The sun had set early, as it does in November, and it was already dark outside. A front had moved through that afternoon, bringing with it a scattering of rain and a cold wind out of the northwest. Whatever brown and withered leaves still clung to their branches were being removed, one by one, leaving only the black, wet fingers of the branch nodes.

The station house was quiet. The shifts had changed at four and the evening patrol was out watching the late afternoon traffic as the residents of Little Penwick returned home from their workplaces. There was dinner to cook, dishes to be washed, kids to be bathed, movies to be streamed, a Celtics game at 8, Jimmy Kimmel at eleven.

Maggie was reading the preliminary report from the state crime lab that had been sent over about an hour earlier. Jess Martin had been able to beg someone at the lab to move with uncommon speed to produce an assessment of the evidence that had been collected from the Ferro garage. The report was preliminary and marked 'still in progress,' but the lab rats had discovered six different human hairs from the evidence bags, so far. They were still running tests to pinpoint gender, nationality and DNA and one of the technicians said she thought she could recover even more hair from the remaining evidence bags. But it seemed that the hair samples would at least prove that there had been several different people inside the Ferro's garage.

Gus, in the meantime, was still thinking about who might have tipped off the Ferros that the police were coming with the search warrant. It was possible, he thought, that after he had cold-cocked the guy outside the garage that night, the Ferros might have realized they were under surveillance and taken steps to clean up the garage. But the whole scene looked like it had been sanitized from top to bottom. On purpose.

"Who else beside you and me knew we were asking for a search warrant?" he asked Maggie, interrupting her reading of the lab report for the fifth time.

She put the paper down and thought for a minute. "Besides you and me?" she asked. "Callahan knew. Buzzy Franklin knew. I think I told Dottie that we were driving over to Newport to see the judge."

"Nobody at the AG's office?" Gus pressed.

She shook her head. "Nope."

"You sure?"

Maggie looked at him, but didn't answer. The look itself conveyed her annoyance.

Gus shook his head in frustration. "I really don't want to think it was Barry Callahan," he said. "But I don't know who else it could have been."

"The judge knew," Maggie said. "After we presented the file."

Gus sat up in his chair. "Yeah," he said, "She did. I wonder if she's got any connection to the Ferro family?"

"No," Maggie said, "The better question is does she have any connection to Preston Knox?"

"Does she?" Gus hadn't thought of that possibility.

Maggie threw out her hands and shrugged. "It wouldn't surprise me," she said. "Preston Knox knows everybody in this state. Especially judges. Especially female judges."

Gus reached over and picked up his phone, punched in a number and waited for someone to answer.

"Buzz?" he said. "Listen, do you know of any past connections between Preston Knox and Judge Maryann Parker?" He listened for a while. "You sure?" he said. Then he nodded while Franklin kept talking. "Okay, thanks," he said finally.

He hung up and looked at Maggie. "Bingo," he said.

"What?"

"Preston Knox and Maryann Parker were undergraduates together at Dartmouth," Gus said. "And their families were close up in Providence. Old friends. Chummy. She coulda dropped a dime on us, called Knox after we left her chambers."

"Wow," Maggie said, "Unethical as hell. What a bitch."

"But much better than having my lieutenant under a cloud of suspicion," Gus said.

"Yeah, there's that," she said. She cocked her head sideways. "How does Buzzy know this stuff?"

Gus smiled. "He's a detective, first of all," he said. "But he also understands how incestuous Rhode Island can be. Everyone knows everything about everyone else. Families are inter-connected in all kinds of ways. It's like the entire state is a small town where everyone knows everyone else's business."

Gus' phone rang, he leaned over and picked it up.

"Yeah?" he said. "Hey, Dottie ... What? The AG? What line?"

"No line," Preston Knox said as he walked into the office. "It's me...live and in living color."

Gus replaced his phone handset and stood up. "General," he said, nodding at the man. "Welcome to Little Penwick. What can we do for you?"

Knox shrugged out of his heavy overcoat and sat down in one of the two chairs in front of Gus Haddock's desk. He nodded at Maggie who was sitting in the other. She was as still as a rock, probably from shock.

"I think the proper question is, what can we do for each other?" Knox said. "And the first thing you can do is find me something to drink. The sun went over my personal yardarm about an hour ago." He nodded at the shelf behind and to the left of Gus, which held some books, a sports trophy or two and a half-empty bottle of a good Tennessee sipping whiskey.

Gus got up, reached back and grabbed the bottle, and took it over to a credenza on the side wall of his office. He opened one of the drawers, took out three lowball glasses and poured a couple of fingers of bourbon into each one. Then he carried the glasses back to his desk, set them down and handed one to each of the people sitting in his two guest chairs. Maggie started to protest, shaking her head 'no,' but Gus stared at her. She got the message and took the drink.

Knox took his glass and knocked off about half of it in a swallow. He closed his eyes and let the amber liquid burn its sweet way down his throat.

"Boy, if that ain't what the doctor ordered, I don't know what is," he said, speaking to no one in particular.

Maggie had placed her glass down on the desk, and Gus left his untouched as well. They both studied the man. He looked exhausted, with dark circles under his eyes. His hair, slightly dampened from the rain falling outside, glistened from the overhead rows of fluorescent lights.

"So," Gus said finally, "How can we help each other?"

"You've got a very interesting investigation going on down here," Knox said, studying his remaining inch of golden bourbon, swirling it around and around. "I want to help."

"If you're talking about Janine Stone, you should know that we've found a possible link between Ms. Stone and the attorney general's office," Gus said. He didn't say "you," but instead used the more passive locution. Knox appeared to be in a conciliatory mood and he didn't want to upset that with anything that hinted of accusation.

Knox pulled one hand off his glass of bourbon and waved it as if he was waving off a pesky insect.

"Yeah, well, what you can do for me is forget all of that," Knox said. "Whether or not it's true, and it isn't, you can deep-six that part of the story."

There was silence in the room as Gus and Maggie digested what he said. They exchanged glances. Each could tell the other was thinking the same thing. In return for what?

"I see," Gus said noncommittally. "And if we forget all that, what will you do?"

Knox sat up straight and knocked back the last of his bourbon. Again, he closed his eyes for the initial burn. Once that passed, he opened his eyes again, put the glass down on Gus' desk and smiled.

"I can get your father out of jail," he said.

"Is that right?" Gus said, feeling a surge of anger sweep through his body. It felt exactly the same as it did one night near Basra when a sniper's bullet had ended the life of a fellow Ranger standing three feet away. The anger, accompanied by a hot buzzing sound in his ears, had taken over his body and all its senses, and made him want to vault the wall and charge at the building from where the shot had come from, to find the bastard that pulled the trigger and make sure he could never kill anyone ever again. Now, that anger and the buzz that came with it made him want to vault over his desk and wring Preston Knox's neck with his bare hands.

But he didn't.

"Since you put him there without cause or reason, I guess it makes sense that you could get him out," Gus said, trying to keep his voice calm. "But how about this instead: You tell us everything you know about Janine Stone and her human trafficking operation through the Ferro place and what role you've played in the whole thing, and Ms. Wells and I will ask the judge to consider your many years of public service before sentencing you to a nice long term in prison. And if you pick up the phone and get my Dad out of the ACI right now, I'll throw in a recommendation that you get the mandatory mini-mum, instead of dropping you in the deepest cell they got and keeping you there for the rest of your sorry-ass life."

Knox stared across the desk for a moment or two and then he broke out in a soft chuckle, shaking his head sadly.

"Chief Haddock," he said, "I appreciate your braggado-cio, really I do. You remind me of myself when I was younger. However, you forget that you are a small-town police chief with less than a year of experience at the job, whereas I am the attorney general of the state of Rhode Island. I believe I have the power and authority to do what I suggested here tonight. But you have none. So your false and meaningless threats mean nothing to me."

"Try me," Gus said.

Knox turned to Maggie. "Miz Wells," he said, "Please tell your colleague here the facts of life, will you? I can make a phone call or two and set this thing in motion. You've got nothing on me other than idle rumor. Please tell this idiot that it would be so much easier if he agreed to my terms."

Maggie listened to his spiel, her head nodding here and there as he spoke, her ringlets bouncing up and down. Then she turned to Gus.

"Chief Haddock, I believe I heard this gentleman proffer what could be construed as a bribery attempt under Rhode

Island General Laws Chapter 11 dash 7 dash 3," she said. "Would you care to read him his Miranda rights or shall I?"

"You stupid little bitch," Knox snarled at her. "You are throwing away what's left of your career here. Nobody is going to believe anything this little twerp has to say. I am the attorney general. I am the law in this state. You both can be swept away. And forgotten. And will be."

"I'm hearing an implied physical threat," Gus said, speaking to Maggie. "You?"

"Oh, yeah," she said. "Should be good for an additional ten to twenty."

"It's the goddam comedy hour," Preston Knox said, shaking his head sadly. "You two children have no idea what you're doing." He looked at his empty glass as if he wished it was full again. "But finc...I'll play along. Why don't you tell me what you want to make this thing go away."

Gus smiled. And he picked up his glass of bourbon and took a small sip. He didn't drink much of the booze, but he wanted Knox to think he had because Knox' drink was gone.

"Like I said," Gus smiled across the desk, "I want the full details on Janine Stone. Who she works for, how you are connected to those she works for, what relationship, if any, she has with you, and what you know about her trafficking operation. After you come clean about all that, Ms. Wells here will decide what action is indicated. That may be your immediate resignation as attorney general. It may mean she shares this information with the other assistant AG's up in Providence to determine if a full-blown investigation is required, or just the immediate prosecution of you."

Knox was staring at Gus, eyes narrowed, face a little flushed.

"Oh, and Julius Haddock is to be released, with a full dismissal of all charges and an official apology, within the next 24 hours," Gus added. "That's not negotiable."

Knox sneered a little, but Gus could tell he was defeated.

"What about your little chippy here?" Knox said, nodded sideways at Maggie. "You forgot to demand that I promote her to deputy AG and give her a raise. Hundred-fifty grand sound about right, sweetheart?" He smiled a fake smile at Maggie in the seat next to his. Gus watched her eyes twitch slightly, and knew that Maggie was fantasizing the same kind of choking death on Knox that he himself had just a minute or two earlier.

"I went into public service to serve the public," Maggie said, her voice low and quiet. "Not to enrich myself at the public's expense. Unlike you."

Knox's face got a little redder. He turned back to look at Gus.

"OK, look," he said, his voice just this side of sounding desperate. "I can't give you much on Janine. She works for the guys who run the strip clubs, not for me. If she's breaking the law, then I'm on your side. Make your case and prosecute and let the chips fall."

"Ricardo Giancarlo runs the clubs," Gus said, "But he's not the owner. That would be The Committee, three or four of the older connected types. We know you report to them. We know they've financed your campaigns. We suspect you've been paid hundreds of thousands of dollars to do what they told you to do. I imagine, seeing some of the things you've done here in Little Penwick, that they wanted you to keep the law off Janine Stone's back. So you sent my Dad off to the ACI and then you sent Maggie here down from Providence to ride herd on lil ole me. But unfortunately for you, Maggie Wells has more honor in her little toe than you do in your entire body. So we're gonna prosecute the law here, including you and anyone else who's broken the laws, and I don't give a pig's fart which one of your crooked friends up in Providence doesn't like that."

"Brave speech," Knox said. He stood up. "But I'd love to see you do anything. That Committee you were talking about? When they get pissed off, you'll know it. At least for the split second before they blow your head away." He shrugged into his overcoat. "But don't say I didn't give you a chance. You're just too young and stupid to understand. Goodbye."

He started to walk out of the office, but then stopped at the threshold and leaned back in.

"Oh, by the way," he was looking at Maggie. "You're fired, effective immediately."

Knox left. There was silence for a moment or two after he had gone.

"Can he do that?" Maggie said, finally. "Fire me without cause?"

Gus shrugged. "Hell if I know," he said. "I don't do HR. Jessie Martin handles all that for us."

"I don't think I've ever been fired before," she said. "Feels weird."

"Oh, hell," Gus said, "I've been fired before. Don't take it personally."

"Don't take it personally?" Maggie repeated. "I just lost my job and maybe my career. Of course I'm taking it personally."

CHAPTER 35

THE DELICIOUS SMELL of a roasting turkey filled the comfortable home of Vera Phillips where Gus had just uncorked a chilled bottle of Gewürztraminer and poured each of them a glass. It was about two in the afternoon on Thanksgiving and Gus had wandered over from his garage apartment to help Miz P with the final preparations. As he poured the wine into the crystal goblets, they heard a car come up the drive, the oyster shells crunching beneath the tires.

"That'll be Maggie," Gus said. He went outside to greet her.

He had invited Maggie to join him for Thanksgiving dinner at Miz P's house after she had been summarily fired from the assistant attorney general's job a few days earlier. Maggie, who usually went home to spend the holiday with her family in upstate New York, had accepted, not wanting to try to explain to her people why she had been fired. She needed time to process the whole thing.

She got out of the car, dressed in fashionable black slacks and a long knitted top in purples and pinks, low heels and a scarf around her neck. She reached into the back seat of her car and came out with a box tied with striped string in a neat bow on top.

"Oh my God," Gus said, taking the box from her. "Is this from Seven Stars?" That bakery was considered one of Providence's best.

"They had some lemon and raspberry tarts with meringue," Maggie said, smiling. "Couldn't resist. I hope Mrs. Phillips hasn't already got something for dessert."

"If she does, we'll have these as appetizers," Gus said. "C'mon in."

Inside, Gus made the introductions, poured a glass of wine for Maggie and sat back and watched as the two women began chatting up a storm. Maggie was making a big deal about telling Miz P what a wonderful home she had, complimenting the decor and design. Miz P, while explaining the provenance of some of her antique pieces, was surreptitiously sizing up the younger woman. Gus was just her tenant, even though she had known him since he was a child, but Vera Phillips could see that he liked Maggie, and so she made it her business to check Maggie out for suitability. After all, she reasoned, Gus' mother was long dead and his father was still outrageously held in prison, so there was nobody else to do this necessary work.

Gus, blissfully unaware of the cross-currents going on around him, was sitting at the counter that overlooked the kitchen, sipping his wine and sampling some of the hors d'oeuvres that Miz P had laid out for the meal: bowls of olives, a plate of smoked salmon on thin slices of baguette, some mixed nuts and some sliced cheeses. The roasting turkey was almost done—the oven timer showed ten minutes left—a big pot of potatoes was boiling on one of the burners and a green bean casserole, topped with grated cheese and onion bits, was waiting to go into the oven after the bird came out. Gus put some smoked salmon on a piece of bread, slathered on a little spicy mustard and popped it into his mouth. He felt content, which was not something he remembered feeling for quite a while.

Mrs. P stopped the conversation and went to check on the progress of the dinner.

"We're eating mostly local today," she told the other two as she checked on the roasting bird and the rest. "The wine is from our local vineyard here in Little Penwick … the Gewürztraminer grapes seem to do well in this climate. The turkey came from Helger's Farm just up the road a bit. The potatoes from Ferrobink, also a local grower on the river near Fogland Beach. I drove over to my cousin's cranberry bog in Mattapoisett. He always saves me a few bags of the choicest fruit every year. They're so sweet you almost don't need to add sugar."

"It all smells divine," said Gus, inhaling the rich scents of Thanksgiving dinner in the making.

"Where's your place?" Maggie asked him.

Gus nodded in the direction of the driveway. "Over the garage," he said. "Not too fancy, but it works for me."

"Maybe I can get a tour later," Maggie said, smiling.

Gus wasn't sure what she meant, but was glad he had taken some time earlier this morning to run the vacuum, empty the sink of old dishes, clean the toilet and bathroom sink and do a little dusting for the first time in several weeks. He had also changed the sheets on his bed, thinking there was an outside chance he might get lucky tonight. But even while plumping up the pillows in their clean new pillow cases, he hadn't given much thought as to whether or not such a thing was something he really wanted. He had finally decided to just let things happen as they would.

Eventually, the turkey came out of the oven, the bean casserole went in, the potatoes were mashed, the cranberry sauce readied and a second bottle of wine was uncorked. The two women were deep into a discussion of online versus in-person clothes shopping, exchanging websites and favorite stores, and Gus was wondering if he should go turn on the TV to watch a football game to air out some of the estrogen flow in the room. But he didn't.

They sat down to eat at about 3:30 and were finished forty minutes later. "That's the thing about a big holiday meal," Mrs. P said, sitting back in her chair with a groan. "Takes days to plan, hours to prepare and minutes to eat."

"But it was all wonderful," Maggie said. "Here's to the cook." She held out her wineglass and Mrs. P clinked it.

"What's for dessert?" Gus said, laughing. "Like the others, he was stuffed to the gills and didn't need anything else to eat. But tradition called for a dessert course.

"Well, Maggie brought those scrumptious looking tarts," Mrs. P said, "And I bought some ice cream from Gray's up in Tiverton. But I was thinking maybe we should adjourn to the living room and have a glass of port before we decide to jump into that."

"I'm down with that," Gus said. He got up and started clearing the table. "You guys get started. I'll do a little cleaning up and be right in."

"Thank you, dear," Mrs. P said, putting her napkin down at her place and slowly rising from the table. She looked over at Maggie who was doing the same. "You can always tell when a young man has been well brought up," she said.

"I've met his Dad," Maggie said with a smile, "Although the circumstances were a little weird, him being in jail and all. But maybe you can tell me all about his mother?"

"Oh, yes, of course," Mrs. P said, grabbing Maggie by the arm and guiding her into the living room. "She was a wonderful woman and a fine mother. Why, I remember ..."

Gus gave Maggie the rolled eye while he gathered up the plates, silverware and serving dishes and began to carry them into the kitchen. But he was smiling.

An hour or so later, the dishes had been washed and put away, the tarts and the ice cream—hand-made and with a butter fat content in the higher stratospheres—eaten and they had moved seamlessly from small glasses of port to some fresh coffee. Outside, the afternoon had transited into early evening.

The streetlights came on and the world eased into the November darkness.

Gus' phone began chirping. He mentally cursed whoever it was d interrupting his life before he saw it was Dottie, the town dispatcher, who was no doubt at her usual place back at the station.

"Hey, Dot," Gus said, "Happy Thanksgiving. I hope you've already had your dinner."

"Naw," she said, "Harold said the girls will be over around eight. We'll sit down and eat something then. But listen, I just got a weird call from somebody who said Janine Stone is bringing in a boatload of inventory at the docks at Little Penwick harbor sometime tonight."

"Really?" Gus said. "Who was it?"

"That's the thing," Dottie said. "I don't know. The Caller ID was blocked on the call. That's supposed to be impossible on our telephone system, unless…"

"Unless it's someone in law enforcement," Gus finished for her. He paused, thinking for a few moments. He wondered if it was Dick Riordan from ICE, giving him a heads up. But why the secrecy? That didn't make any sense. "Did this caller say what time this was supposed to go down?"

"Nope," Dottie said. "Just said sometime tonight. Weird, huh? But I thought you should know."

"Yeah," Gus said. "Well, thanks. I'll take it from here."

He hung up. Maggie was looking at him from her comfortable place on the sofa, her feet drawn up, coffee cup in hand.

"What?" she asked.

"Dispatch got a call, ID blocked, from someone claiming

that our Janine is bringing in a boatload of girls tonight at the harbor," he said.

"Wow," Maggie said, "A hot tip. Is it real?"

"Don't know," Gus said. "But it's the perfect time to do it, isn't it? No one around, and those who are have stuffed themselves full of turkey and probably can't move."

"Do you think it was one of the Ferro boys who called it in?" Maggie asked.

Gus shook his head. "Naw. Too much money at stake for those boys to give it up."

"So who?"

Gus looked at her. "I thought it might be from my friend in the Providence ICE office. But he would call me directly, not play games with an anonymous tip. My next guess is that it probably is your boss," he said.

"Preston?" Maggie was shocked. "Why would he do that?"

"He knows we have the goods on him," Gus said. "We know about him and Janine, we know about him and the Family up in Providence. Since he came to see us last week, he's probably been trying to figure out a way he can wriggle off the hook. I think he's dropping a dime on Janine hoping to get her out of the way. If the Little Penwick police get an anonymous tip, then the Family has no one they can hold responsible. Neither Knox himself or me. Solves a lot of problems for old Preston, doesn't it?"

Maggie thought about that for a moment or two, then nodded. "Yeah," she said, "it does. So, you got a plan? I'm ready for a little head-busting."

Gus chuckled. "Yes, the traditional head-busting came right after the sharing of the maize and turkey at the First

Thanksgiving. But I'm not sure I can let you participate. After all, you're not on the state payroll any more."

Maggie stared at him. "I haven't received any official notice of separation," she said coldly. "So officially, as of right now, I am still as assistant attorney general."

Gus nodded. "OK then," he said. "It will be good to have a state law enforcement official on hand when we bring Janine down. And then we'll deal with Preston Knox."

He picked up his phone and began dialing.

CHAPTER 36

IT WAS NINE o'clock that night and Gus Haddock had his men in place surrounding the Little Penwick harbor. He had called in a half dozen, interrupting their Thanksgiving evenings—from Lt. Callahan to patrolman Freddie Benes—trying not to think about how much overtime pay he was spending. Overtime is supposed to be used on special occasions, he reminded himself, and this—the chance to bust up a major sex trafficking ring and arrest its leader—was definitely one of those.

The old harbor at Little Penwick was half natural and half man-made. There had always been a little indentation in the shoreline along the Sakonnet River where the tides had washed in over the millenia just where the river joined the sea. The old-time locals called the place Church Cove. The installation of a rock jetty on the western edge of the harbor began in 1908 and the Army Corps of Engineers added 400 feet to its length in the 1950s. That jetty defined the boundary of the otherwise circular harbor. Once inside the long arm of the jetty, which extends northwards into the river, the harbor is calm and, once dredged out, deep enough to handle the half dozen or so commercial fishing boats that docked on the wharves along the west side.

Across the harbor, now mostly empty of pleasure boats, which are always hauled off into dry storage during the winter months, there was a long wooden dock that belonged to the Little Penwick Yacht Club, an organization of Old Yankee families that owned summer cottages in Little Penwick and wanted a place to gather, moor their yachts, and have someone teach the kids how to sail a skiff. Gus and Maggie had set up a field headquarters of sorts inside the yacht club building.

The building itself, made of fading gray clapboards and cedar shake roof, was not winterized, and sitting inside it now, feeling the cold wind come streaking off the Atlantic and cutting through the walls like they weren't even there, made Gus wonder if the next big hurricane might take the entire thing down altogether. He suspected that had happened once or twice in the hundred and fifty year history of the yacht club.

He and Maggie were bundled up in winter clothes, parkas, gloves and wooly hats, and both were shivering violently. They kept all the lights off inside so that no one would suspect they were there. Likewise, the waiting police were scattered around the harbor, cars tucked behind trash bins, stacks of lobster cages and Lt. Callahan was waiting inside the dark harbormaster's office above the commercial dock. At least he had central heating.

Gus scanned the harbor. At the commercial wharf, two forty-foot fishing boats were tied up, bobbing quietly. A smaller power boat, black and raked back in its design, also was tied up. Gus wondered for a moment whose boat that might be, then figured it must belong to the harbormaster. Nobody else would keep a pleasure boat like that out in the elements at this time of year.

Gus did a radio check, and everyone signaled that they were in place and ready.

"And now, we wait," Gus said. Maggie shivered silently beside him. He could feel her shaking. "You OK?" he asked, concerned. "Want my parka, too?"

"No," she shook her head, "I'll be OK. But if this takes much longer, I may go find the liquor closet and boost a bottle of Scotch."

Gus smiled. "Good idea. I'll bet they only have single-malts here. No cheap crap for these guys."

She smiled at him and went back to shivering in silence.

It was about an hour later, coming up on nine, when Gus's radio buzzed. He thumbed the button on his mic. "Go ahead, Freddie," he said.

"Ship approaching," Patrolman Benes said. "I can see the running lights."

"Roger," Gus said. He clicked the mic button three times, the pre-arranged signal to get ready.

Ten minutes later, they all saw the boat approaching from the south, from the open ocean, and watched as it traveled up just off the stone jetty, rounded the lighted buoy at the north point and swung into the protected water of the harbor. It was a fishing boat with a short prow, helm station cabin and a long open back deck where the action took place. They couldn't see anyone on board, even on that fishing deck in the stern. Gus knew the type of boat, knew that there was a smallish galley and storage space forward below the helm where any passengers would gather to get out of the cold wind and weather.

"Do we know how many are on board?" Maggie asked, teeth chattering.

"Nope," Gus said. He picked up a pair of binoculars and scanned the boat bow to stern. All he could see was one person in the helm cabin. Nobody else. "But I'd be surprised if they could cram more than about a dozen people down below."

As the boat slowly approached the dock, motoring in behind the two trawlers and the black powerboat, fighting to make headway against the strong southerly wind coming off the ocean, Gus saw someone come out of the cabin, walk around to the bow area and grab a mooring line. He climbed up on the gunnel and waited until the skipper eased the boat into a slip on the dock closest to the harbormaster office. When it was close enough, he jumped onto the dock and tied the line he was holding to a cleat in the front. The guy driving the boat cut the power to neutral, came out of the cabin, walked to the stern and tossed another line over to the man waiting on the dock. He tied that line fast to another cleat at the rear.

Gus thumbed his mic again. "Stand by," he said. "The boat has arrived. Let's see what cargo they're carrying."

The guy on the dock climbed back aboard and the two men went back into the cabin. It was probably warmer in there. Gus picked up his binoculars again. It looked like one of the two was making a call on a cellphone.

"One of them is calling somebody," he said. "Probably calling in the transportation."

Sure enough, five minutes later, Gus and Maggie heard the deep notes of diesel engine and then saw the headlights coming down Penwick Point Road towards the harbor. From their dark and freezing vantage, they watched as a big white fuel oil delivery truck, labeled Ferro Home Heating, made its way around the edge of the harbor. When it neared the commercial wharves, it pulled in and backed up to the edge of the wooden dock. The driver, leaving the engine on, got out of the truck, walked around to the back and fiddled with some controls. Gus and Maggie watched as the entire rear of the oil truck began to swing upward, its hidden hinges connected to some kind of hydraulic lifts, exposing the lighted inside, which showed two wooden benches down each side of the truck.

"That's fucking genius," Gus said, studying the truck through his glasses. "Those Ferro guys are dishonest as hell, but they know how to make things."

"How do people breathe inside that thing?" Maggie wondered.

"I'm sure they've got some kind of ventilation system," Gus said. "Wouldn't be surprised if they installed a porta-johnnie as well."

They watched as the truck driver came over to the boat and banged on the outside.

"OK," Gus said, exhaling slowly, "It's showtime!"

"Have you seen Janine?" Maggie asked. "Is she here?"

"Don't know," Gus said. "Too dark to tell. But we're about to find out."

The door to the cabin opened and one of the two boat operators led a parade out onto the stern deck and pulled open a narrow door in the gunwale that opened onto the dock. The parade was made up of a group of young women—Gus counted twelve—who followed the guy across the back of the boat, onto the wooden dock and down towards the waiting fake oil truck. None of the women seemed to be dressed for a cold Thanksgiving night. A couple had shawls pulled up and over their heads. Several of them were clutching oversized bags that seemed to contain their possessions. The other boat operator trailed after the last woman. Once she was on the dock, he followed and pulled the boat's door closed.

The first guy motioned impatiently and the women began climbing into the back of the fake oil truck. Gus thumbed his mic again.

"Go, go go!" he yelled.

Three police cars, blue lights flashing and sirens suddenly screaming, burst out of their hiding places. Two of them screeched to a halt in front of the oil truck, the other pulled in at the rear. The officers jumped out, guns drawn, shouting instructions. It all took maybe ten seconds.

Gus and Maggie ran for the back door of the yacht club, climbed into Gus's police SUV and sped around the outer circle of the harbor. When they got to the scene, the twelve women had their hands in the air, following the directions of one of the officers. Lt. Callahan and another officer had one of the boat operators on the ground, spread eagled, and were clapping cuffs on him.

"Where's the other one?" Gus yelled as they came up. "There were two guys on the boat."

Callahan looked around as he pulled the first guy upright, and frisked him quickly looking for weapons. "I dunno," he said.

"Shit," Gus said. He went running down the dock, looking into the boat that had delivered the women. He couldn't see anyone aboard. He pulled his Sig Sauer and jumped on board.

"Police!" he shouted. "Come out with your hands up!"

There was no answer. He crept towards the door to the cabin, grabbed the handle, counted to three, and yanked it open, bringing his gun up to the firing position. The helm area was empty. A narrow stairway led down to the lower cabin. Gus, feeling his heart pounding as it hadn't since he left Afghanistan, edged down the stairs then plunged into the galley. Empty.

"Shit," he hissed and went back topside.

Two of his officers had control of the twelve women, none of whom was protesting or resisting. They seemed to know the illegal immigrant's drill: do what you're told and hope for the best. Freddie Benes was standing next to them. There were also two men in handcuffs leaning against the side of the truck: one was the driver of the truck, the other had come off the boat.

"Freddie?" Gus shouted. "Did you see another guy? There were two of them on that boat."

Benes pulled his weapon and a flashlight. "Not yet," he called back. He began to shine his torch underneath the truck and then into other dark corners outside the harbormaster's building.

That's when they heard the roar of a marine engine starting up. It was coming from behind the other two fishing boats. It was the black boat Gus had seen earlier.

"Shit," Gus said again, and began running down the dock towards the sound. Freddie Benes came thumping along behind.

But they were too late. By the time they cleared the bow of the last boat, the little black powerboat was accelerating out of the harbor, fifty yards away. Gus and Freddie both took the shooter's position and fired several shots at the back of the boat, where the three outboard engines were cranking hard, a cloud of exhaust blowing away in the cold wind. But they missed. Gus couldn't be sure, but he thought he saw long blond hair cascading down the back of the boat operator. The boat rounded the corner of the jetty at full speed and turned into the Sakonnet River. It headed due west, away from the harbor and the police bullets and toward the far bank of Aquidneck Island, about a mile away. On the horizon, the orange vapor lights of Newport sent a cozy glow into the night sky.

Gus watched as the boat disappeared into the night. There were no running or navigation lights on it, so he couldn't tell where it was going. It could have continued west toward Newport, or it could have turned in the middle of the channel and headed north to Mount Hope Bay and the city of Fall River, or even on to Providence at the head of Narragansett Bay. Or it could have turned south and headed for open sea. The city of New Bedford and Buzzard's Bay was about ten miles east. Long Island about thirty miles south-southwest. South America, about three thousand miles due south.

"Shit," he said again. Then he turned and walked back to the oil truck. Maggie had herded the women into the back of the truck, out of the wind. There was some kind of heating system pumping warm air into the space, so Maggie had all the women sit down and she was asking them questions, using rudimentary Spanish. Gus only knew enough of that language to order a cold beer and ask where the restrooms were, so he let her continue to talk to them.

Finally, she looked at him.

"They arrived yesterday from Mexico, Honduras and Guatemala," she said. "They've all been promised jobs. They don't know where, or what they are to do. But they'll do whatever, if they can make some money to send home." She shook her head sadly. "Did you get the last guy?"

"Nope," Gus said curtly. "He had that boat stashed just in case. Good backup plan."

"Wasn't no he," said one of the men they had arrested. He was leaning against the back of the truck, arms fastened behind his back. He was smiling. "That was Janine. You'll never catch her. She's like a ghost. Can disappear in an instant. Moves like the wind. Free as a bird. Janine. One of a kind."

Gus went over and pulled the man's cap off his head. It

was Danny Ferro. He grinned at Gus. "One of a kind, that one," he said again.

"We'll get her," Gus said. "In about two minutes, the Coast Guard will be out looking for her. After that, APB. After that, maybe the Fibbie's will put her on the Most Wanted list. So don't you worry, Dan, eventually we'll find her, bring her in."

Danny Ferro laughed and spit in the dirt down at his feet. "I'd make book on that," he said. "No way in hell you'll ever catch that one. No way in hell."

CHAPTER 37

Everybody went home for the rest of the weekend: leftovers and football on the agenda. Gus drove Danny Ferro back to the station, booked him on all the charges he could think of, and the next day one of the patrolmen on duty drove him over to Newport to wait arraignment on Monday.

The next morning, at the station, Maggie took charge of the women, who had all shared the other two cells at the back. She knew of a social service organization in Providence that could take care of the twelve victims and was on the telephone making those arrangements when a TV truck arrived at the Little Penwick station. The producer, who was driving, and a blond woman in a fluffy parka got out of the truck. A third man got out of the back seat and began operating the controls on the back. A boom antenna began rising above the truck.

Gus watched all this from inside the station.

"Who called the TV guys?" he said, wondering out loud. He turned to look at Maggie. "You?"

"No way," she said, shaking her head.

The producer and the reporter came inside.

"Woo," the guy said, "It's a cold one today. I'm Jeremy Winston, TV-5 News. We hear you busted up some kind of trafficking deal last night. We'd like to get you on camera talking about it, and maybe get some shots or interviews with the women. Great human interest stuff for the holidays, right?"

Gus smiled at the man. "Don't think so," he said. "We're pretty busy here. By the way, how did you hear about what went down last night?"

The guy smiled. "We never divulge our sources," he said, "Especially when they come from one of the highest offices in the state."

"C'mon, chief," said the blond woman, giving Gus a toothy smile accompanied by a sideways tilt of the head. "This is a great story. Women rescued from a fate worse than death, plucked off a boat on the high seas ... all on Thanksgiving night. You'll be a hero."

"Where did you get the impression that I want to be a hero?" Gus said. "I'm just a cop."

The TV people started protesting, but after a few minutes, Gus caught the eye of Jerry Hanlon, who was on duty in the squad room and jerked his head. Hanlon jumped up and took control.

"Okay, chief says no," he said, pushing Winston and the woman reporter backwards toward the door. "No comment. Let's move along." He got them outside, closed the door behind them and stood there, arms crossed. The TV crew got the idea and, after lowering their microwave antenna again, got in their truck and left.

"They'll probably head down to the harbor," Maggie said. "Isn't Callahan down there, supervising the techies on the boat? You should call him and warn him."

"Right," Gus said. "I'll do that."

He went into his office and got Callahan on his cell. "You can talk to them if you want," he told the lieutenant, "But I went with the 'no comment' line."

"Ten-four chief," Callahan said. "I'll handle them."

Gus hung up and sat there at his desk for a moment. He was wiped out. After all the excitement of last night, he and Maggie had returned to his place around midnight. They had first checked in with Mrs. P, as they had promised to do when they left her home earlier. She had been waiting up for them, and invited them in for a nightcap while they recapped what had happened at the harbor. After an hour and deep yawns from both of them, Mrs. P. had offered to let Maggie sleep in one of her guest bedrooms.

There had been one of those fraught, meaningful looks between the two, which told Gus that Maggie had been thinking the same thing he had. But after a brief and awkward pause, Maggie had said "It would probably be more comfortable than crashing on your sofa," and Gus had quickly agreed. He got up to leave and Maggie had come over and given him a kiss on the cheek. "Thanks for a memorable Thanksgiving," she said.

Gus had tossed and turned all night, wondering if he had done the right thing.

So now he was yawning at his desk. He wanted to go home and sleep it off. But there were still things he had to do. And then his desk phone rang.

"Yo," he said, picking it up.

"Chief Haddock?" said a familiar voice, "Congrats on the bust last night. I sent a TV crew down to get the full story. It will make you look like a real crimestopper. You'll be getting your fifteen minutes of fame, that's for sure."

"Hello, General," Gus said to Preston Knox. "I already told them I had no comment and that the investigation was continuing. Which it is, since your golden girl apparently got away."

"She can run, but I wouldn't want to hide from the likes of you," the attorney general said. "You did some fine police work, son. Very fine. I'm proud of you. And your department. A credit to our state."

"You wouldn't know who phoned in the tip on Thursday, would you?" Gus said. "I've been wondering."

"No idea whatsoever," Knox said, but Gus could hear a chuckle in his voice as he said it. "Must have been a concerned citizen."

"Yeah," Gus said, "I'm sure that was it."

There was a pause that went on for an uncomfortable time.

"What are you gonna tell the big boppers of The Family?" Gus said. "I got a dozen members of their talent pool in my jail. We're either gonna send them back home or find them a legal place to stay. I can't imagine The Big Guys gonna be happy with what happened. Or with you."

"Well Chief Haddock, I'll take care of all that and don't you worry your little head about it," Knox said. "There are no guarantees in life, especially in the business those gentlemen are in. They'll get over it. And I'm sure, as we continue to work together, we can find, umm, other areas of cooperation that will be mutually beneficial to all of us."

"Yeah," Gus said, "I'm sure you can."

There was another short pause. "Anything else I can do for you, general?" Gus said finally.

"Only one more thing," Knox said. "I've ordered the release of your father. Papers should be over at the ACI by now. I imagine you can pick him up around 2. Does that work for you?"

"How did ..."

"No, Chief, that's the wrong question," Knox interrupted. "Let's just say that upon further review, it was determined that the state no longer has an interest in holding your father. If he wants to come back at us, we will vigorously defend our actions and we can drag that whole thing through the mud one more time. I'm hoping that he, and you, will agree to let bygones lie, and we can all get on with the rest of our lives."

"That's what you're hoping, is it?" Gus said. "Well, you don't know me very well but I'm pretty sure you know my Dad, and my advice to you is to watch your back. Now and for the rest of your life. You fucked with the wrong guy when you fucked with Julius Haddock."

"Which is why I'm now dealing with Augustus Haddock," the attorney general said. "I believe he has a more nuanced view on how things operate."

Gus noticed he was holding the telephone in a death grip, knuckles white, muscles clenched. He also could hear the dangerous ringing in his ears. The one he used to get when some unseen enemy was throwing incoming rounds in his direction.

Maggie Wells came into his office, took one look at Gus' red face and immediately looked concerned. "What the hell is wrong?" she gasped.

Gus reached over and punched a button on his phone.

"Knox?" he rasped, "You are now on speaker phone. I've got Maggie Wells in my office. There's one more thing you need to do. Put this woman back in her job. Immediately. Or I will call that TV crew back in here and give them a real story."

They heard Preston Knox pause, then begin to chuckle out loud.

"I always pegged you as a romantic," he said. "Lothario to the rescue. Very well, I shall be happy to restore Ms. Wells to her position. In fact, I hadn't yet taken any official act to remove her. But I will be glad to have her presence on my staff again. See you Monday, my dear woman?"

Maggie leaned over, getting close to the phone's microphone.

"Preston," she said, "I wouldn't work one more hour for you if you were the last dickhead on earth. Fuck you, fuck your job, fuck your stupid babe parade at the Capital Grille, and whatever political job you run for next time, you can rest assured that I will be working for the opposition. You'll have my resignation on your desk first thing Monday morning."

"Righteous," Gus said and, reaching over, disconnected the call.

AT ABOUT TWO thirty that afternoon, Gus pulled his SUV cruiser into the police parking lot at the ACI in Cranston. The lot was about half full, but there was a group of officers gathered near the entrance to the jail, a concrete walkway enclosed in a cage of chain link fence. Gus parked the car and walked over to the group.

As he suspected, Julius Haddock was in the middle of the group of cops and correctional officers. He was puffing away happily on a fat cigar and holding court. As Gus neared, Julius finished telling a story and the men all broke out in raucous laughter, with a couple men pounding his dad on the back.

"Junior!" Julius caught sight of his son. "You're late! Luckily, this group of reprobates has kept me entertained."

"Or the other way around," Gus said. "You ready?"

Julius took one last puff on the stogie, held the smoke in for a glorious few seconds, and then exhaled dramatically and noisily. "Son," he said, "I've been ready to leave since the second I got here."

He turned to the group of cops. "Fare thee well, gentlemen," he said, tossing the cigar to the ground and mashing it beneath his shoe. "You guys ever get down to Little Penwick, give me a shout. I know a guy who'll sell you a lobster plucked from the sea that morning for five bucks."

"A pound?" one of the correctional officers said. "That's not that great a deal."

"No, you idiot," Julius said. "For the lobster. They usually run three pounds and up."

The men jeered good naturedly at the correctional guy and Julius shook hands all around. Then he nodded at Gus and they walked away towards his car.

The two were silent as Gus started up and slowly drove away from the ACI. Julius turned around to look back at the huge Gothic gray edifice as it faded away behind them.

"What a dump," Julius said. "Son, my fatherly advice to you is to never, ever let them send you there. I don't care if you have to leave the country or eat a bullet. Just never let them send you to that place."

"Good advice, Dad," Gus said. "But kinda obvious, like 'buy low, sell high.'"

"Don't be a smart ass," Julius said. "I'm serious."

"Seriously, Dad, what are you gonna do now?" Gus said. "Do you want me to resign?"

"What for?" Julius sounded amazed.

"So you can get your job back, of course," Gus said. They were on I-95, weaving in and out of the early rush hour traffic as they approached Providence.

"Jesus H. Christ on a popsicle," Julius said. "Are you insane? Did you breathe in some of that Agent Orange when you were overseas? I don't want your job. I'm retiring. No, check that, I'm retired. Past tense. You're the chief of police for Little Penwick now, and I'm sure you'll be a good one."

"Well, thanks," Gus said. "But what are you going to do now? Sit around in your house and do crossword puzzles and cross-stitch? That doesn't sound like you at all."

"Cross-stitch?" Julius said with a bark of a laugh. "There was this guy on my cell block who does cross-stitch. Frankie Pazzola. You know him?" Gus shook his head. "He's doing thirty for criminal assault and battery. He busted the legs of guys behind on their vig. We called him Tiny. He's about six-six, I dunno, maybe two ninety. Three hundred maybe. Works all day in his cell, needle and thread, making these intricate designs for pillows and stuff. Fuckin' Tiny. Actually a pretty nice guy, all things considered."

"OK," Gus said, "Ix-nay to the cross-stitch. So what is your plan?"

"I don't know," Julius said. "hell, give a guy a break, OK? I just got out of the hoosegow. Gimme some time to figure something out."

"Maybe this will help," Gus said. He reached into his coat pocket and tossed an envelope into his father's lap.

"What's this?" Julius said. He fumbled in his own pocket to find his reading glasses.

"It's your private investigator's license," Gus said. "The one you apparently applied for a month or two ago. How you got them to overlook your current address in the Big House is beyond my understanding. But then, you've always been a step or two ahead of the game."

Julius read the papers. He was smiling to himself.

"Julius Haddock, Private Eye," Gus said with a chuckle. "I like it. Or are you going with Little Penwick Investigations … no case too small, even for Rhode Island!"

"I think you need to get back to work catching bad guys and leave the marketing to those of us who know what we're doing," Julius said.

They were now traveling down I-195, the highway that runs between Providence and Fall River, and continues on through New Bedford and almost all the way to Cape Cod.

"Shit!" Gus said suddenly.

"What?"

"I totally forgot," Gus said. "Do you want me to stop and get you something? Food or drink? I mean, you've been inside probably thinking about this minute for months now …"

"You mean, do I want a big steak dinner and a nice whore?" Julius said. They both laughed. "Actually, that doesn't sound too bad. But no, son, I'm fine. Just take me home. That's what I've been thinking about for the last eight months, three weeks and four days, not that I'm counting or anything. Siggi will bring me some dinner later, after I call her and she stops crying. And a hot shower with no one else in the room sounds good. I haven't had a relaxing shower since …"

"OK, Dad," Gus said. "I get it. Home it is."

He reached over to the dashboard and flipped a switch. The cruiser's blue lights began flashing and the siren started whooping. Cars began getting out of the way as Gus floored it. He figured he could probably cut about twenty minutes off the drive this way.

"That's my boy," his father said. And he sounded content.

CHAPTER 38

IT WAS AROUND the middle of December, ten days before Christmas, when Gus returned to Brockton and his monthly appointment with Dr. Susan Maloney. The day was cold and cloudy, but the snappily dressed weather idiot on the local TV channel had assured his viewers that no precipitation, either wet or white, was expected.

"Well, well," the doctor said when he was seated at her desk. The HVAC was softly humming again, this time as it churned hot dry air through the vents in the wall. "From what I've read, you've had an interesting month."

"Yeah," Gus said, "I guess I have. It always feels good to draw a line under stuff, close a case, finish the file. Sense of completion."

"And your father is home," she said, smiling at him. "That must make you feel good too."

"A relief," Gus agreed, nodding.

"Are you two planning something special for Christmas?" she asked.

Gus chuckled. "The usual," he said. "I'll give him a nice new tie, which he'll never wear and he'll give me something like a new pair of gold-plated handcuffs, which I'll never use. But we'll have either lunch or dinner together, and that will be more than enough of a gift for both of us."

"So the case is pretty much wrapped up?" she asked.

Gus nodded. "For the most part," he said. "The state lab finally came back with full details on the hair samples we recovered from the drain. All female. Several nationalities. Once we had that, Danny Ferro rolled over and told us most everything. Janine had set up the network for the goombahs up in Providence who staffed strip clubs everywhere up the East Coast and into Canada. The Ferro place was one of about six or seven different entry points in her operation. It was a pretty big business."

He paused, thinking. "I think we were right in assuming that Angelo Ferro was not in favor of the whole enterprise. Danny says Angelo and Janine were always arguing. She usually won the arguments because of who her backers were. But Angelo made her life difficult. Which is probably why she decided to get rid of him."

"Have they caught that young woman yet?"

"The lovely Janine?" Gus said, "No, not yet. Her motor boat turned up, abandoned down in Greenport, on the North

Fork of Long Island. But no sign of Janine. I figure she probably made her way down to the city, where it's easy to hide out for a while. But she's on a bunch of BOLO lists now, so it shouldn't be long before she turns up."

"Do you think she feels there is some unfinished business between you?" Maloney said. "Something that might lead her to seek revenge?"

"Against me?" Gus was surprised. He had not really considered anything like that. "Well, anything is possible, I guess, but that doesn't sound like something Janine would spend a lot of time worrying about. Now she very well may find a new way to keep her business going … find some new customers and start moving her operations to a new place. That sounds more like what a person like that would be thinking about. But wasting time to come after me? Or the Ferros? Preston Knox? Naw, I really don't think so. I'd be very surprised if we ever saw her face in Little Penwick again."

"Which is why I am suggesting it," the doctor said, nodding at Gus. "From what you've told me about this person, she likes to do the unexpected. She likes to keep people guessing. She has lots of plans and counter plans and strategies. And she seems to have certain psychopathic tendencies. The literature is clear: people like that do not like being thwarted. And you and your department thwarted her, big time." She picked up her pen and waved it at Gus for emphasis. "I would think about this, Gus," she said, her tone serious. "Have a plan ready, just in case."

Gus thought about that for a moment or two. "Yeah," he said, "I guess that does make sense. I'll work something up, make sure the department keeps alert."

"Were you able to determine what happened to the elder Ferro?" she asked, "The patriarch?"

"Not definitively," Gus said, shaking his head. "Danny Ferro said he remembered Janine volunteered to take Angelo down to the harbor the night he disappeared. But what happened after that, no one knows for sure. I still think my theory that she killed him, sent the boat out to sea and swam back to shore is the only one that works. But we'll have to wait until we get Janine in custody to confirm that. Which we will, sooner or later."

"Good," she said, nodding with approval. "Now…what are you going to do about Maggie?"

Gus laughed a little. "I think the question is what is Maggie going to do about me?" he said. "She's setting up a new foundation in Providence for abused women. Right now, she's beating the bushes looking for rich donors to fund it. And I think she's going to make her numbers. The holidays is a good time to raise money for good causes. She's got some pretty important people in town lined up to help. So we've only seen each other twice in the last three weeks."

"And?"

"And it's nice, it's good. We like each other now," Gus said. "But I'm not sure either one of us is ready to push it onto the next phase. We're taking it slow. Wait and see what happens."

"Well, that's perfectly sensible," Dr. Maloney said. Gus caught something in her voice.

"You don't think that's a good idea?" he asked.

She paused before answering to gather her thoughts.

"No, no," she said finally, "That probably is the most sensible approach to take. You two have been though a lot and in a very compacted amount of time. It's probably best to decompress a little before seeing what the next step might be. Or even if there is a next step. Maybe there isn't one."

"Yeah," Gus said, nodding. "I think that's what we're both feeling."

"On the other hand, she seems to be a wonderful person, and you both seem to like each other a lot," the doctor said. "And life is short."

Gus waved his hands in front of his face, as if chasing away a swarm of gnats.

"Yeah, I know that, too," he said. "But I can't think about that right now. Or maybe I don't want to think about that."

"Same thing," she said.

"Yeah, I guess," he said. "My plate is still pretty full. My lieutenant, Callahan, is retiring after the New Year. I gotta get someone to replace him. The town council is still being a total pain in the ass. And now that Dad's home, I gotta figure out how he figures into things."

"Is he going back to the department?"

"Naw," Gus said. "He's officially retired. He says he's going to hang out his shingle as a PI. I'm not sure what I think about that, yet. I'm sure he'll have a grand old time, but I wonder how it might affect his relationship with me and the department and the other guys. It could be fine or it could be a godawful mess."

"Yes," she said, "I can see that. Could be a complicating factor. We can talk about that in our next session. I assume you want to continue meeting with me?"

Gus paused, but not for long. He realized he could get out of mandatory shrink sessions now. Most of the underlying reasons were gone: his father was out of jail, the special master from the AG's office had been canceled. Preston Knox was still Attorney General, but he knew that Gus could easily leak some information that would doom his future political career. Gus hadn't done so, because now he held a marker over Knox. He might be able to use that sometime in the future. Life was pretty much back to normal.

"Have you had any more bad dreams?" Maloney asked. "Or punched out any more walls?"

Gus chuckled. "I had a dream last week," he said, "But it wasn't the one I'd been having. And, frankly, I've been too busy to punch anything, especially a wall in the men's room."

He looked across the desk at his doctor. She was sitting there calmly, looking back at him. Probably sizing me up for a straight jacket, he thought, and smiled.

"Shall we do this again next month?" he asked. She smiled, nodded and checked the appointments page on her laptop. "How about January fifteenth?" she asked. "It'll be a brand new year."

A brand new year. Gus liked the sound of that.

ABOUT THE AUTHOR

James Y. Bartlett is an American journalist, writer, editor and author.

For most of his career, Bartlett worked in magazine journalism, specializing in covering the worlds of travel, golf and upscale lifestyle. He worked on staff as an editor with *Golfweek*, *Caribbean Travel & Life* and *Luxury Golf* magazines, among others.

But he also published hundreds of freelance pieces in publications ranging from *Bon Appetit* to *Esquire*, *Men's Journal* to *Golf for Women*.

Bartlett was the golf columnist for *Forbes FYI* magazine for the first fifteen years of that publication's history and wrote a similar column for nearly 20 years on the golf lifestyle for *Hemispheres*, the in-flight publication of United Airlines, the latter under the pseudonym of "A.G. Pollard Jr."

He began writing his popular Hacker Golf Mystery series in 1991 with the publication of *Death is a Two-Stroke Penalty* (St. Martin's Press). That series, now published by Yeoman House, contains seven novels. In 2021, he published *Year of the Sheep: A Novel of the Highland Clearances*, an epic historical novel of that sad time, that was a quarter-finalist in BookLife magazine's Fiction of the Year contest in 2022.

Bartlett is also the author of five nonfiction books.

Bartlett lives in a small town in Rhode Island.

For more information about the author and his books, please visit his website at:

www.jamesybartlett.com

The Hacker Golf Mystery Series

DEATH IS A TWO-STROKE PENALTY
DEATH FROM THE LADIES TEE
DEATH AT THE MEMBER-GUEST
DEATH IN A GREEN JACKET
DEATH FROM THE CLARET JUG
AN OPEN CASE OF DEATH
P.G.A. SPELLS DEATH

The last four titles are collected in a box set e-book edition titled "THE MAJORS COLLECTION"

The Swamp Yankee Mystery Series

GLITTER GIRL
COLD SECRETS
RAINBOW'S END
FAMILY AFFAIRS
RUM ROW*

** A Prequel/Novella available in e-book format only*

The Bach Musical Mystery Series

THE ORGAN JOB
THE COFFEE GARDEN
THE SONG OF ASAPH

Also available in German translation

Historical Fiction

YEAR OF THE SHEEP: A NOVEL OF THE
HIGHLAND CLEARANCES

Other titles by the author:

CADDIEWAMPUS: LOOPING FOR GOLF'S GREATS
SERPENT POINT: A POLITICAL THRILLER*
THINK LIKE A CADDIE/ PLAY LIKE A PRO
MASTERING GOLF'S TOUGHEST SHOTS

Published under the pseudonym Caleb Clarke

COLD SECRETS

A Swamp Yankee Mystery
Book Two

Read the first chapter of this exciting new novel.

CHAPTER 1

Revenge is a dish best served cold, as the old proverb says. Except, of course, there really isn't a proverb that says that, either in French or in English. I prefer Sir Francis Bacon's variation on the theme: "Revenge is a kind of wild justice."

As a former cop; as a former cop who served eight months at the Adult Correctional Institute, the fancy name for the Big House here in Rhode Island; as a former cop framed by the Attorney General for his own corrupt purposes; I was indeed interested in wild justice when I finally got freed. Any way I could get it.

It was that thirst for revenge—as overwhelming and all encompassing as if I had been marching across the desert for weeks without water— that pretty much dominated my life when I first regained my freedom. I awoke every morning, in my warm and comfortable bed, in my warm and comfortable house by the sea, in the company, usually, of my warm and comfortable partner Siggi ... and could only think of the things I'd like to do to Preston Knox, the afore-mentioned attorney general, and some of the other players who sent me to prison and worked to keep me there. For no good reason other than to protect a beautiful young woman who was running a human trafficking ring right here in my hometown of Little Penwick, the smallest town in the smallest state. My anger and desire for revenge was Texas-sized, and not to be denied.

I was red hot and I would have gladly spooned into the mouth of Preston Knox some heaping servings of revenge flambe if I could. It was Siggi who kept me from doing anything rash and ridiculous in those first weeks of freedom.

"There's too much negative energy coming from you right now," she told me, usually after we had our morning coffee. The elapsed time from waking with a desire to kill someone to having downed a couple cups of joe was maybe half an hour, but despite the caffeine it helped me calm down, reduced the desire to commit mayhem back down to a more manageable level, where maybe some prudent maiming or a couple of painful broken limbs would have satiated my need for payback.

And I suppose my age and position in life helped as well. I was now retired after spending more than thirty-five years on the force of the Little Penwick Police Department, the last twenty-six as chief. My son Gus was now installed in my place as chief, which made me proud and happy. I hadn't decided what to do with the rest of my life, yet, although I knew I wasn't ready to decamp to Florida with the rest of the snow-birds and try to find happiness on a golf course or a sports bar. But I figured I would find something useful after I had taken care of the revenge problem.

"It's not negative energy," I told Siggi, "It's pure, clean, 100-proof anger."

"You must do something to eliminate it," she would say. "It's not healthy to hold that inside you."

"OK," I said. "I will."

Of course, Siggi was thinking along the lines of doing some serious meditation, or Reiki massage or hot stone therapy or something. She is, in addition to being a part-time pediatric nurse, a practicing astrologer, and has been since she was a teenager. She learned the skill from her mother, who was Icelandic, having met and married an American G.I. during the second World War, when he was stationed in Reykjavik. Siggi had grown up in the United States, but was still largely Nordic, a culture that gave us Odin, Thor and the reading of the Runes. She could do that, too, but was still mostly a student of the movements of the stars, the planets, the sun, and the moon, from which she could, quite accurately, determine the probabilities and proclivities of one's behavior and thus, the probabilities of future events.

I grew up as a cop, so I was naturally skeptical of all such things. But as a cop, I had also observed how often Siggi's readings and projections turned out to come true. So I had learned to listen to her. You don't have to be an adherent of the skill to notice if it works or not.

But I was not thinking of therapy, whether New Age or Freudian, to assuage my white-hot rage. No, I was thinking of ways I could put a couple caps in the head of the sitting Attorney General of Rhode Island and watch the light slowly go out in his eyes. Thinking about that part was easy, and therapeutic in its own way.. The hard part was coming up with a way to avoid being sent back to the ACI. Contemplating that aspect of my problem, turning it over and over in my head from the time I awoke until the moment I fell back asleep that night, that was what kept me going in those first few months after I got out.

So my … what? …recovery? … recuperation? … reentry into society? … took a while. It was the holidays when I first got out, so I pretty much laid low. Didn't go out much. Didn't have anyone come over, except for Siggi and my son, Gus. I sat at home and festered.

Towards the end of January, I took some baby steps. Called a few old friends and arranged for a weekly guys lunch at Jack's Diner. That was good: the guys listened to me, sympathized with my anger, told me it was understandable, based on what had happened. None of them believed what had happened to me was in any way justified. But none of them volunteered to help me murder Preston Knox and drop his body at the bottom of the Atlantic, way down deep in the trenches of that part of the ocean bottom they call The Dump. That made me a little angry, but I managed not to let it show. Siggi would have been proud.

In February, there was a get-together at Vera Phillip's place, where Gus was renting her garage apartment, to watch the Super Bowl. Siggi went with me, and Gus' honey, the Providence lawyer Maggie Wells, who had been installed as the Special Master by the AG to oversee the Little Penwick PD while I was in jail, was there as well.

We had a nice dinner and enjoyed watching the Patriots run up the score in the second half on the Bears. I listened as Gus and Maggie laughingly rehashed the Ferro case, which involved the beautiful young Glitter Girl, Janine Stone, who had devised and operated the trafficking scheme, and who had managed to escape arrest at the end. She was still on the loose.

But Gus and Maggie mentioned how a local judge, Maryann Parker, had tipped off Preston Knox when they had gone to get a search warrant from her for the Ferro place. As a result, the Ferro's had cleaned up their act and Janine had evaded our grasp again.

"Did you ever find out why she called Knox?" I asked.

Gus looked at me funny—I think he could feel the anger coming off me like waves of heat from a volcano—and said "They have been family friends for ages, Dad."

"You know what Rhode Island is like," Maggie said. "It's so small that it's almost incestuous. Everybody grew up with everybody else. And everybody knows everybody else's business."

"Yeah, but the judge endangered your investigation," I said. "Not only illegal, and totally unethical, but someone could have gotten hurt."

Siggi reached over and put her hand on top of mine. I got the message and let it drop.

But the next morning, first thing, I was on the phone. I called Gil James, an almost-retired reporter for the Newport Daily News in that small city across the Sakonnet River from Little Penwick. Gil, who had to be even older than me, had been reporting the goings-on around Newport for about fifty years, and the paper, now owned by a big national chain, had downsized almost everyone else on the staff. But they kept Gil around either because he knew where the bodies were buried or because the readers still liked to read his weekend column musing on the changes to the City by the Sea, and how much different, and better, things used to be.

"Chief Haddock," he said when I got him on the blower. "Or, ex-Chief I guess is more accurate. How is your boy doing?"

"Busy as hell," I said, "Arresting every miscreant he can get his hands on."

"Umm-hmm," Gil said. "If I remember the crime numbers from Little Penwick, that adds up to about three or four arrests a year. Am I right?"

"Pretty close," I said.

He chuckled. "So what can I do for you?"

"What's the dirt on Maryann Parker?" I asked.

"What makes you think our lovely local jurist has any dirt?" Gil asked, barely able to keep the sarcasm out of his voice.

"You can't get appointed judge in this state unless you've got some dirt hidden somewhere," I said. "I think there's a state law."

"Ain't that the truth," Gil said. "Let me see. Maryann Parker. Well, she's an old family friend of the attorney general."

"I know that," I said.

"The governor likes her. But then, the womenfolk tend to stick together."

"And who can blame them?" I said. "With menfolk like we have in this state lurking around out there."

"She's quite active at the Ida Lewis Yacht Club," he told me. "She's a big sailor and keeps her boat at the club. She's been appointed Vice Admiral or whatever they call themselves."

"Lots of vice, is there, at the Ida Lewis?"

"Har-de-har," he said. "But I remember hearing that she got the club to approve paying for her anchorage fees. The way my source explained it, she did it on the QT. Didn't want the club membership to know about it, much less the general public."

"Must be a lot of money involved if she was trying to bury it," I said.

"About fifteen hundred a year," Gil told me. "Most people who own yachts and keep them in Newport Harbor, fifteen bills is pocket change. Petty cash."

"But for your average Joe Slobbo, fifteen hundred is a lot of cash," I said. "And her trying to keep it secret sounds like a cover-up."

"Not to mention the other members of the yacht club, each of whom has to pony up membership dues every month— and it ain't cheap, believe me—they would not be happy that their Vice Admiral is getting a benny that they aren't."

"Interesting," I said. "I think I can use that. Thanks Gilly."

"Use it how?" As an old reporter, his ears had pricked up. Those old guys knew a story before it came up and slapped them across the face.

"Not sure yet," I said. "I'll let you know."

"You do that," he said.

ABOUT A WEEK later, Gil James called me back.

"You went to the Projo?" he said, his voice quivering with indignation. "And the TV idiots? What are we, chopped liver?"

"Gil," I said, "You were the one who told me about Vice Admiral Maryann and her special deal. You could have run that story any time in the last five years. So don't go busting my chops."

He was silent. Because what I said was true.

He was referring to a big story in the Sunday Providence Journal—the Projo to us locals—which had been instantly aped by two of the three local TV stations in Providence. "Self-dealing on the Poop Deck" was the Projo's mostly nonsensical headline. They had gone with the narrative that the big, powerful, Superior Court justice had given herself a nice fat annual benefit and then tried to keep knowledge of it away from the other members of the yacht club. At least they had shown some reporting gumption and found three other yacht club members at the Ida Lewis to give them appropriately outraged quotes. Towards the end of the story, Judge Maryann Parker had been allowed to claim the $1500 annual credit she received, which was exactly the annual mooring fee members were charged, was typical for yacht clubs like Ida Lewis.

The TV stations had sent crews down to Newport to photograph the yacht club building, located on a small rock a few hundred yards out into the harbor, connected by a long wooden pier to the mainland. The eponymous Ida Lewis had once been a lighthouse keeper out on that rock, and rowed herself out to work every day, in between brave rowboat rescues of drunken sailors who fell into Newport Harbor from time to time. Nobody, from the judge herself to anyone from the yacht club, would go on camera, so the reporter just re-iterated the Projo story over the images of the club, and the small handful of pleasure boats left on their moorings during the winter months.

"She's not going to resign because of this," Gil told me. "I called her husband last night. She's mad. She's embarrassed. But she's not quitting. No laws were broken. She just acted like an entitled yachty. Which, of course, she is."

"Good," I said. "All I wanted was to fire a shot across her bows. Mission accomplished."

"Geez," Gil James said over the phone. "What did she do to you? She wasn't the judge who sent you up the river. That was Freddie O'Rourke, wasn't it?"

"Maybe he's next," I said.

"Ho-lee crap," Gil said. "Remind me never to get on your bad side."

I FELT A little better after that, so I began doing some much-need-ed repairs and maintenance on my house. Of course, I didn't have a chance to work on the house when I was jailed. And before that, the demands of the job at the police department often left me little time for the small jobs one needs to keep up with at home.

They were mostly small jobs because the house was in pretty good shape. My grandfather, John Edward Haddock, had built the place himself, back around 1930. John Edward had been a merchant marine captain and he found the sliver of land that was a rocky meadow overlooking the shingle beach down below, with a view out across the Rockies, a collection of moss- and lichen-covered outcroppings just offshore. They were pretty to look at, when they weren't being battered and beaten by the wind and tides and occasional storms. The views were great, but everyone in Little Penwick tried to tell John Edward that the lot he chose was probably the most inhospitable lot in town. Underneath, it was all rock and shale. On the surface, the constant winds, the frequent howling winter gales, the lashing rain and snow made it likely that no structure would last very long. And even if it did, they all told John Edward, the cost of heating the place in the winter would be prohibitive.

But John Edward was an onery old cuss who did things his own way. And in building his house, he went about it without care or concern of what other people might think, or even worrying about the way other people built their homes.

In his voyages up and down the Eastern seaboard, John Edward had gotten to know timber men in Maine, the Canadian provinces and even down South. So he knew who made the strongest beams and best boards, and he paid a little extra to have that shipped down to Little Penwick. He dug out his own basement, mostly by hand, with a little mechanical help once he hit the shale, which wasn't that far down. He mixed his own concrete in a medium-size drum mixer, using both the sand and the pebbles he hauled up from the beach below. The roof was double-laid with plywood bolted to the support beams for extra strength. Every part of the house was thickly insulated and the inside was paneled with Southern cypress, noted for its strength as well as its honey-colored beauty. And he made up the architecture as he went. It was mostly a one-story structure with kitchen, living room, dining room and master bedroom and bath all on one level. He added two small bedrooms for kids—who didn't yet exist—over the garage. Then he added a deck outside, to take advantage of those nice views of the ocean.

Despite the naysayers, it all worked. And now I lived here, in a house that was still on the small side, but was as solid as granite, warm, cozy, draft-free and which had lasted all these decades without incident. Turned out John Edward Haddock had known what he was doing and everyone else in town did not.

So I spent the next few weeks working on some of the small to-do items that had built up. Re-roofed the garage. Built a couple more raised-bed planters for Siggi to use to grow veggies in the summer. Trucked in some new crushed oyster shells to line the driveway. Started replacing some of the worn deck boards and added a new coat of stain.

I thought I was doing fairly well. My white-hot rage had cooled a little, and I was able to think about other things, now and then. Preston Knox was not foremost in my mind. But Siggi saw something else. She looked at me one morning over a cup of coffee and said "You need to get going, Julius."

"Going where?" I asked.

"On your life journey," she said. "Jupiter is moving direct into your House of Enterprise. This is a very powerful time and that means you need to get moving."

"Where am I supposed to go?"

She smiled. Then she got up, walked over to my pass-through counter, and picked up a white envelope that had been sitting there, untouched, for months. She came back and put it down in front of me.

"Maybe start there," she said.

I looked at the envelope. It was from some state licensing board and it contained my approved application to be a private investigator in the state of Rhode Island. I had actually made the application when I was still Inmate #GH37-3290. They sent it back to me—approved—just before I was released. The all-knowing, all-seeing state bureaucracy can be pretty dense.

"You need clients to start a business," I said. "I don't have any of those."

"I think the way it works is, you start a business and then begin to prospect for clients," she said. "You have to take the first step first."

"What I really want to do is investigate that bastard Knox," I said. "And then take him out into the swamps and break some of his most important bones."

Siggi sighed. She had heard this before. "I understand your need for revenge," she said. "I feel it, too, quite often. But there are good ways, and not so good ways to get what you want."

"What are the so-called good ways?"

"The best way is for you to become a productive member of society again," she said. "He tried to take that away from you. Only you can put it back. Better, this time. That will show that man that he failed."

I got up and poured myself another cup of coffee.

"And you think this is the way to do it?' I said, nodding at the envelope with my new PI license.

"I think it's a start," she said. "And you'll never get any-where unless you start someplace."

"Aren't we the Adage Factory this morning?" I said.

She laughed.

"You mentioned a few weeks ago that there were some old cases that had never been closed," she said.

"Cold cases," I said. "Yeah, we had a few at the depart-ment. Every police department has a couple. About once a year, we'd drag them out of storage and take another look at them. See if anything jumps out. Or if we might have missed something important."

"Why don't you pick one of those and give it a deep dive?" she said. "It would be police work of a sort. And you might surprise yourself and find something."

I sipped my coffee while I thought about that. It wasn't a bad idea.

"And while you're working on that, you can see if you pick up any other cases or clients," she said. "I think once the word gets out that Julius Haddock is up and about again, you'll have more cases than you can handle."

"Your lips to God's ears," I said. "Of course, all that won't help me destroy Preston Knox."

She shook her head. "There's that negative energy again," she said. "I think you need to focus on more positive things, like helping review those cold cases and then assisting people with their problems. Perhaps it's best to leave Preston Knox to the universe. Most of the time, bad people get what's coming to them."

"That's kind of the policeman's adage," I said with a smile.

She smiled back. "Do you have any idea of which cold case you'd want to take up first?" she asked.

I nodded. "Yeah, the oldest one," I said. "The Dixon case."

"Then do it," she said. "Couldn't be a better time to launch a new venture."